A Measure of Redemption

by

Josephine Howard

It is 1960, just before the Beatles became famous and long before mobile phones and computers. Life was less complicated then and nice girls always said 'No.'

Prologue

Jenny tensed as she heard her father open the front door of the maisonette where they both lived. She glanced at her watch; on time as usual, Charles Warr was never a minute late for anything.

"Hello, Dad," she said as he walked into the sitting room, "shall I make you a cup of tea?"

He stared at her and she felt herself blush.

"What's the matter?"

"Nothing."

"Well then, put the kettle on while I go upstairs."

Jenny shivered and wished she didn't feel so afraid of him. She sighed and went into the kitchen but soon heard a shout and then the thud of his footsteps down the stairs. She stood at the sink and waited.

"What the hell's been going on?" Charles grabbed Jenny's shoulder and spun her round. "Has that boy been in my bedroom?"

"William only wanted to see our home."

"He's seen as much of it as he's entitled to, this room and only when I'm here. He certainly has no right to use my bed."

"We sat on it and talked, that's all."

Charles stepped closer. "You and your so called boyfriend invaded my privacy."

"Nothing happened, Dad."

"You should have done a better job of straightening the counterpane then."

"I didn't ask him to come, he just turned up."

"Don't expect me to believe that. You've the morals of an alley cat, just like your bloody mother."

Jenny winced, he always brought Mum into it. It wasn't fair.

"He'd been swimming and thought he would call…"

"I don't give a tinker's cuss what he'd been doing. But I told you I didn't want him here when I'm out."

"Isn't this my home too? Can't I have friends?"

The slap made her cheek sting and her eyes water. Jenny pushed past Charles, rushed to her bedroom and slammed the door. I can't go on like this, she thought.

She took a piece of paper fom the drawer where she had hidden it weeks ago. She stared at the address. Perhaps now was the time to leave.

Chapter 1

Jenny sat on the green metal trunk and listened to her father clattering the crockery downstairs as he washed the breakfast dishes. Their last row had happened two weeks ago yet it seemed like yesterday and now the day to leave home was here and she was scared.

She looked round the room that had been hers for three unhappy years. Now stripped of her few possessions, it seemed that she had never been there; she was no more substantial than a ghost. She stared at her reflection; too tall, mousy hair, an ordinary face, why should anyone take any notice of her?

"Aren't you ready yet? Christ knows you've had long enough."

Jenny jumped; she had not heard him come upstairs. She didn't turn round in case she showed he could still hurt her.

"Of course I'm ready, I was waiting for you."

She heard her father's intake of breath; her barb had found its mark.

"Do you expect me to get this downstairs on my own while you stand there like Lady Muck?"

Jenny turned and watched as he dragged the large, green, army trunk, that had once been his, towards the bedroom door. She shrugged her shoulders. He was making it so easy; had he shown a hint of kindness she would have broken down. Without a word she grabbed one handle of the trunk. As Charles guided it downstairs Jenny noticed a glimmer of skin through his brown, curly hair. Dad is going bald, she thought, not even the great Charles Warr could stop hair loss.

"The car's at the bottom of the steps, help me get this thing down."

Was there a hint of regret? Jenny could not be sure. She flicked a glance at his face but it was expressionless. Each gripping a handle, they moved together through the front door. It is the start of my new life, Jenny thought, hopefully with William.

*

Lunchtime at the hostel had been quiet. Jenny had unpacked everything and didn't know what else to do; she had expected the business of leaving home to take longer. She wondered what Dad was doing and remembered Saturdays, all those years ago, when he came home on leave and took her to Stamford Bridge to watch football.

She had told William she could not see him this weekend, now she wished she hadn't. Dare she telephone and suggest a meeting? Would that seem too forward? Supposing his mother answered? From what William had said she didn't think she would like his mother. Still, he had promised he would arrange for her to meet both his parents so he must be keen.

It would be six whole days before she saw him again, what could she do? She looked round the bare room that was now her home. She felt frightened. Had she been stupid to leave Dad's flat, was this place any better? She lay down on the bed and listened to the sounds of other residents moving along the corridor, chatting to each other. She heard the occasional laugh. Any of these strangers could become friends, it was up to her.

She sat up. There was no point in wallowing in self-pity, she thought. If she got some postcards she could write to William, say she had settled in and remind him of their date. She could also write to Mum and Gran and give them her new address.

She hurried down stairs and then strode – with a confidence she didn't feel - down the road towards the station and a parade of shops which the hostel warden, Miss Pritchard, had said was not far. The shops looked dusty and rundown but they would provide bare essentials. It was going to be all right, she thought, with just a few friends I will cope.

The only postcards on display in the newsagents were unappetizing local scenes; Baron's Court was unlikely to attract visitors if the cards on sale were the best they had to offer. With no stamps and the Post Office shut she would not be able to post the cards until Monday anyway.

She strolled back to the hostel, found a pen and started.

Dear Mum,

Jenny chewed the end of her pen. It was always difficult writing to Mum but not as difficult as visiting her. Stephen and Ruth, Jenny's half-brother and half sister, did not want her there ever. Of course Mum would never accept that but Jenny knew it was true. Probably Alec, her step-father, didn't want her there either; he found his own children a handful.

What a pity there hadn't been a card with a picture of the Hostel, then she could have put a cross on the appropriate window and written 'I am here'.

When high-pitched screams ricocheted up the corridor Jenny rushed to her door. She looked out and noticed others were doing the same. The screams were coming from the room two doors away. Soon a group of girls had gathered so Jenny hurried to join them.

"It's Laura again," someone said, "always making a fuss."

"Spoilt rotten, attention seeking," another girl added.

Several of the older residents drifted away as the screams became noisy, gulping sobs. How unkind, Jenny thought, as she peered into the room. The girl, who must be Laura, was crouched on the bed.

"There it is," she yelled, "there!" Heads craned and Jenny saw something moving in the corner of the room, a large spider. More spectators departed; perhaps Laura wasn't the only one who didn't like them. Jenny saw the girl more clearly now as her tear-streaked face emerged from the shadows, a pretty face, Jenny thought.

"Shall I get rid of it for you?"

"Please, oh yes do, kill it, anything, I can't stand spiders." Laura's hysteria made Jenny feel flustered. She grabbed an empty cup from the chest of drawers and banged it, upside down, over the spider.

Laura gave a muffled cry. "I'll never be able to drink out of that again."

Jenny stared at Laura, started to speak then stopped, there was no point in telling her not to be so silly.

"I'll open the window if you'll put your hand over the cup."

"I'm not getting off this bed until that thing has gone."

"I don't think it's a man-eating variety," Jenny said and grinned. Laura shivered with disgust and started to protest.

"Got a piece of card?"

"What for?" Laura asked.

"I want to slide it under the cup, keep the spider inside. I'll take it to the window, see if it'll fly."

Either Laura didn't have any card or she wasn't prepared to look.

"Just keep your hand on top of the cup while I go next door."

Laura rolled her eyes but didn't move.

"If you don't the spider might sneak under the rim."

"Don't be long," Laura whispered and without putting her feet

7

on the floor she stretched out far enough to rest her hand on the cup.

Amazing, Jenny thought, pretend you're in control and people believe you know what you're doing. At least I've met someone. She ran to her room grabbed a postcard and hurried back. Laura shuffled to the far corner of her bed and watched as Jenny pushed the postcard under the cup. She looked up and smiled.

"You'll be safe now but I'd better put your chair by the window, I'll need something to stand on."

Jenny balanced herself and listened to Laura's staccato gasps. Leaning out of the window, Jenny turned the cup upside down and removed the card - nothing. She looked inside and saw the spider huddled in the bottom. She shook the cup and the small body, legs folded tightly to its sides, fell down, down past the window. She turned and beamed at Laura. What a wonderful start, a friend already she hoped. She jumped off the chair.

"I hope it lands on grass."

"I don't," Laura said, "it might come back, they always do. I hate this place."

Jenny felt a tremor of anxiety, was it really awful, had she made a mistake coming here? She didn't know what to say so inspected the crumpled postcard. It was the one she was sending to William.

"I'm Laura by the way; I suppose you're new here." She bounced off the bed and gave Jenny a hug. "Thank you so much, I'm really grateful."

Jenny felt herself blush. She opened her mouth to speak but had no chance.

"If I hurry I'll just be in time to change before I meet Tony. He's my boyfriend."

Jenny watched as Laura brushed and combed her wavy, blond hair. She is very pretty, Jenny thought. No wonder she is so confident.

"I'm meeting him in town; he's twenty six and a real dream boat."

Jenny was surprised; twenty six seemed very grown-up for a girl as young as Laura.

"My boyfriend is nineteen." Jenny realized it was the first time she had referred to William as hers.

"Well I can certainly recommend older men," Laura said, as

she started to apply bright, blue eye shadow, "they know so much more about life."

Jenny was fascinated; she had much to learn. Perhaps, if she asked, Laura would help her with make-up. She waited, not sure whether to stay or leave. She didn't want to be on her own, not yet.

Laura applied scarlet lipstick, checked the effect, slipped off her dressing-gown and put on a full-skirted summer dress.

"Zip me up," she said, "and take that cup if you want, I shan't use it. Anyway I've got another one." She glanced at her watch.

"I'd better go, thanks again, you're a star."

Left with no choice, Jenny went back to her room where she brushed dust marks off her postcard. It wasn't the first time she had written to William but this was the first postcard and his parents would be able to read it. That might make things trickier.

'Settled in well, my room is nice (he would never see it). All the other girls are friendly (they will be when I get to know them). See you on Friday. I'll meet you outside the hostel at 7p.m.'

She stopped, unsure how to finish, should it be love, best wishes or nothing, just Jenny? Perhaps she should write a bit more then there would only be room for her name.

She gazed out of her window and watched the trees wave a sad farewell to summer with branches clad in leaves already changing from green to russet and bronze. Sadness gripped her. This is only the beginning, she thought; I shall be staying in tonight and I must accept it. I will read my book. She wondered what William was doing and hoped he was thinking of her.

*

Chapter 2

Iris pushed food around her plate only half listening as George talked to William, their older son, about a new order from Germany.

"It's meal time for God's sake; do you always have to talk business? No-one asks me what I've done, do they?"

Anger bubbled in her throat and the sickly, heavy taste of brandy made her dizzy. They were always ignoring her yet she had been someone once, a top model in Canada; some people in the business had said she was the image of Wallis Simpson. She sighed, that was all so long ago.

She pushed herself to her feet and walked slowly from the room. Swaying with nausea she wondered if she had been wise to drink on an empty stomach but why shouldn't she if she felt like it? She sat on the easy chair in the hallway and closed her eyes. If she sat still she would feel better. Words drifted in and out of her hearing, like sounds of the sea and then she heard footsteps; someone was standing over her.

"She's asleep." It was William, "Why do you put up with it, Dad?"

How dare he? If she hadn't felt so strange she would have given him a piece of her mind. A tear slid down her cheek, all she wanted was her darling Freddie at home.

She listened as husband and elder son cleared the table. She would go to bed for an hour or two, let them do the washing up for once. She struggled to her feet and went upstairs.

*

Iris woke with a start; George had sat on the bed.

"I didn't think I should let you sleep too long; I've brought you a cup of coffee."

Iris nodded and sat up.

"Where would you like to go this evening?"

Iris sipped her coffee. "What about the 'Trocadero? We haven't been there for ages."

George stood up, "I'll go and book."

"Get a table for eight," she shouted as George went downstairs. If only Freddie were here, she thought, he would come with us. George didn't understand, complained that she made a favourite of the boy, he said she'd ruin him. But Freddie would always be her baby.

After a shower Iris felt refreshed and very hungry. She should have eaten more at lunchtime; that must be why she had felt so strange. She took her time selecting what she would wear. She loved dressing in the latest fashion; it made her feel young again. As she walked down stairs she heard George and William talking.

"You're welcome to come too."

"It's O.K. Dad I'm meeting some mates later."

Iris smiled; she found William very irritating.

*

"William's coming to Stockholm with me on Thursday, we'll probably be away a week."

Iris crumbled her bread and pushed the plate away. She wondered who else would be going. That tarty secretary, June, used to figure in dispatches rather too often, now she was never mentioned. He must think I'm stupid, she thought, and took another cigarette from her case. She waited for George to light it knowing he hated her smoking between courses. She exhaled and stared across the room rather than at him.

"So I'm going to be on my own again." Iris drained her brandy glass.

"What do you want me to do? Trade doesn't appear out of thin air."

"Perhaps you should employ someone else to do the donkey work."

"Look, I don't like all this travelling any more than you do."

Iris raised an eyebrow but said nothing.

"Things are difficult with this Common Market business. If de Gaulle has his way..."

"What do I know about that?"

"Since you're happy spending the money I make perhaps you should show some interest in where it comes from."

Iris sighed and ground out her cigarette.

"Scandinavian countries may be our only chance. The other alternative is the States, that's even further away."

"At least I could go there with you, look up some old friends."

"Yes, dear, I know but it's one hell of a time since you left?" He stroked her hand. "You haven't heard from anyone for years."

She pulled her hand away and lit another cigarette, the exhaled smoke swirled about her head. He was smiling that condescending smile that made her want to lash out. She had given up everything for him.

11

"And what about Freddie? I notice he doesn't get a mention in your master plan or is it only William you're interested in?"

"Freddie has exams; he'll tell us his plans when he's ready. We can have a chat with him when he gets back."

"If you hadn't insisted he went to that confounded boarding school we wouldn't have to wait for end-of-term holidays to speak to him." Iris stubbed out her cigarette.

"How long have we been waiting?" She clicked her fingers at a nearby waiter.

"Since your chef's working at half speed, I'll have another Courvoisier while I wait, make it a double."

Iris watched the waiter give a startled glance towards George who nodded.

"Let's change the subject. I've brought you out to enjoy yourself not to talk business."

Iris glared at him; they sat in silence until the waiter returned. She picked up her glass. "Cheers, let's hope you have a wonderful time impressing the Swedes, both male and female."

She lifted her glass; her lips smiled but her eyes were cold.

"Has William told you about this young lady of his?"

"When has he ever confided in me?"

"Recently moved into a hostel," George said.

"Has she no parents?"

"Divorced, lives with her father, a difficult man, William said."

"Not much of a recommendation."

"They met at the swimming baths."

"What kind of girl allows herself to be picked up at a swimming baths?"

"Things have changed. People meet anywhere, none of the formal introduction nonsense."

"At least then you knew what a person's background was."

"Surely we can trust William to be sensible; we've brought him up well."

Iris gave a dismissive shrug.

"Well there's only one way to find out; we'll just have to meet her," George said.

"Oh, and will that be before or after your little jaunt to foreign parts?"

*

12

Chapter 3

Jenny trudged upstairs. After a week in her new job she was exhausted. There was so much to learn and though Professor Walker seemed kind, Jenny was not sure how well she would get on with the other laboratory assistants.

The Tube had been packed as, she'd been warned, it always was on Friday evenings. She hated being crushed together with strangers some of whom could do with a wash. It had poured all the way from the station but at least she was meeting William. She had been surprised to see a letter from him in her pigeon hole in the hall. She would save it until after she had had a cup of tea.

Grinning with anticipation she sprinted up the last flight of stairs, threw her coat and bag on her bed and joined the gaggle of girls outside the nearest kitchen. They were all waiting to use the kettle. As she stood waiting, Jenny remembered the dreadful afternoon when William called round to see her at home. If only she had suggested they went for a walk perhaps things would be different now.

She hadn't been entirely honest with Dad, she hadn't dared to be. William had kissed her that day again and again. It had been lovely, just like in the cinema. She had gasped for air when he released her and she remembered leaning against him. This must be what made Victorian ladies swoon, she had thought. Was kissing so terrible, was Dad jealous? He had no-one to kiss.

She knew things could so easily have gone further, sensed that was what William wanted. But they hadn't, no matter what Dad said. He always thought the worst of everyone. It was just a pity that they had been sitting on Dad's bed. That had been really stupid.

Now, queuing for a cup of tea, Jenny felt her face flush as she recalled how she'd felt that day.

"Got soaked walking from the station."

Jenny jumped.

"You were miles away."

It was the girl in front who had turned to speak.

"Yes, dreadful wasn't it, and the Tube was packed."

"That's rush hour for you, settling in all right?" The girl smiled, "I'm Maureen, my room's at the end of the corridor."

Jenny smiled "I think you're next," she said as two more girls left the kitchen. She wanted to read the letter while she waited but not with other people around.

"Your turn," Maureen said as she left the kitchen, "it's a wonder that kettle hasn't melted. You know where to find me if you want a chat."

"Thanks," Jenny replied. She topped up the kettle and gazed out of the window, listening to the hum of the gas stove and the chatter of the other residents. It's pity you can't re-run life, do things differently, she thought, I should have suggested a walk along the Embankment.

"Come on; show me where my lady rests her weary head." William had said.

She had laughed and led him upstairs. Her room had looked cheerless, dismal, with no carpet - just cold linoleum. Even on a warm day her room always felt chilly. William had said nothing. Embarrassed, Jenny had walked to the landing.

"Dad sleeps here," she had said and opened his bedroom door.

Sunlight had streamed in that afternoon giving the room a welcoming glow. Jenny had moved back to the door, ready to go downstairs.

William had rested his hands on her shoulders, "I do love you, you know."

She remembered blinking away a tear and her heart had felt ready to explode. She had opened her mouth to speak but he had kissed her. Together they had sat on the edge of Dad's double bed and kissed, leaning back until they rested side by side, arms entwined. She had insisted that they went downstairs and soon after William had left.

Jenny's hand was shaking as she made her cup of tea. She walked back to her room. He had only been testing her, making sure she was a nice girl. She had straightened Dad's bed clothes so carefully but still he had sensed that something had gone on. And that is why I am here, she said to her empty hostel room, maybe one day Dad will believe me.

She kicked off her wet shoes, put on her slippers and stretched out on the bed. She tore open the envelope and scanned the letter.

Sorry about Friday…Stockholm….back next week.

Her eyes filled with tears, it wasn't fair. Disappointment overwhelmed her. Her tea grew cold as she lay too heavy-limbed to move.

It was time for the evening meal but she didn't want anything, she would just stay in her room and waste away. The sound of feet tramping along the corridor emphasized the evening routine. Feeding time at the zoo, it is half past five and you will be hungry. Soon the corridor was silent. I'm alone, she thought, Dad is better off without me, Mum's got Alec and the kids and William is going to Stockholm. I've got nobody.

There was the sudden staccato tap, tap of high-heeled shoes accompanied by knocking. Jenny roused herself when she heard Laura's voice.

"Yes?"

"Thank heavens," Laura rushed in, "I'm late and my zip's stuck."

"Going out with Tony?"

"Of course, he's taking me to dinner, none of this hostel muck."

Jenny tugged, releasing the lining that was caught.

"There you are."

"Thanks a million, can't stop, aren't you eating?"

"No, not hungry."

Laura raised her eyebrows and left with such speed she left a vacuum behind her.

Jenny stood at her window. It was still raining and she watched as Laura ran up the road with her umbrella bobbing up and down like a demented daisy.

Jenny sat on her bed, well, it's no good starving, she thought, I can't afford to miss a meal I've already paid for. She slouched down the stairs trying to decide, from the smell, what was on the menu; she hoped it was something tasty. It wasn't.

She joined the queue which moved at a snail's pace round the dining room. When at last she reached the hatch there was only shepherd's pie left. After the grey mash and even greyer mince Jenny decided enough was enough. The pudding was sponge with lumpy custard, school dinners all over again.

She managed some of the shepherd's pie which was tepid, then with heavy heart she went back to her room. She had finished all but one of her books and would have to go to the library tomorrow once she had found out where it was. She would be doing a lot of reading over the next few days.

Several girls in the dining room had smiled and nodded but apart from Laura and Maureen she had not had a conversation

15

with anyone. Now Laura was out having a good time and somehow she didn't feel like talking to Maureen.

She heard crying as she walked along the corridor, someone else having a rotten time, she thought. She listened outside Laura's room but surely she was out. Jenny wondered what to do, was it best to leave people alone in such circumstances? She decided it wasn't and knocked on Laura's door.

A muffled voice said, "Go away."

If Laura had not wanted anyone to know she was crying she should have been quieter about it, Jenny thought, as she opened the door.

"What's the matter, are you all right?"

There was a wail from the figure on the bed. Perhaps the other residents were right, perhaps Laura was always making a fuss about something.

"He stood me up."

So much for older men, Jenny thought. "Do you want a cup of tea?"

Another wail from Laura as Jenny went to the kitchen, Laura would have tea if she wanted it or not. Once she had stopped crying perhaps they could have a chat, get to know each other better. That would be nicer than staying alone in her room.

"Here you are, drink this, I've put some sugar in it, that will make you feel better."

"Nothing will make me feel better, you don't understand. I wish I were dead."

Jenny had often wondered how film stars could cry without suffering devastation of the face. Crying always made her go a blotchy red and she ended with swollen eyes and streaming nose. Laura had the same problem. Jenny felt quite heartened as she sat on the edge of the bed with two cups of tea. Laura snivelled and dabbed at her face.

"I waited for ages in the rain, Tony's an absolute pig. These awful blokes kept leering at me, asking if they could help. Can you believe it?" Her voice was shrill.

"Where were you meeting him?"

"Leicester Square Tube station, it was awful."

"Were you late?"

"Only ten minutes, surely he should have waited."

Jenny didn't know. She was always early when she met William and had to hide until he appeared.

16

"Can't you phone him?"

"I haven't got his number; I'll have to wait until he gets in touch." She started to cry, "Perhaps he never will."

"Maybe you'd be better off without him if he's like that."

Laura's wails increased in volume.

"How long have you known him?"

"Three months."

"My boyfriend's called William. He's had to go to Stockholm on a business trip with his dad. We had a date tomorrow but now he can't make it."

Laura sipped her tea. "I don't even know where he works."

That's strange, Jenny thought, I know a lot more about William than Laura knows about this Tony.

"Where did you meet him?"

"At the Palais."

Jenny looked blank.

"You know, the Hammersmith Palais, dancing."

Jenny knew Dad would never have sanctioned dancing at the Palais.

"Haven't you been?"

Jenny shook her head.

"Tell you what," Laura said, "sod these bloody men, let's go tomorrow."

Jenny hesitated, not sure that was a good idea.

"Come on, it'll be fun."

"I've nothing to wear."

"I'll lend you something."

Jenny laughed as she stood up. She was much taller than Laura and definitely not as slim.

"Anything will do, a summer dress and a cardie, you must have something."

"What about getting back in time?"

"Oh, never mind about that, don't push the sign across when you go out. Old Pritchard'll never know that we aren't tucked up with our hot water bottles."

"But where will we go if the door's locked?"

Laura sighed, "Don't worry. Pat round the corner used to live here, has her own flat now, she always lets people sleep on the floor."

It was all so easy, Jenny thought, but what was she going to wear?

"Well, will you come?"

"Yes, I'll go and check my clothes." That won't take long, she thought, as she returned to her room. She was going out, to the Palais, what an adventure!

*

Chapter 4

Iris roamed from room to room with a cigarette in one hand, a brandy glass in the other. The only person she had seen since George and William left was the cleaning woman – hardly stimulating. If only I had a daughter, Iris thought, I would have a companion and a friend. We could have done things together, gone on shopping expeditions.

She glanced at herself in the long, hall mirror. Leaving the cigarette in her mouth, she put the brandy glass down and smoothed her hands over her hips. Turning sideways she pulled in her stomach muscles. She turned her face to the mirror and exhaled, for a moment the swirling smoke softened her features and she looked young again.

"George is damned lucky," she said to her reflection. Her voice echoed in the black and white tiled hall to remind her of her solitude.

"I'll go into town, I deserve some new outfits," she said and recalled the horrified look her dressmaker's bills would always elicit from George. Iris had told him once that you only got what you paid for. Of course, George in his usual cheese-paring way had pointed out it was not she who paid, he did. She recalled the occasion, years ago, when he had muttered about unnecessary extravagance and she had, with a seraphic smile, suggested the offending items be returned with a note to explain he could not afford them. She had been startled by the vehemence of his response; the breakfast china had bounced as his fist hit the table.

"Don't be so bloody silly, woman," he had shouted. Since then whilst there was bad grace in his acceptance, accept he did. She smiled; it was ages since she had had a day in town.

She went to her bedroom and opened the bottom drawer of her wardrobe. There were the photographs she had taken in Canada, more than twenty years ago, when she was young and had the world of fashion at her feet. In those days her legs were so good she did most of the bathing costume shots. Legs like Betty Grable, that's what she had. It was all so long ago. She wrapped each of the enlarged photographs in tissue paper and replaced it in the drawer.

She took her astrakhan coat from its hanger; it always made her feel special. She would browse through the fashion departments and by the time she got back most of the day would be over. She'd phone Sylvia and arrange for a discussion and a fitting; that would take care of another day. All she was doing was filling time.

She paused, she knew she should go to see her parents but it was such a pain. Sheila would look reproachful and Dad would mutter about how long it was since her last visit and why didn't she come more often? The whole business would be hateful, besides no-one could accuse her and George of not helping out. After all George had paid for Mum and Dad to come back to England as soon as Mum was diagnosed with M.S.

Iris checked her makeup in the mirror.

Of course as Sheila was single it was only natural she should come too. If she'd wanted to stay in Canada, have a life of her own, she could have done. It was unfortunate that mum was now bedridden which did tie Sheila to the house.

Iris touched up her lipstick.

"I've my own family to look after," Iris said to her reflection, "no-one should expect me to take on my parents as well." No, she decided, a visit to the aged parents could wait until George was back, he was so good with them. Iris wanted Sylvia to start on her things before George got back then it would be too late for him to make a fuss. Feeling more cheerful, she went to phone for a taxi, no point in driving to town.

*

Chapter 5

Thank goodness it's Saturday, Jenny thought, as she woke bleary-eyed after a restless night. Her neck ached and the rollers had dug into her scalp. She wondered how girls went through such torture on a regular basis. The beer that Laura had used as setting lotion had made Jenny's hair stiff and sticky and the smell was frightful.

She would have to hurry if she wanted breakfast so she dressed and attacked her hair with determination and a hair brush. After five minutes of vigorous brushing she looked in the mirror. Not bad, she thought. After breakfast I'll go out, have some fresh air to clear my head, get rid of the smell of beer.

Feeling better after her walk, Jenny returned to the hostel to find Laura with her hair professionally folded into a fashionable French pleat. She was inspecting the dress she was going to wear. With its full skirt in deep folds below a fitted bodice it hung like an exotic blossom from the wardrobe door. Jenny saw a froth of paper nylon petticoats on Laura's bed. White winkle-picker stilettos and a white cardigan completed the out fit.

Jenny knew she could never compete with such finery. She sighed as she returned to her room to look again at what she had. There was her best blouse, pale cream, shantung silk which Dad had chosen two years ago. It was suitable for a mature lady, nice, elegant but not what teenagers wore. There were two possible skirts; she chose the fuller of the two. At least she had one decent petticoat and that would have to do.

"It's not bloody fair," she muttered, "some girls have everything, can't even get pretty shoes with my big feet." Had Laura asked her as a foil, pretty girl, plain friend?

It was obvious pretty girls got the boys who never seemed to look beyond face and figure. What about personality, Jenny wondered? Still William must be more discerning than most, he liked her and still wanted to see her. What would she tell him about tonight? Perhaps she should wait to see if there was anything to tell.

After a rushed meal they raced out of the hostel, praying that Miss Pritchard didn't see them. They ran to the station, catching the District Line train to Hammersmith.

The carriage was full of excited girls all with the Alma Cogan look of full skirts and nipped in waists. Embarrassed young men stood in groups near the train doors, ostentatiously smoking and smoothing their D.A.s into place with dirty combs. Their hot eyes surveyed the talent. The atmosphere buzzed and Jenny felt herself swept along by the excitement.

They arrived outside the Palais where there was already a chattering queue of girls. Moody looking boys were trying to disassociate themselves from the crowd, anxious to emulate James Dean. Jenny had seen 'East of Eden' and found Dean delectable, she cried when she read he he'd been killed.

Efficient doormen kept the queue moving, hustling chattering girls into the dance hall first. Tommy Steele's 'Singing the Blues' was belting out and some couples were jiving, others perambulated in a more tentative manner. Jenny felt cold with fear, would she be able to dance well enough? It had never occurred to her that she might not know how to do it.

The noise was deafening and when she looked for Laura she was not there. She must be dancing with someone already. I'll just sit down quietly and watch, she thought, as Laura whisked past in a cloud of petticoats and L'Aimant perfume. Jenny smiled but Laura was too engrossed to notice. The air was heavy with sweat and cheap after shave. Girls were swung round like puppets; their swirling skirts made Jenny feel dizzy. The pounding beat was hypnotic, unnerving.

"Like to dance?"

Jenny looked round. A short, dumpy, young man with bad acne was smiling at her. Oh dear, she thought, I'm going to tower above him. As she rose from her seat the young man seemed to shrink. His smile became fixed and Jenny wanted to giggle, his head barely reached her shoulder.

He would never be able to steer her through the dancers although he seemed determined to try. She wondered if she should offer to lead, she had had plenty of practice at school where she had always had to take the part of a man. Perhaps it would not be tactful to suggest this to a stranger.

"My name's Derek, do you come here often?"

Jenny choked, so people really did say that. According to magazines she had read in her doctor's waiting room it was the least original thing to say. But at least she was dancing, even if it was with a midget and that was better than being a wallflower all night.

"I've just moved into a hostel, at Baron's Court," Jenny said.

Derek looked surprised. "I'm still at home, me, my sister, Mum and Dad."

"I work at the Middlesex hospital and the hostel was easier for getting to work."

"Oh," said Derek, "what do you do?"

"Weigh rats."

"What for?"

"They have their thyroids cut out."

Jenny watched Derek's face turn white.

"You don't do that do you?"

"Oh no, Professor Walker does that, he's working on diets for people who have thyroid deficiency. One of my jobs is to weigh the rats to see if they've lost weight."

Derek nodded, content to continue using Jenny as a battering ram as he steered her firmly through the crowd while she looked for Laura.

*

"How did you know I'd be here?" Laura asked as Tony whisked her round the dance floor.

"Thought you'd probably be sulking after the other night, I can read you like a book, see. Know you like dancing so where better than here?"

"So who was the girl you were talking to?"

"A girl from work actually, not a patch on you."

Laura giggled.

"It was awful, just standing there at the station. I couldn't call you or anything."

"I've just told you, I had to work late."

"Well, why can't I have your number then if it happens again I can give you a call."

"Don't give my number to anyone, doll. It's not allowed, company policy."

"What about your home number then?"

He whirled her round. "You don't want to stay here all night do you? There's a bit of a party back at the flat. Come on, we'll have some fun."

"Well, it's a bit awkward you see, didn't know you'd be here so I brought this girl with me, from the hostel."

Tony sighed then gave Laura a hug. "Let's sneak out when she's not looking."

About to agree, Laura caught a glimpse of Jenny on the far side of the room, she was waving.

"She's seen me, I can't just leave her."

"Go and get her then, I'll wait outside."

*

"What's the matter?" Derek asked.

"Sorry; I'm looking for my friend."

"Want a drink?"

"Oh, yes please." Her mouth was dry with anxiety rather than exertion.

They threaded their way through the crowd to the bar. Jenny was impressed by the way Derek made a pathway, a bit like a terrier going down a rabbit hole. She followed, looking from side to side but couldn't see Laura anywhere.

"What will you have?"

"Orange squash, please."

She noted the look of relief on Derek's face, perhaps girls usually asked for something stronger. Dad had always said don't be a gold-digger and Derek didn't look as though he had money to spare.

Jenny felt a tap on her shoulder, it was Laura.

"Where've you been? You were over there a minute ago; I thought I'd lost you."

"Derek asked me to have a drink."

"Who's Derek?"

"This bloke I've been dancing with."

Laura was glowing, she giggled and hugged Jenny. "You'll never guess what, Tony's here, would you believe it?"

"Wasn't his fault the other night, he had to work late. Anyway it doesn't matter now, he's here and he's taking me to this party. Are you coming?"

Jenny swallowed hard and looked at Derek who had returned with an orange squash in one hand and half a pint of beer in the other. She looked back at Laura.

"This is Derek."

Laura ignored him. "Tony said he'd only wait for five minutes, are you coming or what?"

"I'm really sorry about this but I'll have to go," Jenny said to Derek.

He shrugged and handed her the orange squash. "Might as well drink this, I don't want it."

She gulped most of it down while Laura hopped from foot to foot.

"Thanks ever so much, I'm really sorry."

24

"Perhaps I'll see you here next week."

"Yes, perhaps, that'd be nice." You liar, Jenny thought, next week I hope to be out with William.

She raced after Laura and arrived at the entrance to see an arrogant-looking man checking his watch. Laura touched his arm.

"Sorry it took so long, I couldn't find her. This is Jenny."

Tony nodded then turned and strode out of the Palais followed, at a run, by the two girls. His car was parked in a side street; it was a two-door saloon so Jenny had to clamber into the back. Laura chatted all the way to wherever Tony was taking them; Jenny was ignored. More than anything she wanted to go back to the hostel but she didn't think it wise to say so.

The car was steered into a parking space in a residential area – Jenny knew not where. They stood on the pavement while Tony locked the doors. Jenny shivered although it wasn't cold.

"It's the top floor flat." Tony said to no-one in particular.

Jenny, taut with embarrassment at being, so obviously, the third that makes a crowd, walked up the stone steps. As she looked up she could see lights. That must be where the party was although there was no noise, perhaps it wasn't that kind of party. She paused at the top of the first unlit flight of stairs. She could hear giggling and rustling below, Laura and Tony were following her up. Reassured she went up two more flights and still no noise; she felt frightened.

She tried to see her watch but it was too dark, it must be very late, too late; the hostel doors would be locked and she didn't know the girl that Laura had mentioned. She had nowhere to go but up. She climbed the last flight and stood outside the only door, an attic flat she assumed.

She pushed the door open and saw a dimly lit room with hardly any furniture. Four men were sitting at a low coffee table, playing cards. There was a beer crate on the floor and from the number of empties scattered around, most of the crate's contents had been drunk. The men looked up, surprised.

"Tony said there was a party here."

A man with his back to her swivelled round, eyed her up and down and smirked, "Yes, darling, you're it."

Jenny felt faint, she had to get away but her legs wouldn't move. Tony and Laura burst into the room, she was flushed and laughing.

25

"I want to go home," Jenny whispered.

"Don't be silly, we've only just got here," Laura said.

Jenny felt panic and rage struggle for dominance, this was a nightmare. Also she needed the toilet but where was it?

One of the card players shouted, "Want a beer Tony?"

"Cheers, you too babe?" he turned to Laura. Jenny was ignored. Laura preened and checked her lipstick in a hand mirror.

"Where's the bathroom?" Jenny whispered in an agony of embarrassment.

Laura pointed to a door on the other side of the room while continuing to admire her reflection. Tony stood talking to the card players, there was much guffawing and Jenny realized she was the subject of their hilarity. She opened the door to her left, there was a corridor which she rushed down opening doors to left and right; the first two were bedrooms, the third a bathroom. There was no lock on the door but by now Jenny was past caring. She struggled to raise her skirt, I can't cope with this, I must get out of here, she thought.

She heard footsteps coming down the corridor and clenched her fists. She was ready to hit anyone who came in but the footsteps went past. She took gulping breaths and sat in the dark listening to her heart thudding. Bit by bit she became calmer. Laura only cared about herself and Jenny was angry for being such a fool.

It would not be wise to set off on her own since she didn't know where she was. There was no chance Tony would volunteer to drive them back to the hostel and it was too late anyway. This simplified things, she had no choice, she had to stay here. Perhaps one of these men would let her share a bed with Laura; they would just have to make the best of it.

She straightened her skirt, took a deep breath and headed up the corridor. There was no sign of Tony or Laura. The skin on Jenny's scalp prickled as the four men looked at her. She didn't know what to do.

"Want a beer?"

Jenny wasn't sure which man had spoken.

"No thank you, I don't like beer." She tried to steady her voice. Please don't let them know I'm frightened.

"A coffee then?" One of the man turned and smiled, "I'm Mark."

"I'd prefer tea, please."

"O.K., tea it is." He walked down the corridor with Jenny following him. I'm like a stray dog, she thought, one kind word is enough.

"I didn't know I was being brought here, I really ought to go back to the hostel. I don't think you are supposed to stay out overnight. I wouldn't have come if I'd known."

She realized she was gabbling, words tumbling over themselves. She was amazed that what she said sounded coherent. Yet the words she most wanted to say remained locked away, I'm frightened, very, very frightened.

Mark glanced up as he spooned tea into a battered teapot.

"Don't worry, you can sleep in my bed, you'll be O.K."

Jenny stared at him.

As though reading her thoughts he said, "I'll kip on the settee."

Air whistled out of Jenny's mouth and she wondered how long she had been holding her breath.

"What about the others?"

"Who, Laura and Tony? You won't see anything of them. Mind you, Tony won't be too late away, his wife might ask questions, he'll take Laura home."

Jenny gasped. Did Laura know Tony was married?

"No, I meant the other men, your friends, won't they mind if I stay here?"

"Nothing to do with them who sleeps in my bed, I pay my share of the rent."

Jenny nodded, "You're very kind, do you mind if I go to bed now?"

The sooner she was asleep the sooner it would be morning and she could escape.

"Right, I'll tell the others, don't worry they'll leave you alone."

Jenny gave a quiet sob of relief and with difficulty stopped herself from throwing her arms around him. Better not, she decided, such action could be misconstrucd.

"I really can't thank you enough."

He grinned as he handed her a mug of tea.

"My room's on the left, opposite the bathroom," he said over his shoulder as he left the kitchen, "sleep well."

Jenny rushed to her sanctuary, closed the door behind her and leaned against it trying not to slosh tea over herself or the floor. How could Laura be so irresponsible? No decent girl behaved like that, no-one would want to marry her, men only wanted virgins.

She didn't put the light on; somehow the dark seemed safer. She drew the curtains to shut out the light from the street lamps and lay, fully clothed, on the bed which was under the window. The blankets and sheets had an unfamiliar masculine smell that was not unpleasant. She yawned and realized how exhausted she was. She shuffled round until she had wrapped the top blanket around her. The room seemed to be swaying, rocking her to and fro. Sounds from the street rose and fell like sounds of the sea. She slept.

*

Chapter 6

Iris lay on the settee and wondered if she should have another brandy, the effort of getting up was too much; she closed her eyes. George and William were coming back tomorrow so she would have to tidy the place; heaven only knew what the cleaning woman did.

"I'll sack her, that's what I'll do," she said to the television that murmured in the corner. She lit another cigarette and lay back watching as the smoke drifted upwards; alone, she was always alone. George kept suggesting she should take up a hobby, meet some like-minded women. There were no women in Hendon with whom she had anything in common. None of them had mixed in high society – with film stars in fact. All that was so long ago in a far away place. She wondered if she would ever go back to the States, probably not. She drew on her cigarette and watched the column of ash quiver.

She heard a car door bang, it was close and then there was the scrape of a key in the front door lock and William's voice. Was it part of the watching campaign to return early? She knew George and William were always checking up on her.

"She's in there."

She, not Mother, Mummy, Mum, just she, Iris wanted to slap him for his insolence. Then George was sitting beside her, he eased the cigarette from her fingers.

"Lucky you didn't burn yourself on that."

Iris looked at him, forcing her eyes to focus. "Why didn't you let me know you were coming back today? I'd have killed the fatted calf."

"I phoned but you weren't in."

Iris giggled and closed her eyes. No, she thought, I was with Sylvia being measured.

"Come on, old darling, it's time for bed."

She opened her eyes a fraction, shielding them from the light.

"What time is it?"

"Well past midnight."

"Have you come to take me to bed, my handsome prince?" She took his hand and placed it on her breast. George glanced at William who stood in the doorway; Iris turned and caught the look of disgust on her son's face. Without a word he turned and went upstairs.

"Don't tell me baby William's shocked."

George sighed. "Come on, Iris, I'm shattered, let's just go to bed."

*

Jenny woke with a start; someone was trying to get into bed with her. For a moment she couldn't remember where she was. There was an overpowering stench of beer mixed with stale tobacco. She pulled the blanket around her. She was outraged; Mark had said they would leave her alone.

"Come on, move over, there's room for two. Let's have a good time, don't be shy."

"Go away," Jenny hissed. An arm went round her and she felt herself being pulled towards whoever it was.

"Go away."

"Don't come the innocent with me. You walked in tonight as bold as brass, you were just asking for it."

Jenny realized it was the man who had had his back to her when she first walked into the flat. So he thought she was the party did he, well she'd got news for him.

"I've told you go away."

He tried to kiss her, his hot breath made her want to retch. She pushed him away but he was too strong. What had her mother always said? When threatened by a man knee him in the crutch. It was a shame such sound advice did not take into account being molested whilst wrapped in a cocoon of blanket. But perhaps the blanket would have some use, if she couldn't get out of it he wouldn't be able to get in.

"Go away, Mark said no-one would bother me."

"Well, I'm not Mark and I'm here so stop buggering about."

"I'll scream."

He clamped his hand over her mouth and nose so hard her eyes watered. She tried to push him away with her free hand. He was too strong. She tried to bite him and he grabbed her hair.

"You do that and I'll bite you back, where it shows."

She went limp, too shocked to fight any more. He pulled at the blanket, the bed creaked and groaned. Perhaps someone would hear, perhaps Mark would come. The blanket was yanked off her. This ignorant, drunken slob, his pig of an apology for a man, how dare he? She hit him as hard as she could in the face. As he rolled away from the unexpected blow she wrestled her other arm free. She clenched her fists and punched him again and again, the

30

blows falling on any part of his face and shoulders not protected by his upraised forearm.

"You animal, you drunken, filthy animal, go away, leave me alone."

She sobbed with the exertion. He grunted as he tried to fend off the blows by grabbing her arms. She realised that in the struggle her legs had come free from the blanket. With one final effort she brought her right knee upwards. There was a loud gasp, a thump and he was gone.

Jenny lay still on the bed. Her ragged breathing was drowned by the sound of the man being sick; the sour smell of beer-drenched vomit filled the room.

"You fucking bitch," the voice was thick with venom and pain, "who wants to screw an ugly, evil-looking cow like you anyway?"

Jenny managed a smile in the dark. Well you did for one, she thought.

She heard him shuffle from the room and then there was the heavy click of the bedroom door shutting. She lay in the darkness waiting for her heartbeat to settle. She wondered if he would come back. She grabbed the honour-saving blanket and wrapped herself in it even more tightly. She lay rigid with fear, terrified to go to sleep. At last as dawn was breaking, despite her fear, exhaustion dragged her into a deep sleep.

*

Iris wandered into the kitchen. She looked pale, her eyes were puffy and her hair uncombed. She sat down with a thump as though not in full control of her legs. She lit a cigarette while George poured her a cup of coffee.

"Morning Mother," William said.

She didn't reply.

"I've brought you a little something."

Iris flicked ash from her cigarette and waited as William walked into the hall. George watched her sipping her coffee. Iris sighed.

"Trip went well, had some good news. There's talk about an alternative to this Common Market nonsense."

Iris yawned, business always business.

"A European Free Trade Association, there were hints that it might be set up soon, in Stockholm. That would help things."

William returned and placed a package on the table. Iris put her cigarette down and removed the wrapping paper to reveal a blue box. Her hands were shaking and she wondered if George had noticed. She opened the box and pulled out the tissue wrapped gift, i was a small glass bowl, delicately etched with a tracery of leaves.

"I thought it would look nice on your dressing table."

"Thank you, very nice." She could muster little enthusiasm when she felt so ill. Her head throbbed and she had a sour taste in her mouth She saw William give George a quizzical look.

"I'll give Jenny a ring, let her know I'm back," William said.

*

Chapter 7

Mark knocked then walked into the bedroom. The girl was still asleep, she looked like an Egyptian mummy. The smell of sick was overpowering. He leaned across the bed to open the window. Jenny jumped and opened her eyes very wide.

"You look like a startled rabbit and do you usually wear your shoes in bed?" Mark laughed, "Don't worry; I'm just opening the window to get rid of the smell."

"Where's the other man?"

"Who?"

"I don't know his name but he came in here in the middle of the night, he attacked me, it was awful. I kneed him in the crutch then he was sick. I'm sorry, has he made a mess of your carpet? I'll clean it up."

Mark grinned, "I wondered why Jim looked dog rough, nothing to do with the night of unbridled passion he hinted at."

Jenny gasped, "I wouldn't do that."

"You leave this. I'll let him clear it up later. Would you like some breakfast?"

Jenny unwrapped herself. She was starving hungry after last night.

"I don't believe you, not a single item of clothing removed. What a most determined girl you are."

She grinned at him and her eyes sparkled. A most attractive, determined girl, Mark thought.

"Breakfast, what a good idea," she said, "I'm ravenous."

They sat in the kitchen eating toast and drinking tea. He told her he worked as a trainee estate agent. She talked about what she did at the hospital. He was so easy to talk to.

Jenny was relieved that Jim didn't appear. Although it was Saturday and Jenny didn't have to go to work, she did have to go back to the hostel. She had already missed breakfast without notifying the canteen. She had hoped she and Laura would brazen it out together but if Mark was right Laura had already gone back.

"She left last night, Tony took her back, said she'd see you at the hostel."

Jenny was horrified. If Laura stayed with her friend, she would have gone back to the hostel in time for breakfast. Laura had left without her, what a rotten trick.

"I must go, thanks for being so kind."

"Can I see you again?"

Jenny hesitated, he was so nice and she liked him but what about William?

"I expect you've got a boyfriend already."

"Well, sort of but we're not engaged or anything."

"Would you like to see me, just as a friend?" He smiled, it was a most appealing smile. Jenny thought for a moment, why shouldn't I have a friend who happens to be a man?

"I'll take you out to lunch one Saturday, how's that?"

"O.K. that would be nice."

"I've got to work next Saturday, how about in a fortnight? After all you've slept in my bed; you might as well let me buy you a meal." He winked and Jenny blushed.

"Do you know the Strand Palace Hotel? They have a Salad Bowl Restaurant and you can help yourself to what you want. You can get there by Tube; I'll meet you at 1p.m. We aren't on the phone so I'll just wait for you to arrive."

Jenny felt wonderful, after the horrors of last night the world now seemed a nicer place. "I'll be there."

"If you change your mind, I'll understand but I hope you'll come."

"If I don't sort myself out and get back to the hostel you'll be able to take me to the restaurant yourself. So where am I exactly?"

"Fulham."

"I need to get to Baron's Court."

"I'll walk you to the station; you need the train to Earl's Court then change."

"That's fine, no need to walk me to the station, I'm a big girl now." That was just how she felt, a big grown-up girl who made her own decisions.

"Can I see you down stairs then?"

"Don't worry, I won't run off with the family silver."

He tapped her on the bottom as they walked out of the flat.

"Behave yourself, just because you put Jim in his place doesn't mean you can get uppity."

She giggled, this was fun. She stopped at the front door, uncertain which way to go.

"Down to the end of the road then take the first left, on to the end. That's the main road, the station's about a hundred yards on the right."

"Thanks for everything."

"By the way, you haven't told me your name?"

"Jenny, Jenny Warr, see you in a fortnight."

"I'll look forward to it."

He put his hands on her shoulders and kissed her on the cheek. It felt nice. She strode down the road then turned and waved. Mark was leaning against the door frame watching her.

*

Chapter 8

There was a note in Jenny's pigeon hole from the warden, Miss Pritchard. Jenny took a deep breath, walked to the office door and knocked.

"Come in."

"Did you want to see me, Miss Pritchard?"

The hostel warden removed her glasses and looked at Jenny for a moment.

"Did you forget to indicate on the board that you would be out last night?"

Jenny hung her head; suddenly she was back at school.

"No, I didn't forget, I'm sorry."

"Although I feel responsible for my girls I am not in the habit of checking up on them. However I have had a phone call this morning."

"Oh."

"A young man called, William Martin, your boyfriend I believe."

"Yes." Jenny felt her face flush with embarrassment. He must have come back earlier than planned and would want to know where she had been.

"The world can be a very dangerous place, young girls do not always realize how dangerous." Miss Pritchard paused. "My system is for your protection, I presume you were out all night."

Jenny nodded.

"What you do with your life is your business but, as a courtesy, I wish to be informed if you are going to be away over night. Supposing, heaven forbid, there had been a fire. Firemen could have risked their lives searching for you whilst you were safe elsewhere."

Jenny felt guilt press down on her, this was awful.

"Sometimes girls come here with the idea that they will be able to do what they like. Sometimes they do foolish things and live to regret it. I'm sure your father would not want you to fall into that category and neither would I."

A gentle rebuke, Jenny thought, but more effective than Dad's shouting and nagging. After what had happened last night Jenny wanted to cry; every word Miss Pritchard said was true. She had been foolish to trust someone who thought only of herself. Laura fitted into the dubious category Miss Pritchard had been talking about. She had got away with it this time but might not do so again.

"I'm very sorry; I didn't mean to stay out, I couldn't help it." Jenny's voice wobbled.

"Are you all right?"

"Yes," Jenny whispered.

"Just be careful who you associate with. Now you had better phone your boyfriend, he sounded quite anxious."

*

Laura was in the kitchen talking to Maureen when Jenny reached the third floor.

They were engrossed in discussing the pleasure to be had dancing at the Palais, at least Laura was. Maureen had never been there. Perhaps she would make a more suitable friend, Jenny thought. Then she heard her name mentioned.

"You should have seen the weed Jenny picked up, small, spotty, looked a complete drip."

Jenny bristled with rage, how dare Laura be so dismissive, at least Derek had behaved like a gentleman. Jenny rushed into the kitchen, Maureen smiled and Laura turned round.

"Oh, hello, had a good time?"

It wasn't what Jenny had expected, where was an apology, or some sign of regret?

"No I didn't actually but a fat lot you care." She realized she had raised her voice and Maureen looked nervous.

"I'll see you two later," she said and scuttled away.

Laura turned back to the sink where she was washing underwear; she kept her back to Jenny. The fear, frustration and anger which Jenny had held in check, since last night, exploded. She grabbed Laura's shoulder and spun her round.

"How could you leave me like that, what a rotten trick, how could you?"

Laura shrugged.

"Anyway where did you go? And why didn't you wait for me this morning? Don't you care about anyone but yourself?"

"I only suggested you come with me because you look so damned miserable all the time. I was doing you a favour but don't worry I shan't do that again."

She turned back to the sink and continued rinsing her clothes as though nothing unusual had happened.

"You did me a favour!"

"There's no need to shout, I'm not deaf."

"Who was it that stood you up, the gorgeous Tony wasn't it?"

"No, it wasn't like that, he had to work late."

"I don't believe it, that's what he wants you to think."

Laura turned. There was the slightest frown wrinkling her brow as though Jenny had verbalized something she didn't want to believe.

"Anyway what's all the fuss about, you're all right aren't you?"

"No thanks to you. I was nearly raped last night but don't you give it another thought."

"How was I supposed to know?" Laura stood with her hands on her hips.

"And that isn't all you don't know," Jenny paused, "he's married."

Colour drained from Laura's face. "Who is?"

The words were whispered as though she already knew the answer.

"Tony is."

"How do you know?"

"Mark told me. He's one of the men in the flat, but of course you probably know that since I expect you make a habit of staying out. Anyway, Mark's nice; once you and the wonderful Tony disappeared, Mark let me sleep in his room."

Laura swayed and clung to the sink.

"What's the matter?"

"I'm pregnant."

Jenny put her hand to her mouth and stared. "Are you sure?"

"I've missed two periods already."

"What'll you do?"

"That's why I was so desperate to see him again. I wanted to tell him but I just couldn't." Laura started to cry quietly, unlike previous outbursts Jenny had witnessed, these were genuine tears of grief and fear. Jenny was not sure whether or not to hold Laura, to offer physical comfort. Laura slumped into Jenny's arms and sobbed while Jenny patted her back and wondered what on earth she could say.

"But he'll have to know."

Laura shook her head. "There's no point, I'll just have to get rid of it."

"How?" Jenny's scalp tingled with horror at the matter-of-fact way Laura could suggest the destruction of her own flesh and blood.

"There are ways, what does it matter, what does anything matter? I thought he'd marry me."

Jenny recalled all the veiled warnings her Gran had mouthed, oh so quietly, about girls who got themselves into trouble. So this was it, this was really terrible trouble.

Jenny took a deep breath to steady herself as she relived the events of last night. Had that revolting Jim had his way she could have found herself in the same position in a few months time. What a nightmare that would've been.

"Can't you tell your parents?"

"They're too busy, always too busy. I'm just a nuisance, in the way. I don't think they ever wanted children, too selfish I suppose, they just want each other. They give me money, pat me on the head and tell me to be a good girl. I don't think they've ever really cared."

She's as lonely as I am, Jenny thought. She may have more money but at least I'm not pregnant. All her anger melted away to be replaced by relief. Money or no money she would not want to change places with Laura.

"Let's have a cup of tea," Jenny said, unsure if her presence was a help or a hindrance. She had to phone William but now was not a tactful time to do it.

"I'll put the kettle on," Jenny said but Laura clung to her.

"What am I going to do?" she said.

*

Iris was silent during the short drive home. The visit to her parents had been unsettling.

"You're miles away, my dear."

"I hope Sheila isn't going to do anything rash," Iris said.

"What do you mean?"

"She hasn't seen hide nor hair of this David for years. She'd better be careful."

George said nothing.

"I know you will think I'm being selfish but I don't want my sister to make a mistake."

"Sheila has always struck me as pretty sensible and she does a great job with your parents."

"Yes exactly, and it would be a shame if things had to change, for their sakes."

"I don't think you need worry about that yet. Anyway let's not talk about it now, I want us to have a relaxing evening together. We'll tackle any problems when they arise. By the way has William said anything about this girl of his coming over?"

"No."

"I know he wants us to meet her."

"The girl he met at the swimming baths?"

"Yes, I think so."

*

Jenny dialled William's number. She had her fingers crossed, hoping that he and not one of his parents would answer. She was in luck.

"Where've you been?" William asked.

"Went to the Palais with a girl from the hostel, she asked me to. She didn't want to go on her own."

"So what're you doing tonight, gadding off somewhere?"

"Oh no, let's meet but don't forget I have to be back by half past ten."

"That doesn't give us much scope. We wouldn't even be able to go to the cinema unless we went in the afternoon. Any pubs near you? We could go for a drink I suppose"

Jenny sensed his lack of enthusiasm but dared not flout hostel rules again.

"Would you mind coming to the hostel?"

"If you've got to be back so early, let's meet at half past six."

"Lovely, I'm sure we'll find a nice pub somewhere."

"Let's hope so."

Jenny's feeling of anxiety persisted but at least she was seeing him. Perhaps he was just tired after the business trip. She would ask him about how it went, show lots of interest, which was what girlfriends were supposed to do. As she walked upstairs she thought about all that had happened. How would Laura get rid of the baby? Please God, don't let me ever get into that situation, she thought.

The streets of Baron's Court were dingy and rundown but Jenny and William did find a cosy-looking pub not far from the hostel. Jenny felt nervous. She hadn't been to pubs often and the frosted glass that stopped people looking in suggested to her that what went on in such places must be disreputable. William came

40

back from the bar with a soft drink for her and a pint of beer for himself.

"So what's with the dancing?"

Part of Jenny wanted to tell him everything, all about Jim but then what? Should Mark be mentioned? She thought that might not be wise.

"It was just an evening out, nothing special, but we were too late to get back before the door was locked so we stayed with some friends of Laura's, that's the girl I went with."

"So you can stay out."

"Yes, but we should have let Miss Pritchard know we weren't coming back and we didn't. She was very nice about it but I mustn't do it again. Anyway, what about Stockholm, did you have a good time?"

William didn't seem too keen to talk about it, claimed it was a bit boring really. That's a surprise, Jenny thought, I can hardly wait to get a passport, surely travel can't be that bad?

"Was it just business meetings all the time?"

"Sort of but Dad arranged a guide to show me some of the sights, a girl called Berthe."

"Oh, a beautiful blonde, I suppose."

"She was O.K."

William pulled a small package out of his pocket.

"I thought you might like this," he said.

It was a small, wooden horse that had been decorated with a pattern of flowers.

"How lovely," Jenny said, "I shall call him Alfie and put him on my chest of drawers."

William glanced at his watch. "Suppose we could take a stroll back. At least at this time I will have no trouble getting the Tube back home."

"Have you spoken to your parents yet?"

"It's tricky with Mum but Dad said he'd have a word, don't worry I haven't forgotten. He thought some time next weekend might be O.K."

They walked back arm in arm. The soft evening light muted the stark brickwork of the cramped terraced houses and their feet echoed in the quiet streets. He kissed her at the hostel gates but Jenny felt uneasy as she went up to her room.

*

41

Chapter 9

Barbara Anderson checked her hair and make-up, not too bad, she thought. She heard a knock at the downstairs front door, it would be Gordon and Joan to take her round to Charles Warr's flat.

She had met him one evening in the 'Beehive' when she had gone for a drink with Gordon and Joan. Barbara had found him interesting, intelligent, handsome but decidedly prickly. She recalled his embarrassment when he admitted his home was council property, not his own. She had told him that she too rented her flat and was perfectly happy with the arrangement.

Mr. Charles Warr was very conscious of his image, she thought, she was curious to see his home. Barbara had been tempted to ask her friends about Charles but then decided to make her own judgment

When they arrived the door opened so swiftly that Barbara wondered if Charles had been watching from the window. They were welcomed, with exuberant courtesy, to a small flat that was cosy, unpretentious, with good solid utility furniture, probably bought after the war. Barbara was surprised to see a tablecloth laid out on the floor with cushions spread around. Charles looked nervous.

"What the bloody hell is this Charlie, we could have brought our own chairs; you only had to ask." Gordon grinned as he spoke. Barbara suspected Charles took a lot of teasing from Gordon and probably didn't like it.

"Thought we'd have a picnic...... like Arabs in the desert."

He switched on a reading lamp and turned off the central light.

"That's better," he said, "I would've had some candles but I forgot, anyway wax always makes such a mess."

"We won't be able to see what we're eating," Joan said.

"Might be as well," Gordon replied.

Barbara watched Charles and noticed his face flush. Not much of a sense of humour there, she thought.

"I'll get you a drink," Charles said.

He seemed to be on edge and Barbara wondered if he was always so nervous, "Can I help?"

"Certainly not, you're my guest. Now come on Joan, a glass of wine, I've got a bottle of white, you too Barbara?" He rushed from the room. "Beer for you, Gordon," he called, from the safety of his kitchen.

"I didn't expect this," Joan said, "wouldn't have worn such a tight skirt."

"If we're supposed to be Arabs, perhaps he's tracked down some sheep's eyes."

Joan gasped, "Gordon, you aren't serious are you?"

"Of course he isn't, come on Joan hoist your skirt up and sprawl provocatively, like me. Make the poor man relax a bit." Barbara settled herself on the cushions and smiled. "This will be fun."

Charles returned with brimming glasses. He seemed relieved to see the women seated. "I can easily get the table out if you would prefer it, won't take a minute."

"Nonsense," Barbara said, "it's the most original dinner party I've ever been to."

Charles smiled.

"A drink, my man," Barbara clicked her fingers and Charles laughed.

That's better, she thought.

"Food's nearly ready, I didn't want to do anything fancy so I hope bangers and mash is all right with everyone."

"No sheep's eyes, old chap, what a disappointment."

"Gordon, that's enough, there's no way I'd eat anything like that," Joan said.

"Cheers," said Barbara raising her glass.

"There's lemon meringue pie and cheese and biscuits afterwards. Is that O.K.?"

There were murmurs of approval and Barbara watched the tension in Charles's face lessen, how awful to be so anxious all the time.

*

"But you'll have to tell him," Jenny said, "he's just as responsible as you are."

Laura chewed her lip, clasped and unclasped her hands.

"How can I get in touch with him?"

"Why not go to the flat and see if Mark can pass on a message."

Laura thought for a moment. "Will you come with me?"

"I can't, I'm seeing William. It was bad enough explaining why I wasn't in when he called. I can't alter things now."

The look on Laura's face warned her not to add that she would soon be meeting William's parents.

"Go today, you can't just do nothing, you never know things might work out."

Laura got off her bed and reached for her jacket.

"Good luck; let me know how it goes. I'd better be off as well."

The two girls faced each other, both apprehensive about the coming evening but, Jenny thought, our reasons could not be more different. She patted Laura on the shoulder and left.

*

Iris and George were watching the early evening news. Iris was unconcerned about this meeting with William's girlfriend, what troubled her was that her beloved Freddie, home from school, had chosen to spend the evening with some of his friends.

Iris was hurt.

"Anything I can do in the kitchen?" George asked.

Iris glanced at him; he didn't usually offer to help her.

"No, everything's fine. You seem very anxious to impress this girl; shouldn't she be setting out to impress us?"

George shrugged, "I just want William to be proud of us."

Iris raised an eyebrow and poured herself another sherry before strolling into the kitchen. She heard William's voice and walked back into the hall.

Iris had assumed that Jenny would be small, blonde and pretty. She was, therefore, surprised to see a tall, dark-haired girl being ushered in. She seemed shy, gauche and certainly not pretty in a conventional sense. Iris wondered what the attraction was. George came into the hall and after stilted introductions Iris left George to offer drinks while she checked on the meal.

With some prompting from William, Jenny talked about her job and the hostel. Iris stirred the gravy and wondered what kind of parents allowed their daughter to leave home for a place that sounded dreadful. Pauses in the conversation lengthened until George suggested that William showed Jenny the garden.

Iris joined George at the French window.

"A rather unprepossessing girl, don't you think?"

George shrugged, "Maybe, but she's got a brain, you don't work in a laboratory without some scientific knowledge."

"So you think it's her brain William's attracted to?"

"I've no idea, but I like her straightforwardness, even if she hasn't got your poise and self-confidence." He put his arm round

44

Iris. "The girl's O.K. I prefer someone like her to some sophisticated little piece with a shallow personality."

"So if a girl's got poise and self-confidence, like me I think you said, she's bound to be shallow."

"Look, love, I know you're upset that Freddie isn't here this evening but please don't let's argue. Don't spoil things."

"Well all I can say is she could have made more of an effort." Iris turned and went back to the kitchen, George followed her.

"It doesn't make you feel old, does it, having your son interested in a young woman?"

Iris stirred the gravy with vigour. "Don't be so silly."

"Just think, you could have a lot of fun helping that young lady make something of herself. She could learn a lot from you."

Iris felt George's arms slide round her waist. What was he suggesting, was Jenny to be a daughter substitute? Of course he was right; there was plenty of room for improvement. Iris pulled away from George and stared at him.

"Isn't that what her mother should be doing?"

"I get the feeling she has little contact with either of her parents, why else is she living in a hostel?"

Iris continued to stir the gravy. With George away so much it might be nice to have some female companionship.

"If William is serious about this girl, shouldn't we meet her parents anyway?"

"I think it is early days for that, they are both very young." George sniffed the air.

"I think this meal is just about ready if the aroma is anything to go by. Shall I call the young lovers in? I think they're still in the garden."

"Lovers! I hope you are joking, I don't fancy being a grandmother yet."

*

Laura rang the doorbell again but still no reply, a wasted journey with nothing sorted. What on earth was she going to do? She stepped back onto the pavement and looked up, absolutely no sign of life. She turned and walked slowly back to the station. Once on the main road she became caught up in the early evening crowd of couples and groups of people. There were all on their way somewhere, to have a good time, Saturday night fun. Such fun would be impossible for her once the pregnancy became obvious. She must do something.

45

Deep in thought, she took little notice of the people approaching her, she almost bumped into them. It was Tony with a woman, could this be his wife Laura wondered. Mark was with them. The woman was pretty and she smiled at Laura who was unable to move. She saw panic in Tony's eyes.

The crowd surged around the group as Laura stood in their way. For a split second she wanted to point a finger at Tony and scream to the world, 'I'm carrying his bastard'. That would wipe the smile off his wife's face. Mark grasped Laura's arm.

"Laura, how nice to see you, what are you doing in this neck of the woods?"

Laura opened her mouth but no words came. Her brain whirred. She wanted to lash out, to hurt Tony as he had hurt her but what good would that do? She must clutch the lifeline Mark had thrown her. She must hide her feelings as Tony's unborn child was hidden.

"I was supposed to meet a friend but she didn't turn up."

"Oh, what a shame," the pretty woman said. She looked from Tony to Mark.

"How about spending the evening with us, if these two don't mind? I'm Maggie, by the way, and this is my husband, Tony, Mark you already know."

Laura wanted to laugh, to throw back her head and laugh until her tears flowed.

"Yes, why not?" said Mark, "we are just going to have a bit of supper and a drink at my flat. You'd be welcome."

Tony said nothing and avoided eye contact with Laura. I have become invisible, she thought. They strolled back the way Laura had come. She must try to have a word with Tony alone, but how? Mark linked her arm through his. She wondered if he had guessed the reason she was there. Jenny was right, he was nice and he was doing his best to help. If she had no chance to speak to Tony, she would leave a message with Mark.

She watched Tony and Maggie out of the corner of her eyes and knew, without a doubt, that Tony would never leave her. Why should he? He had a pretty wife who seemed to adore him and a willing mistress, wasn't that every man's dream? What a fool she had been.

She thought about the off-hand way she had talked to Jenny about getting rid of the baby. She had spoken as she did because she had never believed that was how it would end. Now she knew. There would be no happy ending, this tiny life must be dragged from her and the sooner the better.

As they walked down the road Laura tried to join in the conversation, she must present no threat. She sensed that if she were not careful Tony would disappear from her life without a qualm. She must get his help or turn to her parents; that thought filled her with dread.

They clumped up the three flights of uncarpeted stairs. The other men who shared the flat were out, presumably on a normal Saturday night booze-up. Mark put on some music.

"Make yourselves at home. I'll rustle up some grub and a drink, give us a hand will you, Laura?"

Once in the kitchen he turned to her.

"I assume it wasn't a coincidence that you were near here."

Laura shook her head, "I've got to speak to Tony."

"I don't think tonight's the night."

"It's vital, please." Laura's eyes filled with tears.

"Be careful, he can be a hard-faced sod when pushed."

"If I can't speak to him tonight will you give him a message?"

Mark nodded. "It doesn't take an Einstein to work out your problem. Now put on a brave face, we have supper to prepare."

The evening was a nightmare. Laura tried to be natural but it was impossible, everything she said sounded artificial, contrived or downright stupid. She knew she was drinking too much but what did that matter? Perhaps it would solve the problem.

She knew alcohol wasn't good for pregnant women and she had heard that gin and hot baths were used to start a miscarriage. She couldn't manage those right now but perhaps too much wine would do the trick.

She looked at her watch; she would have to go soon otherwise she would be locked out. Of course there was always Pat, round the corner, she was a good sort. If necessary she could always sleep there again, on the floor, good old Pat, yes that was what she would do. Just hang on a bit longer. She had been to the toilet twice, surely Maggie would have to go soon; she must have the bladder of a camel. She'd be bound to go before she and Tony left. Just hang on a bit longer.

The room seemed to be moving from side to side. Perhaps she should eat a bit more, soak up the booze. She felt sick. No, more food was not a good idea. She looked at her companions and

47

didn't know whether to laugh or cry. Maggie was chatting away without a care in the world and Tony hung on her every word. The adoring, faithful, model husband, what a hypocrite, what a sod he was. I've had a lucky escape, Laura thought, at least I will have once I've got rid of this baby.

Laura felt a rush of shame, women were supposed to cherish babies not murder them but what else could she do? He'll find someone else after me, he'll leave a trail of broken hearts and shattered dreams and none of it will touch him. He'll go home tonight to a nice house and a nice wife, because she was nice, Laura conceded. Would Maggie ever know the truth or would she remain secure in married respectability?

Laura sat up very straight. Maggie should know, she was a decent woman who deserved better, she should be told and I should be the one to tell her, Laura decided. I will save her from this selfish, deceitful man; she'll thank me in the end. It is my duty, one woman to another. Laura's mouth was full of words, hateful, spiteful words all jostling to get out but as she opened her mouth to speak Maggie stood up.

"I think it's time we made a move, darling, I'll just go to the bathroom."

"Down the corridor, third on the right," Mark said.

Once Maggie had left the room there was an electrified silence. Tony had half-turned away from Laura so she couldn't see his face. He started to speak to Mark, his voice low. Laura leaned across and almost fell off her chair. She grabbed his shirt sleeve.

"I've got to talk to you, please, I've got to see you, it's urgent."

He looked at her with distaste and pulled his arm away.

"I'm pregnant, don't you understand?" She swallowed hard, the nausea was getting worse.

"What's that to do with me?"

"You're the father." She heard the sound of the toilet flushing. Tony leaned towards her. His bright, blue eyes that had once made her tremble were hard and angry.

"Prove it," he hissed.

Just then Maggie walked back into the room.

*

48

Chapter 10

Barbara undressed slowly, easing her skirt past her overfilled stomach. Charles believed in making sure his guests didn't go hungry. He was not an easy man, Barbara thought, and she wondered if huge portions were his way of expressing his feelings. There was no doubt that Charles was physically attractive and a charming host, if somewhat eccentric. Did she like him enough to continue with a friendship? She wasn't sure.

She enjoyed her life, solitude held no fears, the library work engrossed her and she loved her flat. Did she want anything to upset that? Charles was intriguing but was that contrived? She had sorted out the question of his being an unmarried father, a silly expression that invited enquiry. She also sensed the pain his divorce had caused. But there was his daughter to consider; perhaps he didn't know how lucky he was.

Placing her dirty clothes in the laundry basket she then cleaned her teeth, washed her face and looking in the bathroom mirror said, "Now, my girl, regard it as a challenge, ask him over for a meal."

She slid into bed and, as always, lifted the silver framed picture from her bedside table and kissed the image. "Goodnight, my darling."

*

George was already in bed when Iris entered the bedroom.

"That meal was excellent, as always," George said, "well done, my dear."

Iris sat at the dressing table and creamed her face. She could see George's reflection in her mirror. His dark hair had thinned to a shiny, single layer that he combed into place each morning. He had the well-padded look of the successful business man.

She remembered how slim and athletic he had been all those years ago. We're both going down hill, she thought.

"Quite came out of herself after a glass of wine, didn't she?"

Iris turned, "I still think William could do better."

"Good heavens, I don't suppose he intends to marry her. She's just a girlfriend; it may not last five minutes. How many boyfriends did you have before you met me?"

"Not enough."

"Ouch, that's below the belt."

"She looked so dowdy."

"Now come on, Iris, she explained that her wage at the hospital was poor."

"So why doesn't she get financial support from her parents?"

"I don't know."

"It all sounds a bit odd to me."

Iris removed her dressing gown and got into bed. They were propped up on pillows, side by side, sipping their nightcaps. Physically we are together, Iris thought, but our emotions are worlds apart. She heard a noise downstairs and sat up straight.

"Quick, that's the key in the lock, William's back." Iris emptied her whisky glass in one swallow, turned off her light and lay down.

"Goodnight," she said.

George sighed, "I don't know what all the rush is about."

"I don't want William to think we've been waiting up for him."

She watched as he drained his glass and switched off his light. She felt his arm move across her body and moved away from him, she wasn't in the mood for that. George turned and hunched his back towards her.

It was the end of another unsettling day. Freddie preferred his friends to her and William had picked up a waif and stray. Then there was the business of Shirley and her long-lost boyfriend. She stared at the ceiling; the hum of traffic was soothing and the pattern of lights from passing cars had a hypnotic effect. Sleep wrapped itself around her and she sighed.

*

Mark escorted Maggie and Tony downstairs, on his return he realized Laura was in the bathroom. He listened, with resignation, to the sounds of Laura emptying her stomach. This flat seems destined to smell of other people's vomit, he thought.

He cleared plates and glasses. He'd let her get it over with, no girl wanted an audience in such circumstances. He carried the dirty crockery through to the kitchen and started on the washing up. The noises from the bathroom had stopped.

"Laura," he shouted, "would a cup of black coffee help?"

No reply, he shrugged his shoulders and continued clearing things away. After a while he was aware of movement behind him, Laura stood in the doorway, her face a dingy green.

"Do you feel as awful as you look?"

Laura nodded.

"For heaven's sake, sit down before you fall down. Do you want me to call you a taxi?"

"Please."

"Won't you be locked out of the hostel by now?"

"It's all right; I can stay with a friend who lives nearby."

Mark felt relief, get her a taxi and that was his good deed for the day.

"I've got to speak to Tony about...." Her voice trailed away.

"What are you going to do? He'll never leave Maggie."

Laura began to cry. Dear God, Mark thought, this good deed is turning into a full scale mercy mission.

"I'll have to speak to him; I just don't know what to do. He'll have to help me, after all it is his no matter what he says."

"Listen Laura, take it from me you are unlikely to see Tony again, not after tonight. He wouldn't dare take the risk."

Laura began to wail and moan. He put his hand on her shoulder.

"Crying isn't going to help; do you want me to speak to him?"

"Please, yes please, I would be so grateful."

Mark felt irritated by the whole thing; it wasn't his problem so how come he had landed in the thick of it?

"Jenny said you were nice." Laura gave a watery smile.

Jenny, he thought, let's hope she doesn't behave like this, histrionics I can do without.

"Remind her of our date," he said.

Laura's face crumpled, "She didn't say she was going out with you too. She's already got one boyfriend."

"I know, she told me. I'm just taking her out for lunch, as a friend."

Laura pulled a face. Spoilt that was Laura's trouble, Mark thought, used to getting her own way. With luck this business with Tony should cure her of that.

"Come on, it's time to get you a taxi. The others will be back soon; you wouldn't want them to see you like this would you?"

At such a blatant appeal to her vanity Laura stood, patted her hair into some semblance of order and smoothed her clothes.

Mark grinned at her. "That's better. Now I'll give Tony a ring in a day or two, take him for a beer. I'll do what I can but I'm not promising anything. What will you do if he won't help?"

She whimpered, "Go to my parents, they'll go mad. They would never forgive me."

51

"You'll just have to trust that I can come up with something, won't you?" He hustled her out of the flat, tired of the whole business.

"We'll walk up to the main road and see if there are any taxis about."

As they started down the stairs they heard the front door bang. That was followed by raucous laughter and a crash that suggested someone had fallen up the stairs. The noise got louder as Laura and Mark went down the first flight. As they turned for the next flight they saw Jim and the other flat-mates on their way up.

"Well, well what have we here," Jim said, "poaching Tony's property?"

"Shut up, Jim," Mark said.

"Oh dear me," Jim held up his hands in mock horror, "what will the great lover, Tony, say when he finds his little chick has strayed?"

"For Christ's sake, Jim, piss off. You are not even slightly funny."

"Pardon me, your honour," Jim turned to the others, 'the great and mighty Saint Mark strikes again." He bowed low, wobbled and fell over. "Pardon us miserable sinners." He turned to Laura. "Let me guess, lover boy has stood you up but Uncle Mark has kissed you better."

Laura started to cry. Mark grabbed her hand and dragged her downstairs.

"You really are a prize prick, Jim," Mark shouted as they ran down the last flight of stairs.

"Maybe," Jim replied, "at least I've got one."

Mark and Laura left the house to the sound of drunken laughter.

*

The taxi pulled away leaving Laura standing under a defunct street lamp. The fare had taken the last of her money and she had no idea how she would manage for the rest of the month but that was not her main problem at the moment. The immediate question was where was she going to sleep? She shivered.

The night was cold and after being so sick she felt light-headed. She looked at the house where Pat lived on the second floor. All was in darkness. She hesitated, reluctant to ring the bell. She felt a terrible shame at the way she had behaved with Tony.

Meeting Maggie had been a shock; she was so nice and didn't deserve to have an awful man as Tony for a husband. If Tony could treat his wife so badly he would, without a qualm, deny all responsibility for the child she, Laura, was carrying.

She sat on the top step and leaned against the front door. She wrapped her arms tightly around her body, hugging what warmth there was to her chest. She needed time, time to think, to sort out what she was going to do. Ever since she realized she was pregnant she had assumed that Tony would marry her.

No more boring jobs as a shop assistant, she would be a wife and mother in a nice house with a loving husband. It was incredible that she could have been so naïve. Of course there would be no wedding, no happy ever after, no Tony.

In fact would she have wanted to go on with Tony now she knew what he was like? How many lies had he told Maggie? How had he managed to get out in the evenings? A lie, his whole relationship with that nice woman was based on lies.

Laura shivered again, what was she going to do? The question had gone round and round in her head like a gramophone needle stuck in a groove, round and round until her head ached. I'm eighteen and my life should be beginning, if I have this baby everything will change for ever.

What would Mum and Dad say? She remembered the dreadful rows she had had with them both - particularly Mum. What had she said to them when she stomped out? Terrible things about not needing them, she could manage. They were only trying to stop her having fun. They were old, past it, they were jealous. She had screamed at them. It had been then that Laura had seen the look of deep hurt on her mother's face. They would have the last laugh now. She wondered who would be first to say 'I told you so'.

Fun that was what she had wanted but now, sitting in the dark, she knew she wanted to go home. She must sort out the problem of the baby first; her parents must never know. She got herself into this mess; she must get herself out of it. She sighed and leaned her head against the rough wooden door. A wave of peace washed over her and looking up at the clear, night sky the millions of stars, pinpricks in dark velvet, made her feel very small.

Perhaps once she had got rid of the baby she would be able to make a fresh start. She marvelled at how once the decision was made, mental turmoil vanished.

"I may not know how I'm going to do it," she whispered to herself, "but at least I know what I'm going to do."

She put her hand to her mouth, shocked that she had spoken her thoughts out loud. All she had to sort out now was whether or not to rouse Pat. She did not seem to have any alternative. She stood and with stiff legs walked down the steps to look again at Pat's window. No chance she would be awake now if she hadn't been earlier. Perhaps she had gone out for the evening or, worse still, was stopping out over night.

"Hello, girlie."

The voice made Laura jump, a large man was meandering down the street towards her. The absence of street lighting outside Pat's house made it difficult to judge the appearance and mood of the stranger. The light further down the street outlined his shape and cast a long, menacing shadow. Laura felt a tremor of anxiety, should she stand her ground or run? If she ran, where would she run to? She did not relish waking Miss Pritchard at this time of night.

"What's the matter, girlie, nowhere to sleep?"

"Go away."

"Now don't be like that, I'm only being friendly."

"Leave me alone."

Now he was beside her and the smell of beer almost knocked her over. She felt sweat break out on her forehead and upper lip even though she was shivering. After all she'd been through tonight, this was too much.

"I'll look after you, dearie, come home with me. A nice looking girl like you should be tucked up in bed." He put his arm round her shoulders but she knocked it away with a clenched fist.

"Don't you understand? Leave me alone, just leave me alone."

She could hear the panic in her voice and wondered if she should scream and maybe get help from the occupants of one of the silent, dark houses. The man looked puzzled as he swayed in his heavy work boots.

"Want a fag, girlie? I only want to be friendly, have a fag."

Laura could stand no more. She turned and ran up the three steps and jammed her finger on Pat's bell push. The man stood watching her. With an unsteady hand he got a cigarette from a crumpled packet and after several attempts managed to light it.

Laura kept her back to him reasoning that if she didn't make eye contact he would leave her alone. She listened to the shrill insistent note of the bell as it echoed in the hallway. Please God, she sobbed, let Pat be at home.

She sensed rather than heard the man come closer. Another sob caught in her throat, "Please answer the door," she whispered. Just as she thought she would have to run for it she heard the window above her being thrown open.

"What the hell's going on? Who is it?"

It was Pat's boyfriend, John. Relief made Laura's knees tremble.

"It's Laura I'm so sorry to wake you up, please let me in."

"For Christ's sake," John said and the window was slammed down.

The man behind Laura went back, with hesitant feet down the steps and shuffled off along the road. When John opened the door Laura fell into his arms.

*

Chapter 11

Sunshine streamed through Jenny's window. She lay in bed watching the clouds and reliving the previous evening which hadn't been as dreadful as she had feared. Mr. Martin had been kind and made her feel welcome. Mrs. Martin was something else entirely. Jenny had sensed an unspoken hostility.

William had warned her that his mother was difficult and hinted at a problem. Jenny wondered if it were drink because Mrs. Martin had certainly drunk more than anyone else.. After her experiences with step-father, Alec, she was sensitive to what alcohol could do. Drunken behaviour frightened her, it made people unpredictable.

She looked at her watch, once again she would have to hurry or miss breakfast. She felt happy because William had said if it was a fine day he would call for her. They would go for a walk, what a nice way to spend a Sunday afternoon. She rose, put on her dressing gown and checked the bathrooms, both were occupied. That was the trouble with living with so many girls.

At the sound of footsteps she turned to see Laura shuffling up the corridor. Jenny was shocked by what she saw; Laura had aged years overnight. The vibrant, pretty girl was dishevelled and there was a heaviness in her step that was not caused just by lack of sleep.

"You O.K?"

"I've just got back; I stayed at Pat's place."

"Oh," Jenny heard a bolt slide back and a girl emerged from the nearest bathroom.

"I must have a wash or I shall be late for breakfast, have you eaten?"

Laura shook her head. "Are you going out today?"

"William said he'd call for me later, why?"

"Will you come to my room after you've had breakfast?"

Jenny nodded. She didn't really want to become too involved with such an awful situation. As she ate her cereals and toast she listened to the chatter of the girls crowding the dining room apparently without a care in the world. When she returned to Laura's room the girl was slumped on her bed.

"I met Tony's wife last night."

Jenny gasped. "You didn't go to his house, did you?"

"No, I went to Mark's, as we agreed. I didn't know he had

invited Tony and Maggie round. I met them when I was on my way back here after I couldn't get an answer at the flat."

"What in the street?"

"Yes, I made some excuse but Tony's wife suggested I spend the evening with them. She's really kind. When I had a chance I told Tony about the baby," Laura faltered, "he told me to prove it was his."

Jenny took Laura's hand, "I'm so sorry."

"I'll have to have an abortion, that's all there is to it."

"But how, it's illegal isn't it?"

"Mark said he would speak to Tony, get some money and find out what I have to do."

"How much will it cost?"

"More than I've got, I spent the rest of this month's money on a taxi last night."

"I wish I could help but I can only just manage myself."

Laura gave a weak smile and squeezed Jenny's hand. "I suppose I could always tell my parents."

Jenny watched as Laura struggled to hold back tears. Suddenly she leapt to her feet, "I'm going to be sick," and she raced from the room.

Morning sickness, Jenny thought, the baby is making its presence felt, such a tiny speck of life that would soon be disposed of.

Laura returned ashen-faced and shivering.

"Would some water help?"

"Please," Laura said, "you were right about one thing, Mark is nice. He asked me to remind you of your date."

Jenny blushed, would Laura think William was being deceived? She hurried to get the water. There were so many things Jenny wanted to ask as the two girls sat side by side on Laura's bed. It was obvious that Laura's immediate future would be traumatic; Jenny did not want to make matters worse.

"Is there anything I can do?"

"Not really but thanks anyway."

Jenny stood up, "I'm sorry but I've got to go."

Laura smiled. "Thanks, I'm sorry too but it is my own fault, I know that now; make sure you don't do the same."

*

Mark had had a restless night. Once he had got Laura into a taxi he had been faced by the drunken outbursts of his flat mates.

Finally they staggered off to bed leaving the flat in chaos; he was sick of the whole business. He wasn't a prude but he seemed to spend far too much of his time clearing up after other people.

The vague unease and discontent that had dogged his thoughts for months seemed to crystallize. He did not like living in London, it was too impersonal, too big. He was a Mancunian born and bred and that was where his roots were.

When he had moved down to the Big Smoke two years ago a group of friends had come with him, all intent on making their fortunes. He smiled at their naivety. They had fallen by the wayside and returned to their families. Now only he was left.

As his friends had gone home they had been replaced by young men who had answered the cards he had placed in local shop windows. He had nothing in common with any of them, least of all Jim. Mark felt engulfed by homesickness, he was a city boy but London wasn't his city.

It was a year since Dad died and Mark had offered to return to Manchester then but Mum had insisted he must get on with his life, she would manage. It seemed ironic that it was Mark, not his mother, who felt lost and lonely, lonely in a crowd, the worst loneliness of all.

He decided to get up and have breakfast before the drinkers roused themselves. He went into the kitchen which was littered with mugs, plates and saucers full of dog-ends. At least the sun was shining and the clear, bright light echoed the clarity of his thoughts. He would ask for a transfer to Manchester.

During his time at Rainham's Estate Agents the company had done well. There had been talk recently of opening one or two new branches in the regions. He was sure the North West was being considered, it could be Manchester or maybe Liverpool. He would speak to his boss on Monday. He felt light-headed, the decision was made and it felt as though a boulder had rolled off his back; to go home was the right decision.

Unlike his old mates he wasn't going back with his tail between his legs. He was going back with a job, a job with prospects in an area he knew well. It was the logical thing to do and his mother would be delighted. He looked at the debris around him and laughed, he would have to clear it up but he hoped it would be for the last time. He wrinkled his nose at the pungent smell that was a mixture of stale beer and B.O. He stacked the dirty crockery and admitted to himself that he had long been irritated by his flat-mates filthy habits. Now, at last, the end was in sight. He put the kettle on the stove and whilst he waited for it to boil started on the washing up.

What must he do before he left London? He felt a tremor of anxiety. It's all very well for me to make up my mind but suppose the boss doesn't agree.

"Sod it," he said, "I'm going anyway, feeling as I do this morning, it must be the right decision."

"Bad sign talking to yourself." Jim lounged in the doorway.

"Only person here I can get a sensible answer from."

"Charming." Jim wandered off muttering about sanctimonious sods who should stay where they belong, in the sticks.

Jim's comment reinforced Mark's resolve. Then he remembered Laura and the promise he had made. He'd call Tony on Tuesday. He leaned against the sink and gazed out of the window, how had he got involved and what was he going to say? It was none of his business. Tony could tell him to push off but a promise was a promise, he could only do his best. The whole squalid business with Tony and Laura epitomized all he disliked about London.

Of course the same thing happened in Manchester but he had never been aware of it. Maybe that was the difference, in Manchester he had lived with his parents in a decent, residential area. Here he was a tenant in a rented property with a high turnover of occupants. People had no roots, no standards, no responsibility, they were ships that passed in the night making casual contact before going on their way.

The next problem was Jenny; how would he get in touch with her? Did she live in the hostel with Laura or was she a friend from somewhere else? He couldn't remember what she had said. They had joked and talked nonsense and it had all been so natural and relaxed. The date must go ahead as planned; he really wanted to see Jenny again.

If he did go to Manchester, no, when he went to Manchester they could keep in touch, write to each other. If they hit it off she could always visit. He stopped. I'm day-dreaming, he thought; don't get carried away because it all might come to nothing.

*

William and Jenny sat on the grass and watched couples and families strolling round the park enjoying the warm sunshine. Children were running about, playing games and having fun.

Perhaps one day William and I will have children to bring to the park on sunny days.

"Dad's taken Mum to the Dorchester for lunch, a treat for all the cooking she did yesterday." He stroked Jenny's arm.

Isn't that what housewives were supposed to do, Jenny wondered, particularly when they didn't go out to work.

"Didn't you want to go?"

"Not really, all you can get out of her at the moment is Freddie this and Freddie that. I'm sick of it. Fred's all right but the way Mum goes on you'd think the sun shone out of his bottom."

Jenny looked at him and wondered if that was jealousy speaking.

"What's he like, your brother, do you look alike?"

"No, he's more like Dad; I take after Mum's family."

Strange, Jenny thought and let her mind drift. It was an irony that Mrs. Martin appeared to worship the son who looked like the husband she didn't seem to get on with. Yet Dad and I don't get on because I remind him of the wife he divorced. The difference was the Martins were still married. Perhaps Freddie reminds her of her husband when he was younger, when they did get on. Relationships were a minefield.

"But what's he like as a person?"

"Oh, I don't know, he's just my little brother."

"Will I meet him?"

"I expect so; he's coming home at the end of the week. That's what rattled Mum. Her precious boy decided to spend the first week of his holiday with one of his boarding school chums. She expected him to come rushing home to her."

The bitterness in William's words was clear. Jenny watched his expression and wondered if it was he who needed his mother's devotion. He resented Freddie. Perhaps Mrs. Martin felt she could afford to be less careful with her treatment of William. Maybe she knew he craved her love and attention. Perhaps it was Freddie she wasn't sure of.

With a sudden movement William stood and stretching out his hand helped Jenny to her feet.

"Let's walk."

Jenny assumed the subject of Freddie was now closed.

"Dad wants me to go to Stockholm soon."

"For a visit?"

"No, to stop."

Jenny's heart lurched. "How long for?"

"Not long, I don't suppose." He squeezed her hand. "I'll have to get some orders first," he paused, "I don't think I'm cut out to be a salesman."

He looked at her and smiled. "You're a nice kid," he said, "come on lets have an ice-cream before I take you back."

Jenny wasn't sure she wanted to be a nice kid; it reminded her of when Dad came home on leave and took her out. The day always ended with ice-cream or sticky cakes and then, like today, she was taken back to wherever she lived at the time.

*

Iris phoned her parents' number as soon as she and George returned from the Dorchester. It was so much easier than going round. She couldn't bear the cloying atmosphere of ill-health. She had often wondered if multiple sclerosis was hereditary but had never dared ask. Supposing she ended up bed-ridden, reliant on others for everything; she must not think like that. Sheila answered the call.

"Dad and I were just talking about you, wondered when you were coming round."

Iris gripped the receiver, disapproval from her kid sister again. How she hated it.

"I may not have a job but I do have a family you know."

There was a moment's silence.

"Mum's not too good today, had a bad night and I can't get her to eat much."

"Have you called the doctor?"

"Not yet."

"Look Sheila, why do you think we pay for Mum to have a private doctor?"

"Yes, I know but maybe it isn't the doctor she wants to see."

Iris sighed. "Any news on the boyfriend front?"

"Who, David?"

"How many boyfriends are there?"

"He's coming over."

"Oh." Iris tried to control her feelings of unease. "Where will he stop?"

"Here. Dad's been great; he's offered to sleep on the put-you-up downstairs so David can have Mum and Dad's room."

"Be careful."

"Why?"

"Just be careful, don't encourage him too much, too soon."

"Don't worry, Iris, he's only a friend, I am allowed to have friends you know."

"Yes, well, tell Mum and Dad we'll try to get round soon."

Thoroughly irritated, Iris went upstairs to have an afternoon rest.

*

Jenny walked through the hostel hallway just as Miss Pritchard came out of her office.

"I'm glad I've seen you," Miss Pritchard said, "your father has been on the phone."

"Is something wrong?"

"No, I don't think so; he was just calling to see how you'd settled in."

Jenny smiled, perhaps he does care, she thought, but he'd rather I didn't know about it.

"I think he was calling from a call box. Anyway he was cut off before I could tell him much."

"He doesn't have a phone, says he doesn't think anyone should be able to interrupt what he's doing."

Miss Pritchard laughed. "Sounds like a good idea."

"Did he want to speak to me?"

"Don't think so, just checking you were all right and you are all right aren't you?"

"Yes, thank you, Miss Pritchard."

Jenny turned and walked up to her room. I'm all right but what about Laura? She wondered if she should tell Miss Pritchard.

*

Chapter 12

Although Mark and Tony had joined Rainham's Estate Agents at the same time they had been sent to different London offices once they completed their induction course. Mark dialled Tony's number still unsure of what he would say, only sure that the longer he left it the more difficult it would become.

"It's Mark, fancy a pint after work?"

There was a pause. He's going to refuse, Mark thought, he's scared after what happened on Saturday.

"Don't know, I told Maggie I'd be home early."

"Don't tell me she's got you on that tight a rein."

Another pause, Tony always kicked against the slightest suggestion that he might be henpecked or 'under the thumb'.

"You're on. What time, where?"

Mark grimaced. I've done it again, he thought, if I'd kept my mouth shut he'd have said no. I could have told Laura it was no good and in a couple of weeks I'd be off to Manchester.

"Six o'clock at the 'Crown and Anchor'."

"Right, see you there then, bye."

Mark put the phone down. Now he just had to plan how best to approach the delicate subject of Laura and the baby. Best be direct, no beating about the bush. He looked at his watch, two hours to go. He really must get down to work; he had lots of loose ends to tie up before his transfer.

He had seen the manager yesterday and Mr. Baker had said he would contact Head Office to check how plans for the North West were going. He thought Mark was an ideal candidate for relocation although he would be missed in London. It had all been too easy. Perhaps, Mark thought, life is mapped out for you and it only goes wrong if you kick against the master plan.

Head Office had approved his request, pleased to be saving the resettlement allowance as Mark would be able to live with his mother. It had been decided he could go as soon as he had completed any outstanding work. It had been as simple as that.

His mother had been delighted by the news and was, by now, almost certainly in the throes of redecorating his room. I'm going home but not as a failure like the rest of the gang, he reminded himself, relishing the thought.

*

Iris rushed round in a state of frenzy. Freddie had called to say he was arriving on Wednesday – tomorrow - he hadn't said why he'd changed his plans and Iris didn't care. Her heart swelled with delight, her darling boy would soon be here. She had called her cleaning lady, Mrs. Cartwright, to ask her to come today. There had been no reply, the woman was useless. Iris would tell George to go back to the agency and demand a replacement.

Iris had no alternative; she must clean Freddie's room herself. She stripped the barely used linen from the bed, remade it and placed two hot water bottles between the fresh sheets. Everything must be aired. She dusted, polished and vacuumed the carpet with an enthusiasm she hadn't felt for years.

Leaning against the window sill, she could smile with deep satisfaction at the results of her labours; it had been a labour of love. Now all that was needed now was a vase of flowers. She could go to the florists or get something from the garden. If she called at the florist she could pop into the off-licence and replace the bottle of brandy she had planned to take from George's stock. She hesitated. No, she would be strong, she would not drink today. She must look her best when she greeted Freddie tomorrow. Glancing down she saw several deep red roses in the garden just right for cutting. They would be perfect.

She wondered if she should phone George and give him the good news, no not yet, she wanted to keep it to herself for a little longer. She hummed quietly under her breath as she arranged the roses in her best cut-glass vase. She took them upstairs and placed the vase on the window sill. The blooms glowed as though lit from within, red roses, the symbol of love, how true. Above all others, she thought, I love my son, Freddie.

She wandered round the empty house not sure what to do next. This was her life, always looking for something to do. I won't call George, she decided, I'll go to his office and he can take me out to dinner. She showered and changed into clothes suitable for a managing director's wife. She scribbled a note for William; he would have to get his own meal tonight.

She called a taxi. Let George settle the fare at the other end, she paused, perhaps she should pay herself if she was hoping to be taken out. He always complained about her extravagance, why spoil the evening for the sake of a few pounds.

*

George was at his desk signing letters for that evening's post when Iris walked in. His secretary, June, was standing beside

64

him, her hand resting on his shoulder. The speed with which June removed that hand told Iris everything. The ensuing silence, which could only have lasted a few seconds, seemed to expand to fill all available space, leaving no room to breathe.

In a quiet voice George said, "That will be all, June, see they are posted tonight."

As June walked past Iris the air crackled. The office door was closed with a sigh and Iris felt a great weight crushing her chest. How long had she suspected this? Had she known all along but refused to acknowledge it? She had never looked at another man; she had all the men she wanted, Freddie, George and of course William.

George smiled at her, how he could be so calm?

"This is a nice surprise, my dear."

She wanted to hit him, to wipe that inane and hypocritical smile from his smug face. She wanted to hurt him, tear at his skin, make him bleed as she was bleeding inside.

George continued in a quiet, calm voice, "You look very smart, my dear, been somewhere nice?"

How dare he behave as though nothing had happened, how could he deny the evidence of her own eyes? June had only had a hand on his shoulder but it was more, so much more than that. They had been too close. People only get that close if they have or want to have a physical relationship. Everyone knew that.

How often had he taken this woman away on business trips? He had said less and less about his trips away from home but then he would, wouldn't he, if June was his mistress. Did William know it was going on? That was more than likely which made the whole sordid business even worse.

George didn't get up from behind his desk. He doesn't know what to do, Iris thought.

"I came to give you some good news, there's no point now."

"Surely you'll want to share it with me."

"You've spoilt everything." She could hear the shrill note in her voice but didn't care.

"Don't you dare take me for a fool, George; I've suspected for a long time that something was going on. Don't you deny it."

She noticed that the finger she was pointing at him was shaking but this time it was not caused by alcohol. She gasped for breath as George walked towards her.

"I have never wanted to hurt you, you know that."

He tried to put his arms around her but she moved away. He leaned back against his desk and smiled but she could see wariness in his eyes and she was glad. His nonchalance was a cover. She stared at him willing him to look away, to lower his eyes in shame.

"If I've done anything to upset you, I'm sorry. Let me take you out for a meal and you still haven't given me your good news. Let's celebrate."

He's humouring me, she thought, as though I'm a wayward child. Yet she felt the tension diminish. She wanted to cling to that terrible rage, it shut out the hurt. If she stopped feeling angry she might cry. That was what George wanted then he would be able to comfort her and everything would go back to normal.

She hated his capacity for conciliation. Why wouldn't he fight back? Why wouldn't he shout and scream as she did? That was the aphrodisiac she needed, perhaps then her long dormant desire would reawaken. But George had always been a gentleman. She wondered if he were a gentleman with June or was she his bit of rough? Just the thought of him in bed with another woman made her want to scream. Did June talk about this sordid affair to the others in the office? When I come here, Iris thought, do they all snigger behind their hands?

"You are having an affair with that woman aren't you?"

Iris watched, would he try to wriggle out of it?

"I wouldn't put it in those words nor would I insult your intelligence by denying it."

His words hung in the air between them before sinking like stones into a thick and clotted silence. Without a word, Iris turned on her heel and left the office.

*

When Mark arrived at the pub Tony was already at the bar ordering a pint. Mark stood in the doorway and watched his friend for a moment, the arrogant man with the world in general and women in particular at his feet had vanished, he looked nervous.

"Want a pint?"

Mark nodded and looked for a quiet table.

"We can sit over there."

He indicated a corner of the room not yet occupied by early evening drinkers. They sat side by side, facing the room. Mark was glad they did not have to look at each other during what was

66

going to be a tricky conversation. He took a deep breath.

"I expect you realise why I wanted to see you."

"Laura?"

"She's in a hell of a state."

Tony did not reply or look at him.

"What are you going to do, Tony? She's determined to get rid of the baby but has no idea how."

"How do I know it's mine?"

Mark stared at him.

"What does she expect me to do?"

"Oh come on man, it takes two."

"What does she want, money?"

"Probably, but she needs to know who to go to, to get rid of it. I don't think Mummy and Daddy would welcome her back in her present condition."

"What makes you think I know anyone who will do the necessary?"

"Do you?"

"I might."

"Oh for God's sake, don't play silly buggers."

"How soon does she need to know?"

"The sooner the better...."

"I need to make a couple of phone calls."

"I'll wait here then." Mark felt sure if arrangements were not made tonight they never would be. While he sipped his beer he wondered again how he had got embroiled in all this. After fifteen minutes he wondered if Tony had done the frightened rabbit act.

When he did return he was the old confident Tony again.

"Took ages to get through, first phone box was out of order."

"Well?"

"This is the number she has to ring, the woman who answers will make all the arrangements. Knows some bloke, claims he's a doctor, probably been struck off for doing this sort of thing. But Laura should be all right, he must know what he's doing. It costs seventy five pounds."

Mark stared at Tony who finally, with great reluctance, faced him.

"One of my mates got this girl into trouble, see."

Mark said nothing.

"I suddenly remembered."

"This has happened before, hasn't it?"

Tony took a large swig of his beer and nodded.

"I know it's none of my business but don't you think it's time you learned your lesson?"

"Don't you ever make mistakes?"

"Yes, Tony, but I try not to make the same mistake twice."

Tony looked away and drew on his cigarette.

"Has she got any money?"

"Not seventy-five pounds she hasn't."

"I can give her thirty out of my account but that's all. Most of our money goes into a joint account."

"And Maggie might ask questions." Mark had a sour taste in his mouth. He had been going to tell Tony about his transfer but he wouldn't bother now. He just wanted to get away. It was all so sordid and it was obvious that Tony had no intentions of having further contact with Laura. That was best for the poor kid even if she couldn't see it now.

"Give me the cheque for thirty pounds now, I'll cash it and give Laura the money. Goodness knows where she'll get the rest."

Tony made no comment but wrote the cheque with indecent haste, and downed the rest of his pint in one swallow.

"Must go, promised Maggie I wouldn't be late."

"How the hell does that woman put up with you?"

Tony didn't reply but rose and without a backward glance threaded his way through the now crowded pub to disappear out of the door. Mark sighed. Not only would Laura have no further contact with Tony, Mark thought, neither will I.

*

"There's a call for you, Laura, I transferred it to the booth in the hall."

"Thank you, Miss Pritchard," she said and raced downstairs. For a wild moment she thought it might be Tony but in her heart she knew it wasn't.

"Hello"

"Laura, it's Mark, I've just seen Tony."

"Oh thanks, I'm so grateful; what did he say?"

Mark paused, no point in dressing it up. Tony was making a small financial gesture in order to disassociate himself from a problem he didn't want to acknowledge.

"He's given me a phone number for you to ring and thirty pounds towards the cost. You still want to go ahead with it?"

Laura had known this was how it would be yet the harsh

reality of Tony's callousness still stabbed at her heart. What a fool she had been.

"Thirty pounds, how much does it cost then?"

"Seventy-five."

Laura gasped, where on earth would she get the rest?

"Are you still there?"

"I've got no money, what can I do?"

Mark sighed; here we go, deeper and deeper.

"Look," he said, "I can manage twenty if that would help."

Laura felt her thoughts go into free fall and words tumbled into space, incoherent, disjointed.

"Of course it would help but how can I ever repay you? I'll just have to ask my parents for the rest."

"Will you tell them why?"

"No, I couldn't possibly do that. I'll think of something, I know; I've had my purse stolen, I'll tell them I'm broke. Yes, that's it, I'll call them tonight."

"When do you want me to bring the money and telephone number round? Be quick, I'm out of change."

"Can you come tonight? I've got to get this sorted before I lose my nerve; I haven't got pencil or paper with me."

"O.K."

"Do you know where the hostel is?"

"No."

"Where are you now?"

"In town."

"Come to Baron's Court station, I'll meet you in half an hour."

Laura hoped Mark heard her say thank you before the line went dead.

She stood for a moment and watched as fellow residents moved through the hallway, chatting and laughing. What would they think of her if they knew? She took several deep breaths and tried to sort out what she would say before she rang her parents' number. She needed twenty-five but still had to get through the rest of the month. Better ask for thirty pounds, which should be enough. She dialled their number and crossed her fingers, hoping they would be in. She listened to the ringing tone and prayed.

"9842, Eric Johnson speaking."

"Dad, it's Laura."

There was a pause. "This is unexpected, how are you?"

"I'm O.K., sorry I haven't rung, you and Mum all right?"

"Yes, do you want to speak to her?"

He'd always left things to Mum, never seeming too keen to converse with his only child. Laura had often wondered if he had wanted a son but that wasn't her fault.

"No, er yes, in a minute. It's just that an awful thing has happened. You see I've had my purse stolen. I'd been to the bank and I had all the money for the rest of the month, thirty pounds. I don't know what to do." She paused and leaned her forehead against the cool glass of the booth.

"I see." There was a pause.

"You still there, Dad?"

"Yes. It's just that we haven't heard from you for close on six months. Have you any idea how that's been for your mother? Have you ever given her a second thought?"

Laura gritted her teeth, always the lecture. If they were so concerned why hadn't they called her? They knew where she was.

"I'm sorry, Dad."

"And now you do deign to ring it's because you want something."

"I wouldn't ask if I could manage and I will pay you back."

"I've heard that before and if you could have managed, would you have rung?"

"Yes, I would but you know how things are."

"No, I don't, you could have been dead for all we knew. Have you reported the theft to the police?"

Laura hadn't thought of that. "No, that's because I can't be sure exactly where I lost it."

"That's no reason, it could be one of the girls in the hostel, you never know."

"I'm sure it isn't one of them but I'll report it tomorrow." She clenched her fist and waited, was he going to send the money or not?

"How do you want it, will a cheque do?"

Laura felt faint with relief. "Would you send cash, Dad, you see I'm absolutely broke, I haven't even got the fare to get to work. It would be safe if you sent it by registered post. I can probably borrow my bus fares until it arrives."

"Right, cash it is, I'll sort it tomorrow, should get it by Thursday. Now you'd better have a word with your mother, she's been sick with worry about you."

"Thanks Dad."

*

70

Barbara stared out of the window and chewed her pen. The pale blue writing paper lay before her untouched. It shouldn't be so hard to write a note of thanks to Charles. He seemed to have enjoyed her company on Saturday evening and now was the time to do something positive. She started to write, thanked him for a delightful evening and wondered if she could return his hospitality soon. Was he doing anything this coming Saturday? Would he like to come for a meal?

It would be interesting to see how he responded. Joan had said that Charles was fond of flirting with women but only when there were others present. Barbara wondered if the idea of an evening alone with her would prove to be too daunting. Both her address and telephone number were at the top of the page, he could write or call, which would he do, she wondered.

*

Laura hoped she had enough change; it probably wouldn't be a long call. She dialled the number Mark had given her. She had overcome one hurdle this evening. Mum had been quite pleasant and commiserated with her over her 'loss' and of course Dad would send the money.

Just this one call then she could go upstairs and have a hot bath, as hot as she could stand it. Maybe nature would sort the problem but she was sure she should drink gin as well. That was out of the question.

She listened to the ringing tone. Just as she was about to replace the receiver a woman's voice said, "Hello."

She gave no number and Laura was terrified she might not be speaking to the right person.

"Is that 6264?"

"Yes." Not a voice to encourage confidence, Laura thought.

"I've been given your number by a friend. Please can you help me?"

"How?"

This was awful. "My name's Laura Joh…"

"No names, I don't want no names."

"I'm in trouble, I've got seventy-five pounds; that is what it costs isn't it? Please can you help, I've got to get rid of it."

"Where did you get this number?"

"A friend gave it to me."

"So what exactly do you want?"

Laura leaned nearer the wall aware of movement outside the booth. Girls were walking past and they must not hear what she

71

was saying. She fed her last coins into the slot. Perspiration was running down her face, she wanted to scream and make the nightmare end. She hissed into the receiver, "I want an abortion."

"You've got the money."

"Yes, I will have by Thursday."

"O.K. Thursday evening, seven o'clock, fifty-two Larkhall Lane, it's off Wandsworth Road, Stockwell."

Laura scribbled the address down.

"Make sure you come alone, anyone with you and the deal's off."

"Yes," she replied but the phone line was already dead.

With trembling hands she replaced the receiver and walked upstairs. There was no going back now.

*

Chapter 13

Iris had avoided speaking to George since her visit to the office. She had concentrated all her time and energy on Freddie. She was surprised her darling boy had made no comment on the obvious atmosphere. He had changed and seemed distant. He was growing up and soon he would not need her. Even her efforts to make his room perfect had largely passed without comment. Of course he had removed the roses and put them on the hall window-sill. What had he said? 'Come off it, Ma, I'm not a pansy.' She had laughed and claimed it had been the cleaning woman's idea but his response had shocked her.

What was she to do about George? Coming back from his office she had been determined to divorce him, take him for every penny he had. How dare he? And with a common little madam like June, she was a jumped up nobody who had ideas above her station. But Iris could not ignore her own humble origins. Mum and Dad had been ordinary working folk with few aspirations and less money. What had her sister, Sheila, achieved? She had managed a lowly office job with few prospects not unlike June. Of course Sheila was tied to Mum and Dad now but if she had really wanted to make something of herself she could have.

Now there was this wretched man, David. Iris felt sure that his arrival would have a far from beneficial effect on her life. It was so unfair. She had brought up her family and now just when she and George should have some time and money to do whatever they liked it was all going wrong.

She sensed a new determination in Sheila. She wasn't so young any more; did she think this was her last chance to grab a husband? Iris thought of all the glamorous men she had dated before George. Of course she had been a stunning young woman, everyone had said so. Sheila on the other hand was quite plain.

She opened the drawer under the wardrobe and looked again at the many photographs taken all those years ago, when she was young. She could have had any man. Now when she glanced into her dressing-table mirror the clear light of morning told no lies, years of drinking and smoking had left their smudged finger prints on her face.

If I divorce him who will I have? Her reflection stared back at her. She acknowledged that her relationship with William was uneasy; he was resentful and always sided with his father. What of Freddie? He would leave her, the signs were there.

Already he had mentioned some stupid idea of going into the army. I will be alone, she mouthed silently. The very thought seemed to bounce from wall to wall and back into her head. She shuddered. If she divorced George he would still have June, if that was what he really wanted, the fool.

Once she was alone the way would be clear for Sheila to go off with this David fellow leaving Mum and Dad to her, the older sister; Iris felt her eyes fill. None of this was her fault. Sheila was the caring one, always had been. Iris knew she could not cope with her elderly parents, she had other talents. I'm a good cook, a good hostess, I know how to entertain. I can cope with all George's business contacts, put them at their ease. Sheila could never do that.

Iris rested her chin on her hands and said to her reflection, 'I can't be a geriatric nurse and that's all there is to it so divorce is out, there is too much to lose." She gave a little smile to herself as she added, "But things will have to change, George will not be allowed to get away with it."

Today was Thursday; Freddie was going back to boarding school on Sunday. It could wait until then; she needed more time to think.

She looked at her watch, mid-day and more than time for Freddie to get up. He won't be able to lie abed in the army. She decided she would point that out to him, maybe the thought of such rigours would help him decide on a different career, one that didn't take him away from her.

She hurried downstairs to make him a coffee. She would sit on his bed while he drank it and chat like they had done when he was younger.

*

Laura walked down the unfamiliar street. Although it was still light on this pleasant, early autumn evening, Larkhall Lane had a forbidding exterior emphasized by the absence of children playing or in fact the evidence of any life at all. Some of the houses were boarded up and the windows of the rest stared at her, sightless and dead. That was it, the street seemed dead and all that remained was a decaying carcass.

Litter had been blown into untidy heaps by capricious winds, rain had reduced those heaps to sodden lumps, festering growths which no-one had bothered to remove. Some windows bore scant signs of previous occupation. Shredded lace curtains hung like nicotine-stained seaweed, soot encrusted plants of indeterminate variety clung to life in a few tiny, walled, front gardens.

Laura was frightened, very frightened. Jenny had offered to come with her but Laura explained that was impossible. She checked again the number on the scrap of paper Mark had given her. Number fifty two was over the road. Her footsteps sounded too loud as they echoed to and fro across the grimy street.

She heard a door bang behind her but did not dare look round. Perhaps squatters had moved into some of the empty properties. She didn't want to see who it was; it might be some dirty old tramp hoping to snatch her handbag. There would be no abortion without the money.

She stood outside fifty-two, trembling too much to knock on the door. Take deep breaths, calm down, it's going to be all right. She could hear footsteps coming nearer. They were quick, light steps, not a man's, she glanced back. A hatchet-faced woman was coming down the street. She was dressed in a shabby, nondescript coat that had once been black but now had a greenish tinge to it. She wore an old fashioned cloche-type hat, pulled well down. Her eyes were in shadow. A large, bulging shopping bag hung from her arm and she had a key in her hand. She was in a hurry and her eyes darted up and down the street as though she feared being seen or followed.

"Quick, out of the way," the woman said.

Laura realised it was the voice she had heard on the phone and now this shabby woman fumbled with the key, pushed open the paint-peeling door and hustled Laura inside. She must live in this awful street, Laura thought, she's been waiting and watching for me to arrive.

"Go through to the back, there isn't much time. Doctor will be here any minute; we've got to get ready."

The narrow hallway smelt of damp and decay, it was gloomy after the bright light outside. Laura stumbled against an ancient bicycle, minus one wheel, that leant against the wall.

"Ssh, don't make a noise."

Since the evidence of her own eyes suggested that most, if not all, of the inhabitants of Larkhall Lane had long since escaped to something better, she could see little point in worrying about noise. Under the circumstances, Laura decided, it was in her best interests to do exactly as she was told so she said nothing.

The woman led her through to a room at the back of the house. It was empty with newspaper stuck to the windows. What light there was came from a window in what, Laura assumed, was a scullery. She was surprised. Where would the doctor do what had to be done? There was no bed, no anything.

The woman was pulling wedges of newspapers from her old fashioned bag and spreading them on the bare, splintered floorboards. The middle of the floor was covered with large, dark stains. The room smelt strange, it was a smell that reminded Laura of a butcher's shop overlaid by the sharp stench of cat pee.

The woman ignored Laura and removing neither hat nor coat continued to spread newspapers on the floor. Once satisfied she produced a small bar of soap and a bit of clean towel. These she took through to the scullery which, Laura could see, held an ancient, filthy sink and one corroded cold-water tap.

Laura felt hysterical laughter bubble in her throat, she wanted to run away. This was a nightmare, anything would be better than this. For a split second she wondered if she could have the baby after all, Mum and Dad wouldn't turn her away would they? She stood paralysed with fear and dread; she wanted the toilet but didn't dare ask.

She jumped as the door to the hallway opened. There had been no noise of the front door being opened or closed, the man just appeared. He was short and dumpy. The first thing Laura noticed, because of his silent entrance, was his abnormally small feet. They were like a child's. Twinkle-toes, that's how I shall think of him, a little fat man with a child's feet. Perhaps making him a figure of fun would help her cling to reality and remind her that the whole dreadful business would soon be over.

The shoes, like the rest of his clothes, indicated money. Without a word he removed hat, grey raincoat and the jacket of a navy blue pinstripe suit all of which he hung behind the door. Laura wondered why she was taking so much note of a man she would never see again; at least it stopped her thinking about anything else.

The man seemed anxious and breathed heavily as he rolled up the sleeves of his pristine white shirt. Perspiration shone on his brow as he loosened his tie and stroked into place the thin strands of hair that didn't disguise his pink, naked crown. He walked through to the scullery where the woman waited. The gush of water drowned the sound of their muffled conversation. Laura stood not knowing what she was supposed to do.

She waited until the woman came in.

"Get yourself ready, doctor hasn't got all night."

"I need to go to the toilet."

The woman gave an exasperated tut.

"Be quick, upstairs, first on the left, don't flush it."

Laura raced upstairs as quietly as she could; her breath came in short gasps. The toilet was unspeakable. Laura felt her stomach clench at the nauseating, foul smell of ordure that almost overwhelmed her. In addition to faeces and urine, which almost filled the toilet bowl, there was blood and vomit everywhere. She clung to the door frame and willed herself not to faint. She could not use that toilet but she had to go somewhere.

A voice hissed up the stairs, "Hurry up."

Laura tiptoed into the backroom, beyond the toilet. It was empty except for a pile of rubbish in one corner. With a whimper of relief she pulled down her knickers and squatted. No sooner had she emptied her bladder than she was running downstairs pulling her clothes straight as she went. They were waiting for her.

"Give me the money first."

Laura was startled by the man's voice; it was light and high like a woman's. She fumbled in her bag for the envelope and handed it over. Her hands trembled. He took the money and, with expertise, counted out the notes. He nodded to the woman, then peeled off five pounds and gave them to her. He stuffed the rest into his trouser pocket.

"Lie down," the woman said.

Laura glanced round the room, "Where?"

"On the floor, girl, for God's sake, do you want to get rid of it or not?"

Laura noticed a clean piece of sheeting on top of the newspapers. She hesitated wondering if that was for her, but while she watched, the man lowered himself with care onto the protective plastic. Of course, she thought, he must not get his good suit besmirched by newsprint. What do I matter? I must lie like a lump of meat; I am of no importance now.

"Take your knickers off, pull your skirt up and bend your knees."

His hands on her knees pulled them apart and with no warning he thrust his fingers into her vagina with such force it made her gasp.

"How many periods have you missed?"

"Two."

He pressed on her abdomen and grunted with satisfaction. Laura assumed he was pleased that he could verify the pregnancy was no further advanced than she claimed.

"Right, I'll do what I have to do to start things off. That's the end of my job, understand?" Nodding to the woman, "She'll clear up the mess and see you out. You should start to bleed within twenty four hours. Any problems go to your own doctor."

Laura nodded as tears blurred her vision and she could not speak. There really was no going back now.

"Do not under any circumstances say anything about this place, understand. And the next time you decide to indulge in an adult activity behave like an adult and protect yourself."

The menace in his voice combined with his total lack of sympathy felt like a slap and Laura, now terrified, wept great, shuddering, silent sobs. She dared not make a noise in case they walked out and left her.

"This will hurt but I can't do anything about that. Don't make a noise."

Laura stared at the ceiling while he fumbled with something wrapped in a piece of cloth. The ceiling sagged in the middle and was festooned with cracks like an old man's face. Bits of plaster were missing showing wooden laths that resembled the ribs of a prehistoric animal. The single, flyblown light bulb was moved by some undetectable current of air as it hung from a frayed central flex. Laura concentrated on the bulb, focused all her attention on that; she would not think about what he was going to do.

She clenched her fists as the man leaned over her. Already she was drenched with sweat even though she felt icy cold. She felt pressure on her abdomen again and a violent thrusting as something thin, cold and sharp was pushed into her womb. Searing, excruciating pain radiated outwards, reaching to her finger tips. A hand clamped down on her mouth.

She tried to raise her knees, to curl into the foetal position, to expel this instrument of torture from the secret, innermost part of her body. She couldn't move. His knees were pressed against hers, his hand was pumping backwards and forwards, twisting, thrusting, dragging her flesh, tearing her.

Now the pain was gone. Laura watched what was happening with detachment, nothing mattered. The woman kept one hand on Laura's mouth while the other held her shoulder down. Laura struggled no more. She watched the man, as he squatted like some obscene toad, gripping her legs, holding them down and apart. Why was there no pain? She felt warm and her eyelids drooped. She was floating away from this scene of torment. This was not her lying on the floor, an empty shell, a mere carcass.

It was like a silent movie. Everything seemed far away, disconnected. She wondered if she were dying. Would her parents mourn their loss? She sensed rather than felt the woman's hand release its grip. Laura did not move. The tears on her cheeks were dry now, she could cry no more.

Far away she heard the woman say something, she sounded worried. Laura felt herself being shaken, gently at first. The man must have stopped what he was doing because Laura felt the slender, sharp instrument being withdrawn. She exhaled in a long, drawn out sigh.

The man leaned over her and she felt his breath on her cheek. He slapped her face hard, the shock made her jump. He slapped her again. She moaned aware once more of this terrible pain in her abdomen. She was on fire as sharp daggers of pain stabbed at her again and again.

"She's all right now," the man said as he mopped his brow, "that was a close thing."

He struggled to his feet and Laura noticed rings of sweat under his arms which tarnished his immaculate shirt. He grabbed the piece of towel from the woman and Laura watched as he dragged a knitting needle through a fold of the material to remove the blood.

Laura did not have the strength to do anything but clench her fists and teeth to keep the screams inside. Wave after wave of pain washed over her. She could not move even to pull her skirt down to cover herself. She lay like a puppet that relied on others to control its movements. Logical, coherent thought was obliterated by pain.

She realised the man was getting ready to leave, he had his money and now another successful consultation was concluded he would not give her another thought. Without a word he was gone. The woman had started to gather the newspapers, rolling and folding them to put in her bag.

"Get up, you can't stay here."

Laura struggled to sit up but overcome by dizziness she fell back.

"Get up quick, get dressed, have you got a towel?"

Laura looked at her, a towel, why would she want to wash here in this hell hole?

"A towel, in case you start to bleed before you get home."

"No, no I didn't think."

"No, you didn't think, if you had you wouldn't be here."

The woman groped in her bag for a moment and pulled out a large sanitary towel. She grabbed Laura's shoulders from behind and forced her upright.

"You've got five minutes to sort yourself out then you're out of here, understand?"

Laura most certainly did understand. She struggled to stand, picked up her knickers and leant against the wall to put them on. She felt a thin trickle of blood creep down the inside of her thigh. Her vision was blurred by tears as she dabbed at the blood on her leg with the sanitary towel and then pushed it into place in her knickers.

She tried again to stand upright but was doubled up with stomach cramps. With a great effort she gritted her teeth and with heavy breaths forced her shoulders back until they touched the wall behind her.

The woman continued clearing the papers. Then she hurried into the scullery to retrieve the soap which she wrapped in the bloody piece of cloth. After a final check that everything was now how she had found it she grabbed Laura's arm.

"Off you go now, straight home, have a hot bath and go to bed, not a word to anyone mind. I've never seen you before."

Laura nodded. There was nothing to say. She lurched her way down the hallway and out into bright sunshine. The woman did not follow. Probably she was waiting until Laura had walked to the bottom of the road, turned the corner and was out of sight.

*

Jenny felt dreadful; her throat was getting worse. She had staggered into work ashen-faced and shivering. Both Professor Walker and Doctor Anderson had been concerned. Even Suzanne, the laboratory assistant, had been sympathetic, had made a fuss of her and brought her several cups of tea during a day that seemed endless.

When Jenny left that evening she had been told not to come in the next day unless she felt better. She was not better, in fact she was worse. She alternated between high fever and chilling cold that made her shiver. She must be running a temperature.

Although she had offered to go with Laura to the abortionist she was thankful the offer had been refused. Jenny hoped that a good night's sleep would make her feel better the next day. She was supposed to be going over to Golders Green to meet the wonderful Freddie. Then on Saturday she was having lunch with Mark at the Strand Palace.

She had agonised over how she would explain this to William but it had been easy. She said she was having lunch with a friend. He hadn't queried it. At the time she hadn't known whether to be glad or sorry that he wanted no more information. Did that mean he wasn't bothered or did he just assume it would be a girlfriend?

At this rate it wouldn't matter who it was; all she wanted to do was go to bed. Perhaps a hot bath would help. As she lay soaking in water as hot as she could bear she wondered how Laura was getting on. How long did these things take? She didn't know. How could a doctor do it anyway; she thought abortion was illegal. Laura had said it was being done by a doctor so she was bound to be all right. The steam seemed to be easing Jenny's throat. I'll have a hot drink, an early night and fingers crossed I'm bound to be fine in the morning.

*

Laura walked up the road from the station, every step jolted her insides. She knew she was bleeding; she felt weak and the pain was getting stronger. She stopped every few steps to get her breath and wait for the next dragging contraction to pass. Not far now, only a hundred yards or so then she'd be safe.

She clung to some railings and thought about her parents. Thank God they would never know. She only had to get back to the hostel, have a hot bath and go to bed, that was what the awful woman had said.

She let herself in and staggered up the steps, every one agonising, she rested on each landing. She was relieved no-one was about. Each careful step got her nearer to safety. As she reached the door of her room Jenny came out of the bathroom. She looked flushed. Laura hoped she hadn't taken all the hot water.

Jenny stared at Laura. "You O.K?"

Laura nodded. "I've just got to wait now."

"Can I do anything?"

"Run me a bath, will you, then I'm going to bed."

Jenny nodded, too shocked to speak.

Laura went into her room, undressed and got into her dressing gown. She was alarmed by the amount of blood she had already lost. The towel was saturated. Perhaps that was a good sign, it would all be over quicker. She checked her supply of sanitary towels, there should be enough. She'd ask Jenny to let her have a few extras, just in case. Jenny knocked at the door.

"The bath's running. Are you sure you're O.K?"

Laura nodded and started to weep. Jenny put her arms round the girl's shaking shoulders and held her.

"You'll soon feel better, the worst is over now."

"It was dreadful, Jenny, just dreadful. I wanted to die, it was so awful."

"Ssh, don't cry, you'll feel better after a bath and a good night's sleep."

*

Chapter 14

Barbara enjoyed cooking. Much of that enjoyment came from planning the menu and choosing the ingredients. She believed the amount of care put into a meal indicated the depth of feeling the cook had for those who would eat it. Although what Charles had cooked for them last week had been simple Barbara detected an overwhelming need for him to give.

Here, she thought, was a man in an emotional desert. Yet was it not true that after only a little rain a desert could become an ocean of flowers, flowers that came from seeds lying dormant for who knew how long? Perhaps, like a desert, Charles too would blossom with a little encouragement.

She carried the heavy bags upstairs to her flat. Striking the right balance was important; too complicated a menu would embarrass him, too simple and she would not have an opportunity to show off her culinary skills.

It was a shame she had work tomorrow. The library was always busy on a Saturday and it was her turn to go in. She would have to do a lot of the preparation this evening, make the pate and the coq au vin. Tomorrow there would just be vegetables and fruit salad. She kicked off her shoes and put the kettle on.

Relaxing on the large, comfortable settee she looked round and wondered what Charles would make of it. This main room was light and airy with floor to ceiling muslin curtains which shut out the less than inspiring view of the row of terraced houses opposite. The heavy curtains which protected her from the outside world, when she sought solitude, were a rich golden brown. In fact she had purposely chosen earth colours, ochre and gold that made the room feel warm even on the coldest day.

The cream-coloured walls were covered with an eclectic collection of pictures, prints and photographs. Although there was a central light she seldom used it. She thought a few table lamps gave a more intimate atmosphere. Pools of light glowed on the handmade, embroidered cushions she had taken delight in designing. She loved this room more than any other she had had because it was hers. She had chosen everything with care and thought and the end result was an enduring pleasure to her eye.

She stood up, stretched and went into her bedroom. Once changed into slacks and a blouse she could start cooking. She hummed to herself. Like the living room this too had been furnished with care but it emphasized her solitary state. No man had left his socks and underpants in a heap on the pale pink carpet. There was no electric shaver or aftershave on the dressing table. The large, double, mahogany wardrobe had been part of her parents' trousseau; it was more than enough for her clothes.

All that remained as proof that she had once been a wife and mother was the photograph of Andrew when he was a baby. The silver frame sat on the table beside her bed. This was the room in which she had, over the years, been able to mourn his loss. It was here that she had cried until no more tears would come. This room had witnessed not only her grief but also her anger at the unfairness of life. It had been a sanctuary and repository for all the negative feelings that, if not contained within these four walls, would have destroyed her.

She sometimes wondered if she should leave this flat. Perhaps now the ghost of the past had been laid she could start again. Barbara felt to do that would be like running away and she could not allow that. Besides some happy memories had begun to superimpose themselves on any still able to cause her pain. She had found a measure of happiness.

After Andrew's death her world had been nothing but grief and pain. She had clung to what the young minister had said after the funeral, 'God never gives you more than you can cope with', at the time she had wanted to rail against a god who could be so cruel but in the end it gave her strength. The difficult part had been to develop strategies that enabled her to cope. She did not want to blot out everything because then she would lose precious memories of her only child. It was the physical pain that was so hard to deal with.

Now after so many years she could think about him and not cry. He would have been ten if he had lived and have had dirty knees and pockets full of rubbish that he would have treasured. She picked up his photograph and kissed it. Now she thought, let's get into the kitchen and do some cooking.

*

Laura struggled out of the bath. The water was an ominous pink, the bleeding was getting worse. She put two sanitary towels inside a clean pair of knickers. The pain in her abdomen expanded until it enveloped her, obliterating thought. She was not a person any more; she was a deep, grinding, cramping agony that had no beginning and no end. It invaded every bone, every muscle and every cell of her body.

She swayed and, frightened she might fall, clung to the edge of the bath. She felt dizzy as the next pain radiated out from her womb. She bit her lip and whimpered as she stood with her head down, her arms rigid, her hands still clutching the bath. Just a little longer, she thought, and then there will be a moment's release as the pain eases a fraction before the next one comes. She was panting with the exertion of remaining upright and retaining the cries that jostled in her throat.

I've got to get out of here and into bed, have a hot bath and go to bed - that was what the woman had said. Laura repeated it under her breath like a mantra, do as she told me and I will be all right. She shuffled hand over hand to the end of the bath and pulled out the plug. Perspiration was running down her face and dripping off the end of her nose. Any movement was agonising.

"I can't stay here, I can't stay here, I must go to bed, I must do as I am told." She could hear a voice muttering and wondered if it were hers.

She had no strength to dry herself. Just pulling her nightdress on took the last of her energy; without warning her knees gave way and she slid down the wall. It felt cold and damp with condensation but she didn't care. The nightdress was stuck to her back but what did it matter? What did anything matter? She sat, head back, leaning against the wall. She became aware of a warm, wet feeling between her legs; blood now stained her clean knickers. She sighed, she was tired, so very tired. I've got to get to bed, that was what the woman said, "Go to bed."

She struggled onto all fours and used the edge of the bath to lever herself upright. With one hand she managed to drag her nightdress down far enough to cover evidence of her disgrace and stupidity. No-one must see her, not like this.

The pain was so bad she could not stand upright. She grabbed her towel and slid back the bolt on the door, careful not to make any noise. No sound came from the corridor. She turned the doorknob and eased open the door. Glancing up and down she was relieved that no-one was about. She would make a dash for it but the thought of further movement made her head spin. The bleeding frightened her. I will be found in the morning, she thought, like a stuck pig, alabaster white. I will be an empty shell with all my blood drained from me.

Step by painful step she sidled the few yards to her room using the wall for support. She closed the door behind her and mopped her face. Mustn't sit down, she thought, got to get to bed, get to bed and everything will be all right. She longed for a hot water bottle to place on her pulsating abdomen, anything to get relief from the agony. She knew she didn't have the strength to walk to the kitchen and boil the kettle, she would manage without. Further movement was impossible.

She managed to lift the covers enough to crawl into bed. She knew she should get some new sanitary towels, these were soaked already. She couldn't do it. She was just able to reach the bath towel which lay in a crumpled heap by the bed. With great care, so she didn't fall, she reached out to grab the towel and drag it into bed. She bunched and wedged it between her legs; that would have to do.

She lay still, aware that her abdominal muscles were clenched like bands of iron. Tighter and tighter they squeezed and dragged sending their arrows of pain in all directions. I will lie perfectly still, she thought, I'm in bed now and I've done as I was told. I'm going to be all right, that's what the woman said.

*

Jenny tossed and turned. The sheets felt damp and chill, the beneficial effects of the hot bath had long since worn off. Her throat was on fire, when she swallowed it felt as if she were swallowing broken glass. She shivered even though perspiration rolled off her, her pyjamas were drenched. She wondered if it was worth putting on a clean pair but she would still have to lie in this damp, cold bed.

She pulled her dressing gown over the blankets, if only she didn't feel so cold. Yet at the same time she seemed to be burning up, she must be really ill. She looked at her watch; the luminous numbers glowed, ten past two. She recalled her grandmother telling her that you had to keep your fluid levels up when you had a fever. She wondered if she had the energy to get up, perhaps a cup of tea would ease her throat.

She was shivering as she tip-toed to the kitchen. On her way past Laura's room she thought she heard a noise, perhaps Laura was dreaming. After what had happened to her this evening it was more likely the poor thing was having a nightmare.

While she stood waiting for the kettle to boil Jenny thought about the coming weekend. Friday evening, no, this evening she corrected herself, she was going to the Martins' to meet Freddie. Saturday she was going into town to have lunch with Mark.

86

There's no reason why I shouldn't have a friend who happens to be a man she told herself not for the first time.

What is more important is whether I am going to be well enough to see anyone. Standing, for what seemed an eternity, made her realise how ghastly she felt. With a sickening premonition she thought it was inevitable she would be spending the weekend in the hostel, in bed.

She tip-toed back along the corridor, once again there was a noise coming from Laura's room. She paused and wondered if she should go in, maybe Laura was not well. She tapped on the door.

"Are you all right?"

There was a faint reply. "Help me."

Jenny opened the door. At first she could see nothing then gradually made out a dark shape on the floor.

"What's the matter?"

"Get help, I'm bleeding to death."

Jenny felt a spasm of terror. "Close your eyes," she said, "I'll have to put the light on."

Jenny gasped at what she saw. She had forgotten she had hot tea in her hand, jumping back with shock, she sent scalding tea sloshing over her hand. She yelped with pain, put the cup down on the floor and knelt beside Laura.

"What's happened?" She looked at the bed, there was blood everywhere. The sheets were drenched and so was Laura who lay ashen-faced on the floor.

"I was trying to get help," she whispered, "but I can't stand up. Get Miss Pritchard."

The room looked like the aftermath of a massacre, it reminded Jenny of the reports she had seen on the television after the Mau-Mau troubles in Kenya. Looking around her, Jenny marvelled that anyone could lose so much blood and remain alive.

"Just lie still." Jenny grabbed a blanket and draped it over Laura's limp body.

"I'll go for Miss Pritchard."

She ran down the corridor careless of the noise her slippers made, this was too serious to worry about waking other residents. She banged on Miss Pritchard's door and gasped for breath while she waited for a reply. She banged again.

"Miss Pritchard, please wake up, Laura's dying. Get an ambulance."

87

Her teeth were chattering and she was shivering. She could not be sure if it was shock, fear, fever or the chilly night air. The door opened and Miss Pritchard stood in her dressing gown, composed as though such intrusions to her night's sleep were a regular occurrence. She spoke in her usual quiet, calm voice.

"Now tell me again, what's the matter?"

Jenny took a deep breath and swallowed hard wincing at the jagged pain in her throat.

"It's Laura, she's bleeding to death. I got up to make a hot drink and I heard her. It's awful; I've never seen so much blood."

Miss Pritchard looked surprised. I bet she thinks I'm exaggerating, Jenny thought.

"Something happened to Laura this evening, I can't tell you what but I think that's why she's bleeding so much now."

"Let's go to see how she is shall we?"

"I don't want her to die, Miss...."

"Of course you don't but we don't want to call out an ambulance unless it is necessary."

"There's blood everywhere, Miss...." She raced upstairs in front of Miss Pritchard. Her chest ached with the exertion, her limbs just ached. This won't help me get better, she thought, but that's uncharitable, Laura needs my help.

She rushed into Laura's room followed by Miss Pritchard. Nothing much had changed except that Laura was even paler. Her breathing was shallow and noisy, her skin was translucent. One look was enough and Miss Pritchard turned on her heel.

"Stay here with her, Jenny, while I dial 999."

Jenny listened to the rapid tap, tap, tap of the woman's receding footsteps. It was not the sound of running feet but Jenny knew that Miss Pritchard was moving at considerable speed.

Jenny sat on the floor and held Laura's hand. Now that action was being taken by someone else she realised just how ill she still felt. She was icy cold sitting on the hard linoleum covered floor, her head ached and her throat was raw. This whole business seemed more and more unreal. Laura groaned and moved a little, at least she's still alive, Jenny thought.

"Miss Pritchard's gone for the ambulance, it will be here soon. They'll look after you." She brushed hair back from Laura's face and tried to smile encouragement.

Laura groaned. "Don't let her tell my parents."

Jenny felt as though she were floating. Only the touch of

Laura's cold hand stopped her from drifting away, far, far away.

If only I didn't feel so rotten, she thought. There's no way I can go to work. She glanced at Laura's alarm clock, two thirty, it was only twenty minutes since she woke up, she could not believe it. So much had happened.

At first Jenny sensed rather than heard activity downstairs. Then a few minutes later she heard heavy footsteps climbing the last flight of stairs after which everything was a blur. The room was filled to overflowing by two burly, hearty men in ambulance men's uniform. They were oblivious to the hour and the fact that the rest of the world was sleeping. Jenny stood out of the way by the window. Her body ached for warmth and her need to lie down made her sway with exhaustion.

Laura was lifted onto a stretcher and wrapped in a thick red blanket. Jenny watched and wondered if ambulance blankets were deliberately red to disguise blood loss which would alarm badly hurt patients. She realised she had lost the strength to stand up any more and slumped onto the chair in the corner as she watched the activity swirling around her. Miss Pritchard looked so calm as she supervised Laura's departure.

She smiled at Jenny. "I'll be back in a minute."

Jenny clung to the chair, scared she might fall. Now she was alone she looked round the room that had been defiled by so much blood. It was like that scene from 'Macbeth' she and the rest of her class had watched long ago. What had Lady Macbeth said about King Duncan? Jenny mouthed the words, 'who would have thought the old man had so much blood in him...' Duncan had died, would Laura die?

A deep weariness made Jenny's head droop as she leaned against the wall. Her legs did not want to support her, would she have to sit here for what was left of the night? She did not know what to do. Should she go to bed and leave the carnage for someone else to clear up? How dreadful that this tiny speck of humanity had been wrenched into extinction. Would anyone grieve for this child that would never be?

The world was full of sorrow, a sorrow which now washed over Jenny till she seemed to be drowning. Then the tears came and the pain of them tore at her heart. She cried for what had gone before, for what was yet to come, for herself, for Laura and for the death that had occurred here. Then Miss Pritchard returned and taking Jenny's arm led her back to her room.

"You have had a dreadful shock this evening, my dear. Thanks for your prompt action. I'm sure Laura will be all right but she has a lot to thank you for. It could so easily have ended in tragedy. I'm going to make you a cup of hot, sweet tea then I must contact Laura's parents."

"Oh please don't do that. Laura really doesn't want them to know about this."

"I do realise what has happened you know, Jenny. As Laura is underage I have no choice but to inform her parents."

Jenny tried to speak but what was the point? The matter was out of her hands now; she knew she could do no more. She leaned back on the damp pillows. Her head was swimming and her throat was so sore she could only croak.

"My cup's in Laura's room somewhere."

Miss Pritchard leaned over and placed a cool hand on Jenny's forehead.

"I don't think you are very well, in fict you are running a temperature."

Jenny nodded and tears came again, why was it always worse when people were kind?

"I'll get you your tea and I suggest you stay in bed tomorrow."

Jenny nodded, she craved sleep and then maybe she would feel better.

*

Chapter 15

Iris was in the kitchen preparing the evening meal when William returned after his first day working for George. She turned from the stove as he slumped onto a chair.

"What's the matter with you?"

He sighed. "What a drag. The whole day's been awful, I've trudged up and down Oxford Street all day trying to interest buyers in bloody sweaters."

Iris pulled a face. Of course William was bound to be annoyed at not having much success; he'd had it easy all his young life, not like when she was his age.

"What did you expect; a book full of orders on your first day?"

"You just don't understand, Mum. I thought I'd cracked it when Jaeger's gave me something. It was only small but it was better than nothing. I went back to tell Dad and guess what, he'd had a phone call to cancel the order, the only one I got all day."

Iris turned back to the stove to hide her smile; it was about time William grew up. She continued stirring the sauce she was making.

"Oh by the way I had a call from the hostel, the warden or someone. Jenny's ill, she's running a temperature apparently."

William groaned. "Has she seen a doctor?"

"How should I know?"

"Well shouldn't she?"

"That's not for me to decide."

"Will she be coming over then?"

"I doubt it."

"I suppose I'd better ring the hostel and see how she is."

Iris listened as William made the call. He didn't seem too bothered, perhaps the events of an unsuccessful day were on his mind. She tried to imagine what it would be like stuck in a hostel on her own when she wasn't well, poor girl.

William came back into the kitchen.

"Spoke to someone called Miss Pritchard, I think she's in charge. She said Jenny was running a very high temperature and if she's no better tomorrow they'll get the local doctor to call."

"So who's going to look after her?"

"Don't know." William shrugged.

"Do you want us to get her over here?"

"Don't you mind, with Freddie here as well?"

Iris put down the wooden spoon she was holding. "I am used

to caring for the family you know. I just thought it would be better if Jenny wasn't left all alone."

"Well she can't be too good if they're calling in the doctor."

Iris thought for a moment, Jenny could be a useful additional responsibility. They were all supposed to be going round to her parents on Sunday. Sheila had insisted she would cook a meal for them all. This would give Iris a good excuse to get out of it.

"I'm sure your young lady could do with some home cooking."

"That would be great, Mum. I'm really grateful."

"It'll save you having to take her back tonight, won't it?"

William flushed; she had hit the mark there.

"I'd better call the hostel and tell them to put her in a taxi."

"Thanks Mum." He put his arm round her and gave a quick kiss to her offered cheek.

Iris dialled the hostel and listened as the phone rang with a hollow, echoing sound and Iris imagined the gloomy, institutional corridors. She'd be better here. Maybe I'll have the chance to get to know her; she could be a useful ally.

"Baron's Court Hostel, Miss Pritchard speaking."

"Hello, I'm Mrs Martin. I believe my son, William, spoke to you a few moments ago. I'm calling about Jenny Warr, I think it would be better if she came to us as I understand she is unwell. Would it be possible for you to put her in a taxi, please?"

"That is very kind, we do our best to care for the residents but I am sure she will recover quicker if she is with your family."

Arrangements made, Iris returned to the kitchen.

"She's on her way and I've got a meal to cook."

"What can I do?"

"I'll need to check the spare room, make sure the bed is aired."

"I can do that; shall I put the electric blanket on?"

"Umm," Iris nodded and watched as he left the room. Is he really fond of the girl or just trying to please me?

He always seemed to be in league with George, always so keen to check up on her and report back to dear Daddy. She sipped her sherry. It was her first glass, delicious but never needed in the same way when Freddie was at home. At home, that was a joke, he was using the place like a hotel but that was what all parents said.

She spread the whipped cream over the fruit and covered the surface with demerara sugar. Under the grill the granules melted and bubbled to form a thick, molten crust, fruit brulee, it was her

Freddie's favourite. She heard William clatter down the stairs.

"The room looks fine, Mum. I'm going for a shower, what time are we eating?"

"In about an hour but I'll have to get Jenny settled first. I think I'll phone Dr. Goodwin, perhaps he'd better come over."

"Thanks again, Mum." He paused and she waited for him to speak but he turned and went upstairs.

*

Jenny was shivering and the room seemed to be swaying; she was going to fall out of bed. She had been dreaming, dreaming of oceans of blood. She was drowning in a thick, clotted morass. She fought for air as the snake came towards her. The snake of childhood nightmares was trying to force itself into her mouth. She thrashed at the covers that were suffocating her and managed to half sit, half slump against the wall. Her heart thumped and her nightdress stuck to her, it was sodden and limp with sweat.

There was a gentle tap on the door and Miss Pritchard walked in. She sat on the edge of the bed and took Jenny's hand.

"You look very flushed, my dear."

She rested her other hand on Jenny's forehead and looked concerned.

"William and his mother have been on the phone. He and his parents want you to go to their house; they want to look after you but are you well enough to travel?"

Tears streamed down Jenny's face. She felt so ill how would she get herself over to Golders Green?

"Now looking at you, I'm not sure you should go on your own, not even in a taxi. I'd take you there myself but the rest of the staff are off duty. I can't leave the hostel."

"I'll be all right. I'll have a wash and pack some things. I'll manage."

She gave a watery smile and sat up. Her head swam but she must make the effort. Miss Pritchard helped her out of bed.

"Now you tell me where everything is and I'll pack. You have a wash; it will make you feel better."

Jenny tottered to the bathroom and wondered if this was how it would feel when she was very old. There was no strength in her and she seemed to be moving in slow motion. The bathroom was miles away and when she got there the taps resisted her attempts to turn them on. She shivered. Her bones ached but she gritted her teeth and tried the taps again. Success, she splashed her face

93

and for a moment felt revived. She peeled the drenched nightdress from her clammy skin – like a snake sloughing off a redundant outer layer. She splashed her body with water and made a half hearted attempt to dry herself.

She rinsed her mouth but the foul whiff of infection remained. She looked in the mirror and was shocked, she looked dreadful. What would William think? Her hair was limp and plastered to her head with sweat. She felt too ill to care. She longed to lie down and rest until her body could sort itself out. She went back to her room.

"I've packed for a few days and put out something for you to wear now. You must keep warm. Get dressed while I call a taxi."

Jenny slumped on the bed so weak it was scary. She had had bad throats before but nothing like this. As she dressed she thought about William and his family, it was nice of them to take her in.

She thought back over the years of her childhood, it hadn't been easy. With Dad in the army, even though he had custody of her, life had been disjointed. There had been so many homes but only because people had been paid to have her. But now here was a family that wanted her to go to them because she wasn't well.

Her constant longing to be part of a family brought tears to her eyes; she hated feeling so alone. She wondered who had suggested she should go over, she hoped it was William. She thought it was more likely to be Mr. Martin; he seemed such a nice man.

She wished she didn't feel so wary of Iris but there was something frightening about her. She must have agreed to the arrangement since it was unlikely she would do anything she didn't want to do.

Jenny blew her nose, wiped her eyes and feeling a little better stood up to finish dressing. She checked her bag; everything was folded, Jenny couldn't think of anything else she might need. What a kind woman Miss Pritchard was, Jenny thought, as she heard the brisk footsteps coming along the corridor.

"Taxi's here." Miss Pritchard took Jenny's bag and shepherded her out of the room, down the stairs and into the taxi.

"Now take care of yourself, I'm sure you will soon be feeling better. I've explained to the driver that you are not well, just give him the address and you'll be there in no time."

Miss Pritchard smiled and waved as the taxi drew away. Jenny did as she was told, sank back in her seat and slept.

*

Laura lay still; the pains had receded to a point where they were just a dull ache. The anaesthetic had left her feeling groggy and when she came round she had been violently sick. Now the drip had been taken from her arm she assumed that her blood level was back to normal. She was in a side ward. It was a pleasant room with pale yellow walls and floral curtains.

She had wondered when she first opened her eyes if they were expecting her to die. There seemed little chance of that now even if she did feel like a rag doll that had lost most of its stuffing. Last night had been different. She had wanted death then and had yearned for something, anything that would relieve the agony. That, combined with the horror and shame at what she had done, made death appealing.

Today, as she looked out of the window, there was hope. The sun shone and she could see people walking in the grounds. The past is dead and gone but I am not, she sighed and wondered how everything was going to work out.

She had vague memories of her parents being with her last night but it was all so confused. What would they would be feeling and how much had they been told? Her relationship with them had been so full of anger and resentment. It surprised her that now she felt a great desire to make amends, to start again, to stop fighting and be at peace with these two people that made her.

Perhaps I'm beginning to grow up, she thought. She smiled to herself, I thought I was so grown up but it was all an illusion. She closed her eyes and relished the sensation of peace. She was floating on a sea of sleep when she heard footsteps. Eric and Susan Johnson walked into her room. Laura opened her eyes and smiled at her parents.

Her mother placed a bunch of flowers by the bed and bent to kiss Laura's forehead. Her father pulled a chair to the other side of the bed and sat down.

"Hello Mum, Dad, I'm feeling so much better."

"Are you well enough to talk?" Eric asked.

"Not too much yet, dear." Susan said.

Laura looked from one to the other.

"We thought we'd lost you." Susan dabbed her eyes and

95

clutched Laura's hand.

"We've talked to Dr.Stirling, he was the surgeon who had to patch you up."

Laura picked up the note of censure in her father's voice.

"I'm so sorry. I didn't want you to find out, I've been stupid, I know that now."

"You lost three pints of blood, it was a close call. Thank God you were found when you were, the transfusion you had saved your life." Eric cleared his throat and looked away.

In that moment Laura realised that the thing her dad had always been best at was hiding his feelings.

"You could have told us you know." Susan stroked Laura's hand.

"What that I was pregnant? I don't think so, what would the neighbours have thought?"

Susan wept into her handkerchief.

"Dr. Stirling said he thought you had had something done to make you lose the baby. Is that right?"

"Oh, Dad I did it for the best. I didn't know this was how it would end up."

"Who was it?"

"I don't know, a friend gave me an address, that's all. I went there and this man started things, I was told he was a doctor. I thought it would be all right."

Susan gasped. "A man, some strange man claiming to be a doctor?"

"Yes, Mum, that's how these things are done."

"This friend, was he the one who…."

"No, Dad he wasn't the one responsible. He just wanted to help me out."

"The police should be told before some other poor girl is butchered."

"I can't, Dad. Please don't ask me."

"That's enough now," Susan said, "let's think about what really matters and that's getting you fit and well again. We want you back you know, can we persuade you to come home?"

Laura sighed. "Oh yes please. I promise things will be different."

Eric smiled for the first time. "Let's do our best to patch things up; we've all made mistakes."

*

George walked into the kitchen, rubbed his hands together and sniffed.

"By Jove something smells good, my dear."

Iris knew what he was doing because the pattern never changed. Whenever she gave him the silent treatment he would conduct one-sided conversations that didn't require a reply. To anyone else all seemed normal but not to her. *He hopes I'll get tired of it in the end.*

In the past his crimes had been nebulous, insubstantial compared with the business of June. He must realise, Iris reasoned, *that things would never be the same again. But I will broach the subject when I'm good and ready,* Iris thought.

"I expect Jenny will be here soon, it'll be splendid for her to have such a feast. Don't suppose this is what she's used to."

Iris continued washing up pots, pans and bowls.

"Let me help you with those," George said. Iris glared at him. He shrugged and sat at the kitchen table..

William shouted from the living room. "Hasn't mum told you, Jenny's ill, they're sending her over in a taxi. Mum said she'd be better off here."

"What a kind thought," George said, "it's good of you to take on extra when Freddie's home."

Iris turned. Washing-up water dripped from her rubber gloves.

"Yes, George, it is good of me. I've done my best but then I always do. And a fat lot of thanks I get for it. I haven't just been a good wife and mother."

"No-one would disagree with that."

"I have always entertained your business colleagues and wives, undoubtedly enhancing your career at the expense of my own." She paused, waited for some response. She could feel the adrenalin pumping if only he would reply in kind but they never had blazing rows. George was always the peacemaker.

"Yes dear, I have always appreciated what you have done for me." George stood and moved closer, placed his hand on Iris's arm. She moved away.

"In fact Bergmann and his wife are coming over from Stockholm soon and I am relying on you to do your usual wonderful job as hostess."

"Oh really, thanks for letting me know."

"There hasn't been much opportunity over the past few days."

Iris stared at him. "And whose fault's that?"

"Mine, darling, mine, I know and I'm sorry. We'll discuss arrangements some other time."

The front door opened with a rush.

"Hi Mum, hi Dad, I'm not late am I?"

It had always been Freddie's exuberance that delighted Iris. Here was her baby whose vitality made her shiver with pride and anticipation of all the wonderful things he was bound to achieve. She knew her pride in his very existence, this wondrous fruit of her womb, glossed over any possible flaw in his character or ability but she didn't care. He was her joy now and always. He was the son she had really wanted and she walked towards him her arms held wide.

"Of course you are not late, my darling." She kissed him on the cheek but out of the corner of her eye saw him roll his eyes at George.

At this moment the taxi arrived with Jenny. Iris opened the front door while George told Freddie what was happening. William went out to help Jenny from the taxi and encouraged her to lean on his arm

"Sorry I'm such a sight," she croaked.

She walked slowly to the house and was shaking with exhaustion by the time she had been eased upstairs to the spare bedroom.

"I think the doctor should see her," George said, "I'll call him now."

Dr. Goodwin soon arrived and after a thorough examination diagnosed a severe case of tonsillitis. Antibiotics, bed-rest and plenty of fluids were prescribed. William was dispatched to get the prescription dispensed. George made a large jug of barley water and Dr. Goodwin departed leaving instructions that he should be called if matters didn't improve. Iris caught Freddie in the kitchen dipping his finger in the hollandaise sauce. She tapped his fingers.

"Naughty boy," she said and smiled.

*

Upstairs, Jenny lay still. The bed was like a cloud and she sank into it so she had no sensation of weight. She was floating, adrift on a calm sea, being rocked to sleep. She had drunk two glasses of the delicious barley water and taken the first dose of antibiotics two hours ago.   The buzz of conversation from downstairs ebbed and flowed in and out of her consciousness like

a friendly swarm of bees that would do her no harm. William had popped his head round the door to check she had everything she needed and she had smiled, delighted by his concern.

The nightmarish terrors she had experienced only hours before had faded and Jenny recognised them for what they were – the imaginings of a fevered mind.

She was very concerned for Laura and would call Miss Pritchard for news when she felt better. There was nothing she need do now but rest, let go and drift. She was with people who cared for her. She was lucky. There had been Miss Pritchard and now the Martins.

If your family didn't care there could always be others, nice people like Mark. Suddenly she was wide awake. What about Mark? Today was Friday and she was supposed to be meeting him tomorrow; what could she do? He'd be waiting for her at 1p.m. at the Strand Palace. Could she ring the place and leave a message? What was his other name? He hadn't told her. Her head ached again, there was nothing she could do; she would just have to leave it. Perhaps she would be well enough to go tomorrow if she slept soundly tonight. Instinct warned her that Iris would never agree to that.

*

Chapter 16

When Jenny woke the sun was shining. She swallowed gently, her throat wasn't sore. She stretched, yawned and sat up; there were the noises of people moving about. It was amazing that she felt so much better after last night. She glanced at her watch, half past ten, what would Dad have said at such laziness?

She shuddered as she remembered the countless mornings when Dad got up at the crack of dawn and expected her to do the same. She wondered how he was; she wanted to contact him but feared a rebuff. He always made things so difficult. After the business with William it had been almost impossible to have a civil conversation. Perhaps she should write but he never wrote to her.

At least Mum did keep in touch after a fashion. Jenny knew she would have to pay her a visit soon. That would be difficult but in a different way from Dad. Alec was all right as far as step-fathers went, it was his and Mum's kids that made things awkward, Stephen and Ruth had never accepted her. Families were a problem, particularly parents, even William, with all the trappings of prosperity, had a mother to make your heart sink.

She leaned back on the pillows, there must be some happy families somewhere; perhaps I will have one myself one day. The idea of being a matriarch overseeing this imaginary, delightful, large and happy family made her smile; it was nice to day-dream.

Meanwhile what about Mark and the lunch-time meeting? She slipped on her dressing gown and went in search of the bathroom. She was confronted by Iris with a breakfast tray.

"What are you doing out of bed?"

"I needed the toilet."

"Straight back to bed afterwards."

William was coming up stairs and pulled a face at Jenny. She assumed he was warning her that any argument would be futile. She smiled and hoped her appearance was less cadaver-like than it had been the previous evening. Once again she was spellbound by his astonishing good looks with his golden hair and blue eyes. He had a slow-moving, languid grace that suggested confidence. What does he see in me Jenny had often wondered? I rush about like a headless chicken, I have no poise, I'm not pretty yet he likes me.

She locked the bathroom door. Her legs still felt wobbly but she thought she'd survive. She washed her face and hands, and dampened her hair which was a disaster. It stuck to her head at the sides but stood upright on top.

"I look like Stan Laurel," she said to her reflection. She gave up trying to flatten and tidy it. She would have to wash it soon but wondered if Iris would sanction such a reckless activity.

She went back to her room and got into bed. Iris placed the tray on her lap; there was fruit juice, boiled egg, toast and coffee.

"You look better this morning, did you sleep well?"

"Yes, thank you, I feel tons better."

"You must stay in bed today and maybe get up for a little while tomorrow."

Jenny's heart sank; this was not going to be easy. She swallowed hard, the lump in her throat was there but this time it was not caused by tonsillitis. What about Mark? Dad had always said it was wrong, selfish and irresponsible to let people down; she was going to let Mark down and there didn't seem to be anything she could do about it.

"It's a bit difficult, Mrs. Martin."

Although she had been told to call William's parents Iris and George somehow she could not bring herself to do it.

"There's nothing difficult about it; you're a friend of William's."

Jenny noticed with dismay that she was a friend and not the girlfriend, a subtle but significant distinction, she thought.

"We can't have you being ill on your own; you must stay with us until you are completely better."

"It's very kind of you but I'm so much better and you see I had arranged to meet this friend." She paused. "I can't get in touch to cancel the arrangement."

Jenny watched as Iris swelled with indignation.

"You see I don't like to let people down."

She stopped; it was pointless, Iris's expression made that very clear.

"No I'm sure you don't want to let people down so you should not even think of letting us down. We have taken you in because we are concerned for your welfare. We paid a consultation fee to our doctor, private I should point out. If you leave this house to keep an arrangement with a friend and so put your health at risk you will not come here again. You can make your apologies next time you see this person, any true friend would understand."

That was it. Jenny felt she had just run headlong into a brick wall.

"I'm sorry," she whispered, "I don't want to be a nuisance."

"You won't be as long as you do as you are told."

Iris gave a tight smile and left. Jenny sighed and smacked her teaspoon down hard on her boiled egg. Sorry Mark, I did try, I hope I will be able to explain another time. William poked his head round the door.

"How's the invalid?"

"Tons better, thanks, you don't want an egg do you? This is soft-boiled and I just can't eat them like that."

William plonked himself on the bed making the tray lurch.

"Shall I ask Mum to do you another?"

"Oh no, don't do that, toast will be fine."

He raised his eyebrows. "Crossed swords with my old lady, have you?"

Jenny wondered how Iris would react to William calling her that.

"Sort of," Jenny squirmed. She felt disloyal to William, what would he think if he knew she had arranged to meet someone else - even if it was innocent?

"I just thought I was well enough to get up."

"Whatever you do don't try to stop Mother when she's got her Florence Nightingale cap on. She loves it. There's nothing like a captive patient to get her going, watch out or she'll have you in bed for a week."

"But I've got to go to work on Monday."

"I wouldn't bank on it, don't let her phone your boss. He'll think you are about to peg out with typhoid and order a wreath."

Jenny giggled, he really was lovely. As he leaned forward his hands brushed her breasts before he rested his arms on her shoulders.

"Give me a kiss you bug-ridden brute."

She tingled as she leaned towards him and their lips met.

"Just you wait until you are better."

Her heart thumped and she could feel colour suffuse her neck and face. She looked away, all at once shy.

"Eat your breakfast, I'll explain to Mum about the egg." He closed the door and left her in a state of confusion.

*

Mark had shaved with extra care and had his hair trimmed, he would still be in plenty of time. He walked to the Tube Station in bright sunlight, it was a beautiful day. He felt an inner peace; life was sorting itself out rather well. Confirmation of his transfer had come through and he would be moving north, to Manchester, in two weeks. He had told Jim et al. that they would need another flat mate, very satisfying that had been. Let Jim do the donkey work in future.

This meeting with Jenny would decide whether they should see each other again. She seemed such a nice girl. Of course since he was moving away it would not be ideal but if they hit it off he could arrange to see her again before he left London. He wondered if he was placing too much importance on this date. But wasn't there supposed to be chemistry between people that was evident from the start?

He'd thought that about dear Denise who had blown into his life like a tornado and left it with equally dramatic effect once she had achieved the desired level of chaos and heartache. Time will tell, he thought, meanwhile the sun is shining, I've got a date with a nice girl, what more could a bloke ask for?

He whistled under his breath as he approached the station. If things went really well perhaps she would want to move north too. He shook his head in disbelief at his own capacity for romancing but perhaps that was what he was ready for now, a new romance.

On the platform the noise grew and a rush of air blew along the platform as his train arrived. Unlike during the week, it was almost empty; no strap hanging today.

Because he was so early and the weather was fine he decided to get off at the Embankment and walk the rest of the way, cutting through Villiers Street and up the Strand. The streets were busy with tourists and youngsters in town for the day. There was a light-hearted, holiday atmosphere which suited his mood.

He reached the Strand Palace at twelve forty, stood to one side of the main entrance and lit a cigarette. He enjoyed people-watching and speculated on the lives of the stream of people walking past. What were they like, where were they going, were they happy? He felt relaxed and more content with life than he had for many months. It was only now the heartache was diminishing that he realised how much Denise had hurt him.

He glanced at his watch, one o'clock, Jenny would be here soon. He started to look above the heads of people hoping to get a glimpse of her. Which way would she come? She was unlikely to have walked as far as he had. Charing Cross was her nearest stop and then, like him, she would come up the Strand. No sign of her yet. He would have predicted that she was the sort to arrive on time.

He checked his watch again, ten past. He felt a tremor of disappointment, perhaps she was waiting inside. He walked into the foyer and upstairs to the Salad Bowl restaurant. It was very busy but he couldn't see her. This is stupid, he thought, she's stood me up.

He went downstairs again, twenty past, I'll wait until half past, he decided, then that's it. He lit another cigarette. He was just a fool, taken in again, he was bloody sick of it. Women let you down every time, can't trust any of them, he pulled hard on his cigarette. But Jenny had seemed different; they were the worst, the ones who led you on.

He paused, unwilling to accept that his judgement could be so faulty. Supposing something had happened, she wouldn't have been able to let him know, would she? He heard a clock somewhere above the sound of the traffic; it was chiming the half hour. He hesitated, no point in waiting any longer but somehow he would have to try to find out where she lived. Something must have happened.

*

After a light lunch of home-made soup and French bread, Iris was making coffee in the kitchen, she had asked Freddie to help her carry it through. She could hear the buzz of conversation between George and William in the living room. Jenny was asleep upstairs. Iris was pleased to have exerted her authority over the girl. Freddie might use the house like a hotel but Jenny would not. With the extra work of making meals suitable for an invalid, Iris felt she had pulled out all the stops and Jenny had better realise it. She placed cups of coffee on a tray.

"Take it through now will you, darling?"

Iris followed Freddie through and caught the end of what William was saying.

"... I've tried I really have."

George looked up from his paper.

"When I was your age, my lad, I was out every day for months, in all weathers. Woolux was in its infancy then"

"Yes, but Dad."

"You should listen to your father, William; you've only been with the firm five minutes."

"Mum, you don't understand. I'm just no good at selling, I have tried."

"So what do you think you would be good at?" George folded his paper

"I don't know."

"Your trouble is you have no fire in your belly; you've never had to struggle."

"What do you think it was like for me in Canada?" Iris said as she poured coffee.

"Oh, it's the united front now is it, that makes a change," William said.

"Don't speak to your mother like that. She's worked hard to make things nice for you." George turned to Freddie, "For you both, so don't you sit there smirking."

"And for this friend of yours," Iris added as she handed William a cup of coffee.

"But selling is a special skill, everyone knows that."

"Listen lad," George leaned forward. "I wore my feet ragged traipsing from shop to shop. It didn't do me any harm."

"Why can't I work in the office?"

"Because if you want the people you employ to respect you, you have to show you can do the same as them. I assume you do still want to be in the business." George looked at William for several seconds, waiting.

"Yes, of course, but not as a salesman."

George sighed. "Things are changing. It's the young who dictate fashion now. I need younger salesman and I want my son to be one of them. We must adjust or die."

"And you wouldn't like that would you William. The trouble is you've had too much." Iris sipped her coffee. It was time, she decided, that William had some home truths.

"But if I'm no good at selling, I could no more harm than good."

"I'll send you round with Johnny Wilson; he can sell ice to Eskimos."

"That reminds me," Iris said, "when is Bergman coming over?"

"Next week, with his wife...."

"I see. You aren't expecting them to stay here are you?"

"Of course not but I'll need to entertain them and....."

105

He smiled at her but Iris looked away. She wondered if that was how he beguiled that slut, June. She would have to be got rid of, there was no doubt about that. Iris got up and collected the crockery before striding from the room. George followed her.

"Shut the door," she said, "You and I are going to have a very serious talk because I've had enough. I'm not prepared to upset Freddie as heaven knows we see little enough of him. So it'll have to wait until tomorrow evening. But I warn you things are going to change."

She turned to the sink and with considerable vigour started on the washing up.

Freddie ambled into the kitchen. "Mum says we're going to Granddad and Grandma's tomorrow."

"Yes, your Aunt Sheila's putting on a meal," George said.

"Don't know why we can't have it here," Iris said.

"Because you know your Mum wouldn't be able to come. Sheila wants us all together."

"I'll get the late afternoon train tomorrow, then," Freddie said, "If I pack and leave my stuff in the car boot will you drop me at the station, Dad?"

"Certainly, old lad, I suppose you'll be glad to be back with your mates."

Freddie grinned and slouched out of the room.

Iris bristled but at the same time a pang of fear made her blanch. Why did he always seem so glad to be gone?

"I won't be able to make the meal at Mum and Dad's," she said.

"Why not?" George asked.

"Well in case you've forgotten there's Jenny to consider."

"But she says she feels so much better, surely by tomorrow she will be well enough to go back to the hostel."

"There's no guarantee and if she is well enough how's she going to get back? I thought she could either stay here for an extra day or I'd take her back myself."

"Shouldn't I do that? Your Mum and Dad will be sorry if you aren't there."

"They aren't fussed about me."

"Let's wait until tomorrow shall we?"

*

Chapter 17

The table was set, the candles ready to light. A bunch of anemones that Barbara had bought on her way home now sat in the middle of the table, in a pottery vase she had made years before at evening class. The rich purples, blues and reds of the blooms were reflected in the crystal wine glasses placed on an immaculate, white tablecloth. Matching napkins had been folded simply, Barbara was anxious not to overwhelm Charles with too much grandeur.

Everything in the kitchen was under control as Barbara mixed herself a small gin and tonic. She glanced at her watch, he would be on time, to the minute; he was that type. She was about to sit down when the doorbell rang, she smiled and hurried downstairs to let him in.

Charles did not speak as he looked round Barbara's living room. She watched his face and wondered if he felt as uneasy as he looked. He fumbled in the pockets of what Barbara assumed had been his army trench coat. Did he need to cling to his identity as a military man, did it give him confidence?

He produced a bottle of wine and a box of chocolates which he offered with a small bow and a click of his brown, brogue heels. Barbara smiled and gave a mock curtsey.

"Thank you kind sir; white wine, that's good, we are having chicken. I'll put this in the fridge. Now what will you have to drink, sherry or gin and tonic?"

He paused and Barbara realised she should have bought some beer; he was bound to feel that beer was a real man's drink.

"Sherry would be fine, not too sweet."

Tension crackled between them and Barbara remembered what Gordon and Joan had said after their evening at Charles's flat. Perhaps he was scared of women. Drink in hand, Barbara moved towards the sofa and indicated that he should join her.

"Food won't be long, I hope you are hungry."

"If it tastes as good as it smells I'm in for a treat."

"I confess I love cooking, it's the one creative thing about being a housewife."

"I hope you haven't spent too much time on all this."

"Why? Aren't you worth it?"

He looked at her and she realised he wasn't sure if she was serious or making fun of him.

"You'll have to decide that at the end of the evening," he said.

There was a pause and they looked at each other. This is like walking on egg shells, Barbara thought.

"I'm not very good at small talk," Charles said.

Barbara pulled a face, "No neither am I, so let's get down to business; tell me about you."

"I work for the Post Office; I live alone in that dreary flat. There's not much else to tell."

"Nonsense, what about when you were a child? Where were you brought up, do you have brothers or sisters?"

He held up his hands. "I surrender. Gordon didn't warn me to expect the third degree, have you ever thought of being an interrogation officer? I'd give you a good reference."

She laughed. "Sorry, but I am interested."

"O.K. I grew up in Camden Town, not a particularly nice part of north London. I have an older sister and my parents are dead. Actually I did have three older brothers but they all died as babies."

Barbara shivered; the ghost of her own child swirled in her head and clouded her thoughts.

"How tragic, it was so common then, so much suffering."

"I suppose so; it must have knocked the stuffing out of Mum and Dad. They never talked about it but I found the memorial cards for each of their dead children after Mum died."

They sipped their drinks in silence, each reflecting on the tragedy of life.

"What about your sister, what's she like?"

Charles paused. "I don't know what she's like now, we lost contact."

Barbara raised her eyebrows. "What a shame."

"Not seen her since before Mum went into hospital, that's seven years ago."

Barbara waited.

"You see I phoned her; I told her Mum was dying, she was so frail by that time, like a little bird, struggling for every breath."

He stopped and looked away and Barbara patted his hand.

"It's the role reversal that's so hard to cope with. They care for us when we're small then as they become vulnerable we care for them."

Charles snorted. "Connie never came you know, never one to put herself out, she just couldn't be bothered. I wanted nothing to do with her after that."

It's obvious, Barbara thought, that people who cross Charles or who don't live up to his standards do so at their peril.

"That was her loss," she said.

Charles sat back. "What about you? It's my turn to do the questioning."

"Oh, very boring, I'm an only child and I lived in suburban bliss in genteel Bromley until I came to London and qualified as a librarian. But went back often to see my parents."

"I envy you that; the army gives few opportunities for family visits. I wish I'd seen more of my parents as they got older."

"Mum died three years ago, cancer. Dad coped for a bit but he had a stroke last year. It was a blessing he did not live long after that; he hated being an invalid. I'm glad he was spared the living death some poor souls have to endure for months and sometimes years."

Charles nodded, "Mum was ill for years and she never really got over my Dad dying."

Barbara stood up, "I had better go and check the food, you wouldn't want burnt offerings."

She felt him watching her as she walked to the kitchen. Assured that all was well, she returned with a basket of Melba toast and pate.

"Grub's up, grab a chair."

She lit the candles which made the curls of deep-yellow butter glisten. Charles sat down and draped the large, white damask napkin across his knees. He looked across at her and smiled.

"Cheers," she said as she raised the remains of her gin and tonic.

"Cheers, this looks truly wonderful."

*

Mark had left the whole day free in the hope that he and Jenny could have a leisurely time together after their meal. Now he had time to kill. On impulse he went to Euston to see when the next train to Manchester was. He felt an urge to go back home even if it was only for the weekend.

The train journey was uneventful and Mark had watched as the hectic jostle of cramped terraced houses melted into a more spacious suburbia with its neat semis and well-tended gardens. At last the train was moving through open country. Mark sighed and leaned back in his seat wondering if this was what he had missed.

109

He recalled the times he had spent living in Greenfield, one of Saddleworth's villages. Mum and Dad had rented a weaver's cottage on the main street but soon after that Dad had decided they would buy outright even though the price was five hundred pounds. That had been a princely sum after the war. Dad had been an engineer and worked at Fletcher's Mill where cigarette papers were still manufactured.

It had been an idyllic childhood with the grandeur of the West Riding hills sheltering the village from the excesses of Yorkshire's winter weather. Mark smiled. He and Tommy Barraclough had roamed the fields and spent glorious days building dams in Chew Brook, which ran through the village.

Hot summers had bronzed their skins and they had pretended to be Red Indians on the war path. Mark wondered what Tommy was doing now, the last news he had heard was that his friend had gone into the army, the Cheshire regiment.

When Mark was twelve his Dad had taught him to shoot and on many a crisp morning the pair of them had gone out to tackle the thousands of rabbits in the area. The mill owners supplied the pellets because rabbits did so much damage to the water course the mill workers relied on. Sometimes Mark and Dad had indulged in a little poaching of game birds but they always managed to evade the game-keeper.

It had all changed when Dad decided to move nearer to Oldham. He had wanted the best of everything for his family and a neat semi-detached house in Chadderton was their next home. Going up in the world had led to a small car too. By now Mark was at the local grammar school and Mum had a job managing the clothing department in Oldham's Co-op.

Perhaps it had been his teenage years in Chadderton that persuaded him to go to London to make his fortune. Mum and Dad had encouraged him but he had sometimes seen a wistful look in his mother's eyes that suggested how hard it would be to have her only child leave the area. But she never said so and now her only son was returning, to his roots. He was going to get on with his life away from the choking fumes and frantic noise and bustle of the Metropolis.

The other passengers were dozing or reading their papers as Mark stood up. He needed to stretch his legs and left the compartment to go to the buffet car. Yet again he wondered what had happened to Jenny. He chided himself for dwelling on an insignificant episode with someone he had only met once. He'd been so sure she would turn up even if it was only to tell him she didn't want to have lunch with him. He felt sure she was a decent girl who wouldn't have left him in the lurch.

He leaned against the corridor window and stared out, trying to recall her face. It was the eyes that he remembered, so green, like the green of trees reflected in still pools. He shrugged.

"Don't be daft," he muttered and swayed his way to the buffet car.

"Can I help you Sir?" A spotty-faced youth in a British Rail jacket asked as Mark looked at the unappetising selection of sandwiches on display. Everything said about British Rail food was true, he thought.

"A cheese sandwich and a cup of tea, please," he said. He bit into the sandwich which was as dry as it looked; it would be good to have some of Mum's cooking.

*

Jenny was finally allowed to join the Martin family for the evening meal. She had had a warm bath, washed her hair and dressed. She was alarmed by the weakness she felt after one day in bed and wondered how people recovering from protracted illness managed to get fit again.

She wished she felt more comfortable in this house. There was such a strong undercurrent of antagonism, surely the Martins must be aware of it too or had it gone on so long that they ignored it? She felt apprehensive as she walked downstairs, not only was there Iris to face, she would also meet Freddie.

She went into the kitchen where Iris was putting the final touches to what would be the final meal the family would have together for several months.

"Is there anything I can do?"

Iris looked both surprised and pleased, neither William nor Freddie often made such an offer.

"Thank you, dear. Would you carry the plates through and tell the men the meal's ready."

Jenny smiled, the 'dear' felt nice, perhaps Iris had a softer side. Having done as she was told she waited until everyone was seated and then slid into the vacant place indicated by George.

"Good to see you looking so much better," George said. "This is our younger son, Freddie." He added, "Freddie this is Jenny, a friend of William's."

Jenny felt William's leg press against hers and she blushed.

"Pleased to meet you," she said to the young man who was the image of his father.

Iris pushed the laden trolley with a huge joint of beef and many vegetable dishes into the dining room. Jenny watched as George carved the meat while Iris transferred the other dishes from trolley to table. It reminded Jenny of Grandmother Cardew's house.

Although her memories were clouded by time she did recall the grandeur and elegance of that house and all that was in it. Jenny realised with shock that despite all the finery and expense that was evident in the Martin's home the grandeur and elegance, the birth right of the well-bred, was missing.

Grandmother had often scathingly referred to the 'nouveau riche' and Jenny knew now what she had meant. Jenny felt less apprehensive as she looked at Iris perhaps she too felt insecure. Perhaps all the bluster was a contrived carapace designed to protect and deflect attack.

"Jenny kindly offered to help." Iris looked around the table as her remark fell like a stone into the pool of silence. She watched as ripples of discomfort spread and Jenny stared at her plate. To be praised to the detriment of the rest of the family embarrassed her, she wondered if that had been Iris's intention.

George and William exchanged glances and Freddie laughed.

"Come off it, Ma, you just love being the queen bee, lording it or should it be ladying it in the kitchen. Anyway that's a woman's place everyone knows that."

Jenny watched as a huge smile appeared on Freddie's face. Everyone around the table was included in his joke but the smile was aimed at Iris. The atmosphere relaxed at once. Iris chuckled and ruffled Freddie's hair as she sat down. This was worse than walking on egg-shells, Jenny thought, she was staring into the crater of an active volcano.

"You mustn't let Ma bully you, you know." Freddie grinned at her. "Her bark's worse than her bite."

Jenny had no idea how to respond without upsetting the harmonious atmosphere which Freddie had created. She felt herself blush and nodded.

"You are definitely looking better now," George said, "but

how do you feel?"

"Much better thank you, it is so kind of you to take me in like this and care for me." She turned to Iris. "I must have made so much extra work for you."

So far so good, Jenny thought, Iris looked pleased.

"I think I shall be well enough to go to work on Monday so I had better think about getting back to the hostel."

"We'll see." Iris said.

"What's the hostel like?" Freddie asked.

"Not bad, a bit Spartan, nothing like as comfortable or luxurious as here, of course." Jenny sensed the increased level of conviviality. Lots of compliments, flattery, sycophancy, that seemed to be the answer.

"Can't be much fun shut up with a load of women," Freddie speculated.

"Some people wouldn't mind, I don't suppose," Iris said. She watched, wanted to make sure George registered the remark. He is like a fish on a line, she thought, just when he thinks he can swim away I jerk the line taut. Tomorrow, when we are on our own, is going to be interesting.

*

Chapter 18

There was little conversation as Iris drove through town on Sunday afternoon and Jenny wondered if she would ever feel comfortable in this woman's company. She had said she would be happy to go back to the hostel on the Tube particularly as the whole family were expected to dine with Iris's parents but Iris would have none of it.

"My son will be going to Stockholm soon to gain experience before he takes up a post with Woolux."

Jenny felt her chest contract with alarm; William was going away but no-one would say how long for.

"I expect he'll enjoy that," she paused, "I hope I'll be able to travel one day. My father travelled all over the place when he was in the army. He said it was exciting."

"You should get as much experience as you can before you meet Mr. Right."

Iris turned towards Jenny and smiled briefly. The message was both given and received. In her view Jenny was not Mrs. Right. Jenny looked down at the directions to the hostel that she had worked out using the Martins' A-Z and decided to say nothing.

"I should have done more before I married George."

"What would you have liked to have done?"

Jenny suspected that after Freddie, Iris was Iris's favourite topic of conversation.

"I was a model, you know."

"Yes, William told me. That must have been wonderful."

"But soon after I met George we decided to get married and he made a public announcement of our engagement."

"How romantic," Jenny said.

"Well that was the end of my freedom."

"How?"

"He had to go back to England for months on end and I was left high and dry. No decent young Canadian would try to date an engaged woman."

"Oh, it must have been lonely for you."

"That was that and I was stuck at home. I did have my work but it started to dry up and there didn't seem much point in trying anything else – not if I was coming to England."

"It must have been very different here, from Canada that is."

"I could have been the Jean Shrimpton of my day."

Jenny watched Iris from the corner of her eye as she told her tale of lost opportunity and thwarted ambition. I wouldn't mind if William wanted to announce an engagement, she thought, at least I'd belong to someone who really wanted me. The sunlight of a beautiful autumn day caught the down-turned mouth and the lines of dissatisfaction carved into Iris's face.

"Couldn't you take up a hobby or interest now, something that you would enjoy, that would give you satisfaction?"

There was a lengthy pause during which Jenny realised how stupid she'd been. Iris would never be one to take advice from a teenager. She felt her skin prickle with apprehension.

"My husband would never agree to my doing something that suggested he wasn't a good provider and I must always be available to act as companion and hostess to the wives of his business colleagues. That is what is expected of a managing director's wife."

That's put me in my place, Jenny thought. Not only did Iris assume I didn't know what was expected of a managing director's wife but that I'd never be one.

"Of course that must make it very difficult for you," she said.

The final instructions given, Jenny closed the A-Z and sat in silence until she could see the hostel.

"It's the big building on the left."

Iris stopped the car and switched off the engine.

"Thank you very much, Mrs. Martin, you have looked after me so well. I do appreciate it."

Iris smiled. "Do you like living here?"

"It's O.K. but it's not like having a proper home."

"What do your parents think?"

"I'm not sure. I think Dad was happy to see me becoming independent and I've not lived with Mum for some time so it doesn't make any difference to her."

"Don't you see either of them?"

"Not often."

This was awful – like being a fly on a pin. Jenny wanted to get away but she mustn't upset her, she was William's mother. Whatever I do, Jenny concluded, I've got to keep her happy.

"Don't you mind?"

"Pardon?"

"Not seeing them."

"I didn't spend much time with them when I was little so I'm

115

used to them not being around."

"I see. You'll be all right now won't you? I'd better get back. I want to see Freddie before he goes."

She switched the engine on and put the car in gear. Jenny picked up her bag, closed the car door gently and waved as Iris pulled away from the kerb.

*

Mark sat on the top of Indian's Head, the distinctive crag that looked down over Greenfield valley. He knew he was out of condition; life in London had made him soft. As he looked across the fields and meadows he knew he had made the right decision.

He wondered if Mum missed the countryside as he had. Perhaps he'd buy a little cottage in Greenfield or one of the other villages then he could go walking whenever he wanted, straight out of the front door and away. He poured another cup of coffee from his thermos and listened to a solitude that was broken only by the chirruping of birds.

Mum had been delighted to see him and they had spent the previous evening reminiscing and catching up on news of the people Mark had grown up with. His mate, Tommy Barraclough, had left the army and moved to Norwich. Mum said he was courting a girl there. Mr. and Mrs. Barraclough still lived in Chadderton; Mark would go round and get Tommy's new address.

Mark had told his Mum about Jenny. He'd wondered if she would think he was being silly. She didn't. He had been surprised when she said "You know it is possible to fall in love at first sight, I did with your Dad. If you really think this girl is special you'd better track her down."

Mark bit into the apple Mum had put in with his sandwiches. It was easy to say track her down but how? He didn't know her surname, he didn't know if she lived at the hostel or if she was just someone Laura had met at the Palais, perhaps Laura was the answer. He knew she did live at the hostel so he could contact her there. First decision made, he thought, as he repacked his rucksack. That's what he would do as soon as he got back to London.

*

By the time Iris got to her parents' house the meal was over, that was as she had hoped. Walking in on them had shocked her; they all seemed so damned cheerful. She had kissed her parents

116

and talked about Jenny but the mood had been shattered simply because she had arrived. Once again she felt she was the outsider and after all she had done.

George had left almost at once to take Freddie to the station and she'd told William to stay with his grandparents for a while. Now, back home, she was ready. She stood in front of the French windows where she could see her reflection and that of anyone who came into the room.

She heard the key in the lock and waited. George walked into the room, glanced at her and slumped into a chair. She noted that he looked tired. She felt adrenalin flow through her, she felt alive, vibrant. June would go, of that she was certain.

She turned and stubbed out her cigarette in the overflowing ashtray.

"You do realise this can't go on."

"What can't go on?"

Iris lit another cigarette and exhaled noisily.

"This business with your bloody secretary cum bed mate."

She watched as he closed his eyes.

He struggled to his feet. "Where're the aspirins?"

"In the medicine cupboard."

She stared at him, his face was grey and she wondered if she might be pushing him too far. Men of his age had heart attacks; he was overweight and drank too much wine, smoked too many cigars. He looked better when he returned, was it just an act to avoid a scene?

"Has it never occurred to you to ask why I might have leaned a little on June, as a colleague and a friend?"

"I presume you just fancied a bit of rough but didn't fancy kerb crawling to get it. You men are all the same. A tarty piece with a tight sweater can lead you by the balls like a bull with a ring through its nose."

"That's totally unfair. June is a good secretary and a decent woman."

Iris's face flushed.

"You bastard, how dare you sit there and defend that woman to me in my own home?"

George sat forward and tried to speak.

"I know you've been screwing her, you admitted it. Even if you hadn't, I'm not blind. If you don't get rid of her, I'll show your staff a thing or two. I'll go down there when you least expect it and I'll tear her bloody hair out."

"For Christ's sake, Iris."

She brushed his words aside. "She looks as though butter wouldn't melt in her mouth. Yes, Mrs. Martin, no, Mrs. Martin, he's busy in a meeting, Mrs. Martin. Shall I ask him to call you as soon as he's free and all the time laughing behind my back. How many other people know? Tell me that. I will not be made a fool of, not by a cheap little trollop like her!"

Iris realised that by the end of her performance she was a shrieking banshee but what did she care, she felt alive for the first time in ages. She gave a sharp gasp of pain as the cigarette clamped between her fingers burned her. She threw the dog end towards the ashtray on the coffee table, missed and watched as it rolled onto the carpet.

George leapt to his feet, scooped it up and crushed it out in the ashtray. He straightened up and they stood inches apart.

"I've had enough of this," he said, "living with you is a bloody nightmare."

He stepped nearer and the expression on his face made Iris pause even though she was tingling with excitement. She had his full attention for once. Then she stepped back suddenly frightened. What if he left her? She only wanted to be the centre of his world was that so terrible?

"So why should I look at someone else? Why would I? Oh yes, the grand hostess, Lady Bountiful, you are so bloody gracious. How often have I been told how lucky I am to have such a wonderful wife? If they only knew what you are really like." He paused turned on his heel and left the room.

Panic clogged Iris's throat as she ran across to the door, ears straining, mind willing him not to walk out, praying that she would not hear the click of the front door closing behind him. It was all going wrong; somehow he was different. She heard him returning and moved to the centre of the room. He held a brandy glass in each hand, both a third full.

"I presume you will join me in a drink," he handed her a glass. "I've never known you refuse."

She glared at him. The moment's panic disappeared as though it'd never been. Of course he would never leave, not this beautiful home and all that went with it. He could not bear to make himself a laughing stock and that is what he would be, just another middle-aged fool running off with his secretary. It was

118

the action of a man in the throes of a mid-life crisis; how laughable, how pathetic, how insupportable. She took a large mouthful of brandy, holding it on her tongue to feel the warmth spread around her mouth. She swallowed slowly breathing in the heavy vapours with a sigh.

"So it's my fault you can't keep your flies done up is it?"

George opened his mouth to speak.

"I've been a bloody good wife to you and well you know it. Look around you, see the evidence with your own eyes."

"At a price, Iris. Yes, you choose nice things but who pays?"

"Look at your two sons, they weren't found under a gooseberry bush."

"Yes, two sons as different as chalk and cheese and by God you've made sure William knows he means nothing to you."

"Are you surprised? How would you like it if I got Freddie to spy on you? He'd have had a pretty tale to tell me wouldn't he?"

"For heaven's sake, Iris, what do you think it's like for me not knowing what state you are going to be in when I am trying to make an impression on business colleagues?"

"Is it obligatory for men in the woollen garment trade to have the sparkle, wit and social repartee of a three-toed sloth? Or do you hand pick them for my benefit?"

"Materialism, possessions and fucking status, that just about sums you up. What about love? Where's the tenderness? I come in after a God awful day, and believe me I do have God awful days, only to find you in one of your moods and off we go again."

Iris backed away. The whole thing was getting out of control. She was the one who'd been badly treated, she was the wronged wife. What right did George have to start complaining?

"Do you know I can't remember the last time you put your arms round me and kissed me with any show of warmth?"

"Well, we both know where you went for a show of warmth."

"I can't remember the last time you made advances to me, actually instigated making love. In fact, when you have condescended to allow me between your legs I have felt as welcome as a dose of the clap!"

Iris gasped, colour drained from her face and with shaking hands she placed the brandy glass on the coffee table.

"How dare you, how dare you use that foul language to me, is that what June likes? My background may have been lowly compared with yours but that doesn't give you the right to speak

119

to me like this."

She stepped towards him and raising her arm brought her hand crashing down on his cheek. His head snapped back, then he grabbed her wrist so tightly that she cried out. He jerked her towards him and thrust his face into hers. His eyes glittered; he enunciated every word as though speaking to an idiot.

"You are a fucking bitch."

Iris tried to free her hand but he held her tighter.

"Yes, I will use that word."

She raised her free hand but he grabbed it and forced her to face him.

"In fact I will go so far as to say that if there had been more fucking in our marriage we might not be in our present situation."

She whimpered as his grip on her tightened. This should not be happening; this was not how she had planned it.

"You are so full of what you want."

Iris closed her eyes to shut out George's face, made unrecognisable by rage.

"It never crosses your mind to think of anyone else, least of all me."

"But...."

"Shut up woman and listen. I'll correct what I just said."

"And so you should, I never thought I'd be a battered wife."

"Don't tempt me. Where was I? Oh yes, you do think of someone else, Freddie. The poor bloody kid can't cope with your endless adoration."

"He loves me, you're just jealous."

"You are an embarrassment to him. You are choking him, driving him away."

Iris sobbed. "Never."

"Listen you'd better believe me. You...are...driving...him ...away."

With each word Iris felt her arms being jerked downwards until she was half kneeling, half slumped against him. Finally he let go of her wrists. I'll be bruised in the morning, she thought, that will be something to show the police.

She realised that George had sat down. She watched him take a large mouthful of brandy. And he complained about her drinking. She could hear his teeth rattle against the cut-glass brandy balloon, one of a set. Serve him right if he broke it.

She mopped at her eyes with her handkerchief but George

ignored her. Now she was terrified, was this was the end of everything? George had never been like this.

"What are we going to do?" she whispered and realised with surprise that she really was crying. "What are we going to do?" She felt like a small child crying in the dark.

"I don't know," George said, "I just don't know."

She knelt in front of him and watched as he leaned back and closed his eyes.

"I didn't mean to hurt you Iris, I never have. All I know is that this will happen again and again and I haven't got the stamina any more."

"No!"

"We agree about nothing, ours is a dance of death, the death of our relationship."

"No!" Iris clutched at George's knees. It frightened her that he had fought back; she had thought that was what she wanted. She leaned against his legs and let the tears continue unchecked. Her future looked bleak.

"All I ever wanted was you but you always had something else - work, clients, business deals. I was nothing, just the little woman left at home to wash nappies and cook meals."

She choked back a sob.

"Even when the children were born, where were you?" She felt swamped by sorrow. She had always done her best and now this, another woman.

She felt George's hand rest on her head and then gently stroke her hair.

"I thought I'd given you everything you wanted," he said.

"I just wanted you. Then William came along so quickly and I was ill all the time I carried him. Your life went on as usual but I was just William's mother."

Iris flexed her knees and tried to alter her position.

"You can't be very comfortable on the floor." He looked at his watch. "It's quite late; perhaps we should go to bed."

Iris looked up and as their eyes met she nodded. George stood and helped her to her feet. Together they went upstairs but they undressed, as usual, with their backs to each other. Iris felt sad that this was how things were but she had hated what pregnancy had done to her body, both during and after.

She wondered if George had thought she was rejecting him when what she really felt was shame at the sagging flesh that had once been so firm. He turned her round and their naked bodies touched as he put his arms round her.

"When did we last make love?"

She wanted to scream at him 'You'll have done it more recently than I have.'

Instinct kept her teeth clenched to stop angry words escaping. He led her to the bed and throwing back the covers helped her slide between cool sheets. She leaned across to turn out the bedside light.

"No, leave it on," he said.

She turned and looked at him. They'd invariably made love in the dark and she didn't want him to see how little she felt, it had always been so messy, sweaty and utterly undignified. At least in the dark you didn't have to look as though you were enjoying it.

She lay back on the pillows and waited. He kissed her and his hand move lightly, stroking her breasts, then her stomach crisscrossed as it was with stretch marks. She longed to pull the covers over the imperfections. In her modelling days her stomach had been as flat as a board. Who would look at it now? His hand slid down her thigh, first on the outside then across and up towards her groin, it was pleasant. Was this what he did to June?

"Relax my dear," he said, "let's just enjoy being close."

She closed her eyes but all she could see behind her eye-lids was a picture of George thrusting and poking at an abandoned and squealing June, legs waving in the air, moaning and grunting as she surely would. Suddenly the stroking hand became unbearable, why didn't he just get on with it? After the row this evening she did not dare tell him to leave her alone. She reached out and pulled him towards her. George smiled.

After what Iris hoped was a convincing performance she heard the front door being closed, William must be back. George rolled off her, at least he was satisfied. They moved apart and now Iris did turn out the light. She lay back and was thankful for the dark which allowed her to separate herself from the evening's events. Her body felt bruised. George had been rough, so unlike himself almost as if he wanted to hurt her. She felt a tremor of alarm but she knew what she had to say and say it she would.

"You will get rid of June, won't you?"

George did not reply but Iris knew he was still awake.

*

Chapter 16

Iris sat in her dressing gown, cup of coffee in one hand, cigarette in the other and watched George as he ate his breakfast. He looked sad, defeated. It was his own fault but if he had learned his lesson so much the better. Iris smiled; everything would be so much better once June had gone. Iris shifted on her chair, aware of tenderness, the result of last night's sex. She could not regard it as love-making; it had been too violent for that. If it was the price she had to pay for a continuing marriage she would pay.

"Are you telling her today?"

George looked up. "Probably."

"You'll give her an excellent reference no doubt."

George stared at her. "Of course I'll give her a good reference, why wouldn't I?"

Iris shrugged. "Have you thought about Sheila's friend, David; couldn't he be your personal assistant or secretary?"

"You're assuming he can type."

"I don't know, it's just an idea. You always complain I don't do enough for my sister. I should have thought offering some work to this fellow of hers who turns up like a stray dog would meet with your approval."

George sighed. "I suppose I could find him something."

"Hasn't Bergman got a P.A.?"

"Yes and that reminds me he's coming over on Thursday so I must get June to arrange some accommodation."

Iris exhaled cigarette smoke, "That's the sort of thing David could do."

"That would work really well, a Canadian P.A. who knows bugger all about London hotels etc. etc. That would be really clever."

"So you're going back on your word are you?"

"For Christ's sake, woman, give me a chance, I've a business to run, a son who couldn't sell snow in the desert and you on my back morning, noon and night."

"So how is it that Bergson or whatever his name is can manage to delegate? He's the owner but he can trust his manager to do the travelling around. That's what managers are for or is it that you can't wait to get away from here?"

"When you behave like this can you blame me?"

Iris shuddered. The fear she felt last night, when she thought he might walk out, made her skin prickle.

"Don't you realise I'm lonely?"

Her voice had lost its edge but George did not seem to notice. He glanced at his watch and stood up.

"You'll never understand. I have to work to keep you in relative luxury, I've got to keep expanding, replace any customers we lose. It's a treadmill. If I stop I'm dead, is that what you want?"

Iris looked away, she knew he was right.

"Have you thought about some sort of companion or friend that you could spend time with? I don't want you to be lonely."

"Old women have companions."

"What about Jenny? She seems a nice enough girl and it must be pretty grim living in that hostel. Take her under your wing, help her to make the best of herself, you'd be good at that."

Iris gave a tight smile.

"She works so when am I supposed to spend time making her look as though she knows how to dress - at the weekends?"

"Well, think about it anyway."

"Isn't that when I should be spending time with my husband?"

George sighed, "I must be off. There's been a problem with the over-locking machines and the maintenance men need a boot up their backsides. We've a big order to send off at the end of the week."

"That's the sort of thing a personal assistant could sort out."

Iris watched as George opened his mouth to speak, changed his mind and leaned across to give her a perfunctory kiss. She listened as he called upstairs to William who, as usual, was too late for breakfast.

"See you, Mum," he shouted as he hurried after his father. The front door closed behind him as Iris lit another cigarette and poured herself some more coffee. It was not a bad idea of George's, but was Jenny the sort of girl she would want to treat as a surrogate daughter? On the positive side, if Jenny were to live under their roof the relationship with William could be closely watched. Yes, Iris thought, a most satisfactory suggestion. They could all discuss it tonight when William came home.

If George was going to send William to Stockholm both she and Jenny would be in need of companionship. The whole thing would have to be discussed with the girl and her parents but from what Jenny had said they were hardly doting. Probably welcome someone else being responsible for their daughter.

124

Iris started to clear the breakfast things; as usual George had left her to do the menial tasks. It amused her that George insisted on William making his own way to work as if it made any difference; everyone knew he was the boss's son. If you had privileges why not use them? She hummed to herself as she worked. Last night had cleared the air; she had done George a favour and stopped him from making a fool of himself.

*

Jenny walked through the hospital's main entrance. Miss Pritchard had told her that Laura was in Ward 3. It was Jenny's first day back at work and she was exhausted but after all that had happened she wanted to see Laura for herself. She toiled up the three flights of stairs and once at the top held onto the rails while she got her breath back. She looked at the small bunch of violets that were all she could afford; still they were better than nothing.

It was five minutes before visiting time and people were milling around the ward doors, waiting for the stampede to patients' beds. Jenny wondered if any of these people were Laura's parents. Would they object to her being there since she knew the circumstances that led to Laura's brush with death? She decided she would not stay long, just long enough to assure herself that Laura was going to be all right.

The doors opened and the crowd of visitors streamed in. Jenny hesitated; she didn't know where Laura's bed was.

"Who are you looking for, dear?"

"Laura Johnson."

"Side ward one on the left. She's feeling much better today." The nurse smiled encouragement and bustled off.

Jenny stood in the doorway of Laura's room unsure of what to say. Laura was sitting up in bed reading a magazine; her parents hadn't arrived yet. Jenny didn't know what she had expected but surely such a trauma would leave its mark. Then Laura looked up and smiled.

"Hello, the nurse said you were better."

"I didn't expect you.....thanks for coming. Yes, I feel fine; I might even be able to go home tomorrow."

"Home?"

"Yes, to Mum and Dad's." She blushed and Jenny wondered if Laura remembered all the uncharitable things she had said about her parents in the past.

"I don't want to go back to the hostel."

"Oh." Lucky Laura, she has a choice.

"We've had a long talk, you know, about everything. I'm going to try to make a go of it at home. I don't know if it'll work but I feel I have to give it a try."

Jenny nodded. "I'm pleased for you," she held out the violets which were looking tired, "shall I get something to put these in?"

Laura smiled and held the flowers close. "They smell lovely."

Jenny felt her eyes fill. It must be because I'm overtired, she thought. I just wish one of my parents would ask me 'to give it a go'. There was no point in travelling down that road, it was a dead end.

She found a small vase in the sluice room and placed it by Laura's bed. The violets drooped a little but their heavy perfume filled the room. The two girls looked at each other but recent events hung between them like a curtain. Jenny cleared her throat.

"Does Miss Pritchard know you won't be coming back?"

"I don't think so, perhaps you would tell her."

Jenny stared out of the window. She would be on her own again, she thought, but it was wrong to think like that, she should be glad for Laura.

"But you might change your mind."

Laura shook her head. "I've learned a lot, all this has been a nightmare and perhaps I'm beginning to grow up. I do owe Mum and Dad a great deal so I must try to make it work."

Jenny wondered if the abortion would come back to haunt Laura in years to come. She had killed a child, her child. Perhaps to shut out what happened was the only way to cope.

"Are your parents coming tonight?"

"Yes," Laura glanced at her watch, "they should be here any minute."

"I don't think I'll stop then, you must be feeling tired. I'm just glad to see you looking so much better; you gave me a terrible fright."

Laura gave a brittle laugh, "That's nothing to the fright I gave myself."

She gripped Jenny's hand for a moment and both girls had tears in their eyes.

"You must come to see me once I'm settled in at home. I'm sure my parents would love to meet you. I've told them what you did."

"Yes, that would be nice; you can always leave a message for me at the hostel."

She stood up, ready to leave, anxious not to be in the way when Laura's parents arrived.

"I'd better go. I've been poorly myself, had a bad dose of tonsillitis and I still feel a bit groggy."

She remained standing by the bed unsure whether to kiss, shake hands or hug her friend. Laura held out her hands and gripped Jenny's.

"Thanks for everything, I'll be in touch, honestly I will."

Jenny nodded and waved when she got to the door. She won't be in touch, she thought, we have a shared memory that has to be buried. I would be a constant reminder to her of Tony and what that relationship did to her life. Surely this was goodbye.

She walked towards the stairs and noticed the couple coming towards her. The woman had fluffy blonde hair and the vulnerable look that Jenny had so envied in Laura. Jenny smiled as the couple passed her on the stairs. It must be Mr. and Mrs. Johnson anxious to see their daughter.

*

Iris rang the hostel; she couldn't wait until later tonight. She wanted to speak to Jenny now, sound the girl out. If she didn't want to live with them Iris wanted to know before anything was said to William. It took several minutes for Jenny to come to the phone.

"Hello."

"Hello, Jenny, I was wondering how you got on at work."

"Not bad but I feel very tired. Had to call on a friend… she's in hospital, went straight after work. Perhaps I've done a bit too much so I'll have an early night."

"Very sensible, actually I want to make a suggestion to you. George and I don't like the idea of one of our son's friends living in a hostel. We have a spare room and thought it would be nicer for you to live with us."

Jenny was stunned. Still clutching the phone, she took a deep breath.

"That would be very nice, Mrs. Martin, you are so kind to me. Are you sure I wouldn't be a nuisance?"

"We wouldn't have asked you if we'd thought that. Of course we'll have to have your parents' approval since you are under age."

Jenny felt perspiration break out on her forehead. She didn't want the Martins to meet either of her parents. After the business at the flat Dad had definite views on William and none of them were flattering. Not only would he make his feelings clear he would interrogate the Martins in the process.

She knew she could predict how Dad would behave but the same could not be said about Mum. On a good day she was passable but good days were few and far between. Her manic depression had blighted the family's life. If she were manic she would be belligerent and argumentative. If she were depressed she would neither speak nor acknowledge the world around her assuming she managed to turn up at all. What a dilemma, life was just too complicated.

"Jenny, are you there?"

"Yes, sorry, I don't know what to say. I'm sure Mum and Dad would be happy with the arrangement."

Yes, thought Iris, I'm sure they would be. After all they are happy for their daughter to live in a hostel. What kind of parent does that? She felt virtuous and caring, a Good Samaritan in fact.

"Yes, Jenny but George and I do feel that the matter must be discussed with at least one of your parents,

"I'll have a word with Mum then shall I?"

"A good idea, now will we be seeing you this weekend?"

"I think so. William said he would call me tomorrow or Wednesday." She paused. "I don't know how to thank you enough, Mrs. Martin."

Iris laughed. "Lets suggest Saturday to your mother; we could meet for a meal."

"Yes, I'll call her tonight."

Goodbyes were said and Jenny replaced the receiver. Her hands were shaking and wet with sweat, everything was happening too fast. She slumped against the wall, I can't cope with this. I want to belong, I want a family but if they meet Mum will they still want me?

She walked up the endless stairs listening to the thump of each funereal footstep. She sat on her bed and glanced around the bare room. This couldn't be home because it would never be hers. She thought about all the material benefits of the Martins' house but what about the atmosphere, could she cope with that? She would be near William and that would be lovely but he was going to Stockholm. Freddie was away at boarding school. She would be alone with Mr. and Mrs. Martin most of the time.

She sighed and rubbed her aching forehead then checked her purse for plenty of change and went downstairs to the phone to call her mother, Rachel.

The phone rang and rang and just as Jenny was about to give up a breathless voice answered.

"Hello, who is it?" It sounded like Ruth, Jenny's younger half-sister.

"Ruth, it's Jenny, is Mum there?"

There was a pause then Jenny heard Ruth shouting.

"Mum, Mum it's Jenny."

There was a sudden piercing whistle down the receiver and as Jenny took it away from her ear she heard a boy's laughter. It was Stephen and just the sort of thing he would do. Never had his dislike and rejection of his older half-sister wavered; Jenny knew it never would. She waited and thought she could hear footsteps.

"Darling, how are you?" The voice leapt out of the phone as though the disembodied voice had been made flesh.

Jenny always found this intensity of response, verging on the melodramatic, embarrassing and impossible to cope with.

"Hello Mum, I'm fine. How are you all?"

"Splendid, now when are you coming to see us?"

Jenny heard a commotion in the background and then her mother placed a hand over the receiver but it didn't stop Jenny hearing the chorus of wails from Stephen and Ruth. No, Jenny thought, they don't want me to visit; they have never wanted that.

"We'd all love to see you, darling."

Jenny smiled to herself. Mum would not even acknowledge the animosity between her children.

"That's why I'm ringing. You remember William, my boyfriend."

"You've mentioned him, now isn't it time I met him?"

"Yes, Mum, that's it, you see I want you to meet him and his parents."

"Darling girl that would be wonderful, are you bringing them here?"

Jenny gasped in horror. Mum's flat always looked as though a hurricane had blown through it. Alec was often drunk and always spent the weekends in bed and the kids were unspeakable. It had always amazed Jenny that no matter what Mum's mood she seemed never to register the mayhem around her.

"They want us to go out for a meal with them, just you and me."

"All a bit sudden isn't it; you've not done anything silly have you, you're not pregnant?"

Jenny groaned. "No Mum, I'm not pregnant. It's just that they want me to go to live with them. They don't like me living in a hostel."

There was a pause and Jenny waited for the storm to break.

"I see, I suppose you would rather live with strangers than with your own family. How long is since I saw you?"

"Yes, but Mum, you know how Ruth and Stephen are."

"Don't be so silly, you imagine it, of course they want to see you."

Jenny listened to the chorus of denial in the background. The receiver was put down and Jenny could hear shouting and general uproar. For a second time Mum must have placed her hand over the receiver while she shouted at the other two. Then there was a sudden bellow of rage and Jenny recognised the sound of Alec, her stepfather. Once the noise diminished Mum came back.

"So what are they like, darling, William's parents?"

"They're all right; they were very kind to me when I was ill recently."

"Ill, what do you mean you've been ill? Why wasn't I told?"

"I didn't want to worry you, anyway I'm better now. The point is they want to meet you. They don't think it's right for me to just move in unless you or Dad have met them and approved."

"Your father, what's he got to do with it, what has he ever done for you? If he's there I shan't be coming, the bastard. And I'll never know why you went to live with him in the first place."

Jenny leaned back against the wall, closed her eyes and waited. It was always the same. Why didn't Mum realise how difficult it made things. If she can't say anything nice about Dad why say anything at all?

"No," she replied, "Dad won't be there. I think they want to take us out for a meal, somewhere nice, probably on Saturday. Would that be O.K.?"

"Yes, Alec can look after the kids."

Thank goodness, Jenny thought, at least Mum hadn't wanted Ruth and Stephen to come too. That would have been more than flesh and blood could stand.

"I'll give you a ring later in the week to confirm arrangements.

Bye Mum."

Mum was in her manic phase, Jenny thought. Saturday, if that was to be when the meeting would take place, was going to be tricky.

*

Axel Bergman, his wife Helga and Brigit Bjoerling had arrived in London on Thursday as planned. George and his chauffeur had met them and taken them to the hotel in Hendon which June had booked for them. They were expected at the Martins' house for an evening meal and Iris had suggested that Jenny be invited too. If she were to be a member of the family, as seemed likely, she might as well start now. An extra pair of hands in the kitchen would be useful.

She and George would be taking Jenny and her mother to lunch on Saturday as a treat. There was no reason why the girl shouldn't earn the privilege of dining at the Dorchester. Iris wondered why Jenny had been startled by the choice of restaurant. From what the girl had said her mother came from a wealthy and upper middle-class family. Therefore if Iris had to impress, impress she would.

Jenny had set the table and folded napkins as Iris had shown her. She had changed into clean clothes and put her discarded ones in the bedroom that would soon be hers. Beneath her calm exterior she was in turmoil and went through the conversation she had with her mother the previous evening. She had explained that they were to meet at the Dorchester and suggested that Mum wear something nice.

That had been a mistake. Rachel had shouted down the phone that no-one was going to tell her how to dress. It wasn't what people wore that mattered, it was what they were. And why should she dress up for people who were trying to take her daughter away? Jenny could feel anxiety tighten in her stomach, by Saturday, she thought, I'll be a gibbering idiot.

She checked the table and walked back into the kitchen where everything seemed to be under control. She was unsure of what to do next. William had gone with his father to collect the dinner guests. She stood watching as Iris stirred sauces, basted meat, whipped cream and drank sherry. She looked flushed and Jenny wasn't sure if it was heat from the stove or the effects of the alcohol. After living with Alec and his drinking, Jenny had a

131

healthy regard for the power of drink. Still Iris seemed in an amiable mood.

"Pour yourself a glass."

Jenny hesitated, would sherry on an empty stomach make things better or worse? Things could only improve so she poured a glass and sipped it slowly. Living here was going to be very different from anything she had experienced.

The front door opened and there was the sound of several voices. Iris wiped her hands and removed her apron, ready to greet her guests. Jenny followed and stood on the periphery of the group while introductions were made. Mr. and Mrs. Bergman were in early middle age, prosperous and confident. Their clothes were expensive but understated, well cut, elegant with no hint of flamboyance.

Mrs. Bergman wore enough jewellery to proclaim her husband was a good provider but not enough to appear ostentatious. The personal assistant, Brigit Bjoerling, was young and dressed in a sombre, professional style; Jenny had never mixed with people like this.

William winked at Jenny over the heads of the group; she smiled and felt herself relax. She wanted William to be proud of her so she mustn't make a fool of herself. She would watch what everyone else did then there would be no mistake. She realised with a start that Iris had spoken her name.

"This is Jenny. She's a friend of the family and has been kind enough to help me in the kitchen."

Jenny felt a prickle of irritation. Why didn't she introduce me as William's girlfriend? Iris had reduced her to little more than a kitchen maid. She said nothing, just smiled and shook hands.

Everyone went into the living room where drinks were poured and the vagaries of the weather and air travel were discussed. Iris excused herself and gave Jenny a look that indicated that she too was to go to the kitchen in her role of chef's helper. As she walked past William he grabbed her hand. She felt the colour rise on her face and neck, her heart thumped and she hoped no-one noticed.

*

Jenny glowed with the effects of wine and good food. She felt light-headed and found it difficult to follow the conversation but that didn't matter as it was mostly concerned with business. She let her mind wander into a future that seemed rosy and it was so nice to have William sitting opposite her his feet entwined with hers under the table. Provided Mum doesn't behave too badly I'll be able to move in and make a fresh start, like Laura.

William was talking to his father and Axel Bergman about his wish to go to Stockholm. It was a shame that was what he wanted to do just as she was coming to live under the same roof. I mustn't be selfish, she thought, he has his career to think of.

"I think we can find plenty for this young man to do." Bergman said, "And I know someone who will be pleased to see him again."

"Oh?" said Iris.

"Ah yes, the lovely Berthe, William made quite an impression on her. She is a charming girl and acted as a guide when your husband and son visited before." He beamed at Iris.

"She asked most especially to be remembered to you, William."

Jenny felt a great weight press down on her chest. She looked across at William but he avoided her gaze.

"How kind," Iris said and stared hard at Jenny.

She's looking for a reaction, Jenny thought.

*

Chapter 20

Mark got off the train at Baron's Court and looked round. It was a dismal, depressing area and just to make everything look even more miserable, it was raining. Not for the first time he wondered what on earth he was doing.

Since leaving London he had settled into his new job at the Manchester branch of Rainham's Estate Agents. The people he worked with had made him welcome and life with Mum was comfortable. He had contacted some of his old friends and it felt like he had never been away. Head Office had arranged for him to attend a training seminar and at first it had seemed a great opportunity to trace Jenny. Now he felt stupid.

He was chasing about trying to find a girl he had met once who might live in a hostel whose name he didn't know, he didn't even know Laura's other name. He turned up the collar of his raincoat and started walking. He would just have to ask the first person he met. The rain was lashing down now and the streets were empty.

"This is hopeless," he said and turning on his heel went back to the station. As he got nearer, a flock of people surged past him all intent on getting home and out of the foul weather as soon as possible. At the entrance to the station an elderly woman was struggling with her umbrella. Perfect, Mark thought, she's probably lived here all her life.

"Can I give you a hand with that?"

"Umbrellas are more trouble than they're worth, young man, see what you can do."

Mark managed to loosen the jammed release button, opened the umbrella and handed it to the woman.

"Well that's your good deed for the day, thank you so much."

She turned to leave.

"Actually you might be able to help me. I'm looking for a hostel, somewhere round here. You don't know it do you?"

The woman paused. "Hostel? Yes, there is, just let me think."

Mark crossed his fingers and waited.

"Of course, it's in Westbrook Grove. It's not far from here but it's for women I'm pretty sure of that."

"Oh I'm not looking for accommodation; I'm trying to trace someone."

"I see," the woman smiled, "go out of here then straight on

then turn left into Princess Avenue. I'm sure Westbrook Grove is the first on the right."

"Thanks a lot; I didn't fancy wandering round in this."

The woman gave Mark a knowing sidelong glance as she walked away.

"I hope you find her."

"So do I," he said and watched her hurry down the street.

The rain had eased so at least it wasn't bouncing now. He smiled as he strode down the road, I think I'm meant to find Jenny, he thought.

He turned into Westbrook Grove and saw the hostel at once. It was a tall, imposing building, austere rather than cosy. He wondered if it had always been a hostel or if it had once been a workhouse, the kind of place that his grandmother had spoken of in hushed tones, a place to be dreaded.

He opened the gate, walked to the front door and knocked. After a lengthy wait the door opened. Mark hadn't known what he was expecting but the woman standing in the barely opened door was a surprise. She was dressed in grubby overall and had a cap on her head.

"Yes?" she said as she eyed him up and down.

Mark felt himself blush. "I'm sorry to bother you but I'm trying to trace someone."

"Miss Pritchard's out, been called away."

"Miss Pritchard?"

"The warden."

Rain was trickling down Mark's neck but from the look on the woman's face he didn't think there was much point in asking to be allowed in.

"When will she be back?"

"How should I know, I'm in the kitchen, Cook told me to answer the door."

"I see. I'm trying to trace a girl called Jenny."

"Don't know nothing about that."

"Do you know a Laura?"

"I told you I don't know nothing, I'm in the kitchen."

"Can I write a letter then?"

The woman shrugged and went to close the door.

"Thank you so much, you have been really helpful."

His last few words were said to the closed door.

*

135

Mr. and Mrs. Martin, William and Jenny had arrived at 'The Dorchester' at twelve fifty; they had been shown to the lounge. George had ordered aperitifs while they waited for Jenny's mother, Rachel, to arrive.

At ten past one Iris looked pointedly at her watch. Jenny, crimson with embarrassment, said that her mother was not a very good timekeeper. She explained that there were two younger children and maybe there had been an emergency. Perhaps she had tried to ring the restaurant, maybe there had been a delay on the Tube. George had patted Jenny's hand.

"Don't worry, I've had a word with the Head Waiter; they will hold the table until half past one. She's bound to be here by then."

Jenny offered up a silent prayer that he would be proved right. She looked at Iris and looked away, her face was like thunder. I knew this would happen, Jenny thought, why didn't I tell Mum to meet us at twelve thirty? Then I would have stood a chance. At twenty five past one Iris stood up.

"Well, I for one am not waiting any longer. George, are we going through to our table now or I shall call a taxi and go home?"

The lump in Jenny's throat threatened to choke her. She looked for support to William who shrugged his shoulders and stood up. In desperation Jenny turned to George. "Shall I stay here and wait a little longer?"

"No, my dear, we had better go through and start to order before it's too late. I'll have a word with the receptionist, when your mother arrives they will bring her through."

Jenny felt tears gather behind her eyes. She could cope with Iris being angry but the combination of George's kindness and William's disinterest was unbearable.

Things had not been the same with William since the dinner party with the Bergmans. He had denied anything untoward between him and this Berthe woman but Jenny was uneasy, particularly as William was leaving for Stockholm in two short weeks. Was it her imagination or was there coolness in his behaviour? She was too frightened to ask. She felt helpless, hurt and at a loss and now this, why couldn't Mum be like other mums?

They walked through to the restaurant with Iris leading the way. She reminded Jenny of a ship's figurehead as she cleaved her way to the table indicated by an obsequious waiter. The Head

136

Waiter hovered as menus were distributed and crisp white napkins were unfurled by an underling who then, with much bowing and scraping, placed one on each diner's lap.

Jenny was shaking so much she could scarcely hold the heavy embossed cover of the menu, listed inside was a cornucopia of gastronomic delights. Jenny's appetite had withered but she knew she must make an effort or cause further insult to the already nettled Iris. She wanted to see if there was any sign of Mum but as her back was to the door this was impossible.

Her eyes skimmed the menu which was in French. She blessed her GCE 'O' level which meant she did not have to ask what everything was. She chose melon followed by chicken in a cream sauce and having made her choice shut the menu and left it on the table in front of her. The Martins were arguing over the relative merits of oysters and smoked salmon with shrimps. Jenny prayed in silence for the ordeal to be over.

It was then that Jenny noticed Iris looking past her as a frisson of surprise rippled through the restaurant. Jenny sensed rather than saw the turning of heads. With a sickening lurch of her stomach she assumed Mum had arrived. She watched as Iris's expression showed disdain, distaste and finally disbelief. She turned to George who was ordering wine and whispered something that Jenny could not hear.

George smiled and stood to greet his guest. Jenny turned and swallowed hard. In this elegant room full of wealthy, well-dressed people her mother looked as though she were dressed for a hike across Hampstead Heath.

Jenny felt a surge of anger, why hadn't she made an effort? She had asked Mum to dress nicely, it wasn't fair. At that moment Rachel saw Jenny.

"Hello, my darling," her voice reverberated across the dining room, "how lovely to see you. It's been far too long."

She bent and gave Jenny an extravagant kiss on the cheek. She held out a hand to George. "You must be Mr. Martin, so pleased to meet you. I'm not late am I?"

William choked on his bread roll and Jenny cringed.

"I don't wear a watch, you see, why should I be governed by time?"

"As a courtesy to others," Iris said.

"Of all God's creatures only man straps a watch to his wrist so he can account for the passing of minutes and hours. All we need to know is that when it is light we enjoy the beauty of our surroundings. We should live, love and create new life and when it is dark we sleep to replenish our souls. That is all."

No-one spoke.

Finally George broke the silence. "We're all glad you were able to come."

Rachel took the empty seat, removed her duffle coat and draped it over the back of her chair.

"Allow me, Madam."

The Head Waiter had arrived, on silent feet, to stand behind Rachel's chair. He eased the coat away. His expression was unreadable as he held the garment between fastidious finger and thumb before handing it to one of the waiters.

A menu was produced as Jenny introduced everyone. It can't get any worse, she thought, as Rachel glanced at the menu.

"It's such a glorious day I thought a picnic would be nice. What do you think? I've just walked across the park, it was a delight. Couldn't it be arranged? It seems a shame to be stuck in a stuffy room when the sun is shining and good fresh air is just outside." She beamed at everyone around the table.

Iris took a cigarette from her case and lit it. "I don't think we are dressed for such an arrangement."

Jenny felt the air chill.

"Would you like an aperitif while you decide what you are going to have?" George asked.

"How nice but I rarely drink. Do you remember that holiday we had in the caravan, Jenny? I had a glass of cider and became quite tipsy. That was the year we ran out of money and had to get on the train with no tickets." She turned to George. "Alec, my husband had to rescue us at the station as the ticket collector wouldn't let us leave. So silly, I gave him my address. Anyway Alec brought enough money to pay all our fares. It was quite a hoot."

Jenny gave an inward groan, it could get worse.

"Sherry?" George enquired.

"Yes please, sweet."

Rachel studied the menu.

"Can you read French or would you like me to translate?" Iris's tone implied she had little confidence in Rachel's ability to cope in any way with the social situation in which she now found herself.

138

"I speak and read French fluently. I lived in Paris for six months and taught English to anyone prepared to pay for lessons."

"You didn't tell us you'd been to Paris, Jenny," George said.

"I haven't." Jenny whispered.

"So where were you whilst your mother was on her travels?" Iris asked.

"She was with my ex-husband's parents, weren't you darling. I just took my son, Stephen. It was a wonderful experience for him and one that Jenny would have shared if her wretched father hadn't done his best to keep the girl from me."

The waiter came to take their orders and Jenny blessed the intervention. Once the waiter had gone Iris returned, like a bull terrier, to the kill.

"So you and your husband were in Paris for six months, on business I suppose. What is his line of work?"

"Oh no, I went on my own with Stephen."

There was a pause while Iris digested the unexpected reply and the wine waiter gave Rachel her sherry.

"Didn't he mind you going off like that?"

"Why should he, he doesn't own me."

Iris lit another cigarette. "I imagine your son must have missed his father."

"Oh I don't know, children are very resilient, they cope with most things."

Rachel drank her sherry too fast for Jenny's peace of mind. Please don't let Mum become argumentative, she thought.

"Has Jenny told you of our suggestion?" George said.

"About coming to live with you?"

"Yes."

"I am pleased that you have taken the trouble to ask although I want to make it clear that I would prefer Jenny to live with me. I am her mother after all." Rachel looked from face to face daring anyone to object.

"But Mum you know it's difficult with Stephen and Ruth and what would Alec say?"

The first courses arrived and conversation was stilled. The same old argument raced around Jenny's brain, Mum would never accept that she could not live with Alec and the kids. It would be mayhem – particularly with Stephen.

Jenny slowly picked at her melon which was splayed into a fan and garnished with jewel-like berries. The coolness of the fruit calmed her agitation as she let each spoonful rest on her tongue before chewing. She glanced at her mother who was spooning soup into her mouth; she was responsible for the slight slurping sound that Jenny hoped she had imagined. What must Iris think?

"It's a long time since I ate out," Rachel said between mouthfuls of soup, "but the prices here are exorbitant. Do you realise a poor Indian family could live for a year on what this meal will cost?"

William and Iris exchanged glances.

"I sponsor two Indian children you know. Most people in the western world eat far too much, pure gluttony most of it." She spread her arms wide to encompass the whole restaurant. "I don't suppose any of these people have ever known a single pang of hunger."

There was a disapproving murmur from the nearest table and Jenny realised that other diners were listening and hard glances were being directed towards them. William choked on his spaghetti carbonara which was his first course.

"You seem to have a very healthy appetite, William; you will have to hope it doesn't turn to fat." Rachel smiled at him.

Iris put down her knife and fork and leaned forward. "I believe that if one works hard one is entitled to the fruits of that labour."

"Yes Iris, may I call you Iris?"

Iris opened her mouth but Rachel ploughed on.

"But if you were working in the fields all day for the whole of your life you would never be able to afford a meal like this in such a sumptuous setting."

An elderly matron with blue rinsed hair in an extravagant bouffant style was sitting at the nearest table; she gave a loud, disapproving tut.

"If I were such a person would I want or even appreciate what you see before and around you?" Iris said.

"Are you equipped to judge what a poor person would want or appreciate? That seems condescending to me." Rachel paused.

"I think I should tell you I am a fully paid up member of the Communist Party and it is my belief that all people should be given the same chance to have the best for themselves and their families."

"I'm sure you are right," George said, "In an ideal world we would all prosper and enjoy life however we choose.

Unfortunately it is not an ideal world so we must all do the best we can."

"How many third world children do you sponsor?"

"I must confess none at the moment so I am glad you have drawn my attention to such a grievous omission. We will have to do something about it won't we, my dear." He turned to Iris whose expression was icy. William continued to eat and avoided looking at anyone.

"Of course," said George, "there are other ways of spreading the good things of life." He smiled at Rachel. "I like to think I do my bit by providing work for some fifty-odd people. That supports more than fifty when one includes their families. I believe I am a fair employer and pay the best wages the company can stand."

"Do any of your employees eat here?"

"I doubt it but if they didn't work for me they might not eat at all." With that George signalled to the waiters to clear the first course plates away.

While waiting for the main course William talked about going to Stockholm and what he hoped to learn about the business. Jenny tried to think of other safe topics but when Mum was in her present, manic mood that was well nigh impossible. In desperation, Jenny did say a bit about her new job but avoided the subject of rats in case it upset Iris. After that conversation became more and more artificial and laboured.

"I think we should discuss the offer we have made to Jenny regarding her coming to live with us." George smiled at Rachel.

"I do appreciate that you have not met us before and are bound to have reservations."

Rachel nodded and placed a hand over Jenny's.

"Perhaps that is what we should talk about." George continued. "As a mother who cares for her daughter I know you will want what is best for her. Although we love our two sons dearly," he turned to Iris, "we have both longed for a daughter."

Iris stared at Rachel who had waltzed into a top class restaurant looking like a bag lady with her hair dragged back into a rubber band for God's sake. And all she could do was sit in judgement on all that she and George represented. How dare she?

Iris indicated to George that her wineglass was empty. She had suspected there was something odd about Jenny which was hardly surprising when you met the mother. Who knew what

141

other skeletons there were in that family's cupboard?

"Perhaps we should ask Jenny what she thinks," Iris said.

Jenny blushed, whatever she said was going to upset someone.

"Mum, I know you want me to live with you but it wouldn't work. You know what it was like before; that was why I went to live with Dad."

Rachel bristled.

"It would be worse now you know it would, Stephen and I have never got on."

"Whose fault is that? If you hadn't gone to your father's you and Stephen would have sorted out your differences."

"Would we?"

"He's your brother."

Jenny looked in mute appeal to George.

"There are always problems when families split up," he said, "but that is in the past and it is the future, Jenny's future we are thinking about now. I promise you we will make sure Jenny keeps in touch with you on a regular basis."

Rachel looked at George and smiled. Iris watched and was both startled and alarmed by the transformation of this strange women who now looked beautiful. Too beautiful by half, Iris thought. Jenny has inherited her mother's eyes and who knows what else.

Rachel placed her hand on top of George's, "You will look after her won't you?"

"Of course, my dear, trust us."

Jenny's legs had turned to jelly. She took a deep breath and felt dizzy with relief or was it the alcohol? The rest of the meal passed in a daze and she realised that she was more than a little tipsy. She concentrated on coping with the chicken without dropping cutlery or in any other way drawing attention to herself. George kept conversation going by encouraging Rachel to talk about her childhood.

They were regaled with tales of her life in a large house with many servants. Iris took satisfaction in remembering how she had risen above her own very humble beginnings. Yet this woman, full of righteous indignation had squandered her chances of comfort, probably through wilful fecklessness. Who was she to criticise?

At last the meal was over and a silver tray with a folded bill was presented by the Head Waiter. George, puffing on a large cigar, took the proffered pen and signed his name. Rachel looked puzzled.

Iris said, "Expense account."

"What does that mean?"

"It means that George includes this meal as part of his business expenses which he is perfectly entitled to do."

"How so? Surely this is a social occasion, shouldn't he pay himself?"

William gave a nervous laugh and Iris glared at him.

"Of course, if you would like to pay for what you have had I'm sure that can be arranged." Iris gave an anaconda smile as George took her hand.

"I'm sure, my dear, Rachel would not want to cause any difficulties." He turned to Rachel, "We take this facility for granted. Please don't give the matter another thought; it is a perfectly acceptable method of payment. As long as you have enjoyed the meal and are prepared to lend us your daughter for as long as she cares to stay we will be both happy and grateful."

There was nothing more to be said so the party stood and left the restaurant. Jenny was aware that many eyes followed them as they threaded their way through the tables.

"Can I drop you anywhere?" George said.

"No thank you I will enjoy the sunshine and fresh air. So much nicer than being cooped up in a car don't you think?" She smiled at George, kissed Jenny and with a cheery wave set off at speed up Park Lane.

*

Chapter 21

Barbara was tired. Everyone assumed that being a librarian was a peaceful occupation as books can't answer back but the borrowers can. I'm getting older, she thought, as she ran a bath adding a liberal sprinkling of bath salts to the steaming water. She stripped off her clothes and said to her reflection, before condensation covered it, "I deserve a drink." She padded through to the kitchen and mixed a gin and tonic. Drinking alone was a bad sign her father had always told her. "Sod it," she said, as she took a large mouthful.

Returning to the bathroom she balanced the glass on the side of the bath and stepped into the scented water. She lay back with the glass in her hand and felt the stress of a hectic day seep away. She closed her eyes and let her mind wander back to happier days when she and Paul married. That had been a glorious day. Then there was the day Richard was born. She sat up. Perhaps gin was not such a good idea, mother's ruin guaranteed to make you weep. She put the glass down and started washing herself.

"This won't do, my girl, what's gone is gone."

She stopped scrubbing her feet and listened, it was the telephone. Why did people always ring when she was in the bath? She scrambled out, grabbed the towel and sprinted to the phone.

"Hello Barbara, it's Charles."

She laughed, "Sorry I took so long to answer but I was in the bath. It's a good job you can't see me standing here dripping."

She waited, expecting a risqué comment but there was silence. He's embarrassed, she thought.

"Hello Charles, are you still there?"

"Yes, sorry to disturb you, I won't keep you long. I wondered if you would like to go out for a meal sometime, thought we might try the new Italian restaurant on the Kings Road."

"That would be lovely, when had you in mind?"

"When are you free?"

"Tomorrow or one evening next week maybe."

"Tomorrow it is. Will seven thirty be O.K.?"

"Yes fine, I'll look forward to it."

Barbara clutched the towel around her and went back to the bathroom, the water had cooled and she couldn't be bothered to get back in. Charles was an enigma. On the surface he seemed confident, bossy in fact. But she felt sure there was more to him than that. He was handsome, intelligent and good company yet he was burdened by a sack full of emotional baggage. She knew he was divorced and had a daughter because Gordon had told her, yet when he came round for a meal his child was not mentioned. She pulled a comb through her damp hair. I will get him talking tomorrow.

*

"That woman is extremely odd."

George nodded his agreement, "But that is hardly Jenny's fault."

"But it's in the blood; manic depression isn't that what Jenny called it, that's a polite word for madness isn't it?"

"I really don't know but does it alter your feelings about Jenny coming here? After all she seems normal enough."

Iris thought for a moment. "You're probably right but I want it clear now, I'm not having that woman here."

"I don't think that will be a problem. We'll give the girl plenty of encouragement to see her mother in her own home." George put his arms round Iris.

"I do think you'll enjoy having Jenny around particularly as William is going away."

"Have you spoken to David yet about working for you?"

"Briefly, he's coming in with me on Wednesday before June leaves."

Iris raised her eyebrows. "Leaving so soon?"

"Yes, my dear, so soon."

Iris pulled away from George's embrace. The 'my dear' had sounded more like an insult than a term of endearment. "I presume she's got a new job."

"Apparently her sister and brother-in-law run a hotel in Bournemouth. She's going down there to help out."

Iris smiled. That was ideal, not only was June going but she was going soon and out of London. That was perfect. She decided to change the subject; it would not do to gloat too much.

"How do you think this thing between Sheila and David is going?"

"Very well I hope, I think they are good for each other."

"But won't they want a place of their own? We've got to think about Mum and Dad, they can't be left. Mum isn't going to get any better."

"Well we can't let that stand in the way can we? After all

Sheila has done a hell of a lot over the years, now she deserves a life of her own."

"So what are you suggesting?" Iris asked.

"Nothing yet, it's early days and I can't see Sheila just walking away."

"I suppose not. Now when is Jenny bringing her stuff?"

"Friday, after work."

"Will she need our help or would it be easier if she gets a taxi?"

"I think she has a large trunk so a taxi would be best."

Iris stood up; she had an empty brandy glass in her hand.

"I'm having a night cap, shall I get you one?"

"No thanks."

Iris knew George was watching her as she walked from the room. She wondered if he was waiting for her to stagger, make a fool of herself. Then he would be able to moan about her drinking. With care she negotiated the coffee table and went through to the dining room. Her hand shook as she poured a generous measure of brandy but she managed to put the stopper back in the decanter and then retraced her steps.

"Here's to June's departure and David's arrival, cheers." She saluted George and drank.

*

Barbara checked she was ready for Charles's arrival, he wasn't likely to approve if she kept him waiting. She smiled when she heard the bell and checked her watch, seven thirty to the second. She hurried downstairs and beamed at Charles as she opened the door.

She had chosen a bronze coloured silk shirt with a brown linen skirt. She had brushed hair until it shone and used just a touch of make-up. Charles looked startled.

"You look lovely, Barbara, truly lovely."

Barbara relished the pleasure that his compliment gave her and realised she could not remember the last time she had been made to feel attractive, desirable. I have cocooned myself away for far too long, she thought. She stood aside for him to enter.

"Do you want a drink before we go or have you booked a table?"

"I've booked for eight so we'd better go, perhaps we can have a drink after."

"Why not, I'll just get my jacket." She ran upstairs, grabbed the brown linen jacket and hurried downstairs.

"Right, I'm all yours." She linked her arm through his as they walked down the street.

The final flourish of summer was over. Window boxes and hanging baskets were past their best and autumn gave a chill to the evening air. Barbara shivered.

"Come here, woman, put that jacket on properly." He lifted it from her shoulders and held it while she slipped her arms in. Then they walked in companionable silence picking their way through cheerful crowds all intent on enjoying a pleasant Sunday evening.

The Italian restaurant, with the obligatory red and green decor, was busy. As was to be expected each table had a Chianti bottle plus candle, encrusted with melted wax dribbles. The clientele was young and noisy, so were the waiters.

Charles and Barbara were shown to the last empty table and decided on spaghetti and red wine. The clatter of plates and the animated chatter of the other diners made conversation difficult but there was ample opportunity for people watching. Most of the diners were sitting in groups of six or eight. Waiters raced up and down the aisles bearing vast trays, heavy with plates piled high with pasta and pizzas. The atmosphere was heady with good cheer, camaraderie and laughter.

"You look very serious," Barbara said.

Charles shrugged. "I'm just feeling a touch of regret for the lost years of my youth." He squeezed her hand and smiled.

The waiter arrived and Barbara gasped at the quantity of spaghetti placed before her.

"If I get through this lot you will have to carry me home."

"So who's going to carry me?" They grinned at each other.

"We're just like a couple of kids," Charles said.

"And quite right too."

The meal over, they sat back and gazed at each other. Barbara felt there was an intimacy in the look. Charles signalled to the waiter, paid, left a tip and helped Barbara into her jacket. He grabbed her hand and almost dragged her into the street.

"It's a long time since I've felt like this," he said as he put his arm round her shoulders. They walked along the road, the metallic click of his heels interspersed with the rapid tap, tap of her high-heeled shoes. She giggled.

"Slow down, I've only got little legs."

Charles stopped and stared at her. "Someone else always used to say that."

Barbara wanted to ask who but looking at Charles' face decided not to. Charles offered his arm for her to link. She looked at him aware that something had changed his mood, everything was different.

"You'll come in for a coffee or a night cap won't you?"

"Thank you that would be nice."

There was a silence that created an uncomfortable void which Barbara tried to fill with talk of her work but the magic had gone and she didn't know why.

*

Jenny had packed her trunk and was waiting for a taxi to arrive. This weekend was William's last one for at least three months. What an irony; one week in the same house was all they would have. Jenny checked again the cupboards and drawers remembering how anxious she had felt when she arrived. It seemed so long ago yet it was only a few weeks. Now here she was embarking on a new life yet again, she felt nervous but for different reasons.

Miss Pritchard had been kind and assured her that there would always be a bed available if she needed one. That was a comforting safety net which she hadn't had when she left Dad's. He hadn't replied to her recent letter informing him of her new address, she hadn't expected him to.

There were brisk footsteps in the corridor as well as the heavy tread of a man's feet. Miss Pritchard knocked and entered followed by the taxi driver. He viewed the trunk with disapproval and pursed his lips.

"I'll give you a hand with this," Jenny said grabbing a handle. They walked along the corridor and down the stairs with the trunk bumping against Jenny's hip. She wondered how many more times she would have to lug the wretched thing around. Miss Pritchard followed carrying Jenny's coat and handbag. While the taxi driver manhandled the trunk into the boot Jenny said her last goodbye.

"Don't forget there's always a bed for you even if it's only a camp bed in the corridor."

Jenny grinned, it was a nicer goodbye than Dad had given her when he dumped her trunk and drove off without a word. She sat back in the taxi feeling quite grand. The last time she had been in

one she had felt too ill to care about anything, this time she was
going up in the world. To have a warm, comfortable bedroom
with carpet and central heating would be a joy, no more bed socks
and thick jumpers in bed. She was contented with her lot even if
William would not be there. She decided she would not even
think about how she would cope with Iris. Why spoil the
moment?

By the time she reached the Martins' house, in Golders Green,
it was dusk. The house looked both grand and inviting. George
opened the door and together with the taxi driver lugged the trunk
into the hallway. George insisted on paying Jenny's fare and after
shutting the front door said, "Welcome to your new home."

"Leave the unpacking until after we have eaten." Iris called
from the kitchen.

William bounded downstairs and gave Jenny a hug as he
kissed her on the cheek.

"Hi ya," he said.

How silly, Jenny thought, I thought he was getting tired of me
but everything is going to be fine.

*

Barbara sat drinking her coffee and wondered what it was
about Charles that was so intriguing. She had felt sure they
would end up in bed after their Italian meal. She wouldn't have
objected, she had few hang-ups about sex. It was an expression
of desire, sometimes love and sometimes not, but she could not
regard it as a sin when two unattached adults chose to indulge
their passions.

What went wrong? One minute he was dragging her out of the
restaurant and the next it was like being walked home by a
circumspect vicar. He had come in for coffee but had chosen to
sit in an armchair not the settee. They had made polite
conversation and then he had left.

She could not recall what had been said before he switched off
his feelings for she was sure that was what he had done. There
had been nothing of significance only that he was walking too
fast. Joan had said he was still screwed up about his ex-wife and
there was his daughter too, another enigma. 'I'm going to find
out more about you, Mr Warr, you see if I don't.' She got paper
and an envelope.

Dear Charles

Thanks for the meal, your turn to come to me next.

I'm free next Saturday, are you? Give me a ring to confirm arrangements.

Yours Barbara.

It was a nuisance he wasn't on the phone. She looked outside; it was a pleasant evening and not quite dark. She'd walk round and maybe pop in for a drink with Gordon and Joan on the way back.

What is it about council flats, she wondered, they always seem to have a desolate, rundown air about them. Her footsteps echoed on the concrete stairway. There was a light on in Charles's flat, she hesitated, not sure whether to knock or just push the letter through the letter box. The decision was made for her when Charles opened the door.

"What a surprise, what are you doing here?"

"Just delivering your mail," she handed him the letter.

"Come in a moment, I was only going for a walk."

"I'll come with you if you like or are you the cat that walks by itself?"

He smiled. "Oh I think I could cope with your company."

She looked round the room while he read her note, everything tidy but nothing personal like family photos.

"Saturday will be fine. Shall we walk down to the river then along the Embankment and I'll drop you off on the way back?"

"Sounds good."

They clattered downstairs and linking arms walked in the now deepening dusk. The Albert Bridge was festooned with lights like sparkling diamonds on fine silver chains.

"I love the river at night and just look at the Moon. I could reach out and touch it."

Charles stopped. "Men will go there one day; I wish I could go with them."

"Why?"

"I would look down on Earth and all mankind's problems would look small and insignificant."

Barbara squeezed his arm, "That sounds sad, are you sad, Charles?"

He shrugged and started walking again. Barbara took a deep breath.

"I know you have been married, Gordon and Joan told me before I met you, and that you have a daughter. Tell me about her."

"Not much to tell. She's eighteen and went to live in a hostel after she left me. Now she has moved in with her boyfriend's family. Can't say I approve but she isn't likely to take much notice of what I say."

"Why not?"

"Wilful, undisciplined, like her mother."

"She must have missed you when you were away in the army. How long was it?"

"Fourteen years."

"I suppose she was with your ex-wife."

"Good God no! I got custody you see, there was no way Rachel was a fit mother."

"So where did she go?"

"Lived with my parents for four years but then Dad died and I had to make other arrangements. Not easy I can tell you."

"Couldn't have been easy for her either, she must have felt like an orphan."

"I always did my best you know."

"I'm sure you did but children need stability."

"That's my point, Rachel was far from stable and that's why the whole burden fell on my shoulders."

They walked on in silence and Barbara considered that last statement. Burden was such a strange word to use, had he thought of his only child as a burden? If so no wonder the girl had left, a child is for loving. The old familiar pang of loss squeezed her heart; it was not like the first sharp agony but it was still there. She could live with it and accept it without it destroying her peace of mind. We remember the past, she thought, and learn from it but we must not live in it.

"I'd like to meet your girl, does she have a name?"

"Oh." Charles sounded surprised. "It's Jenny."

"I bet she could tell me a thing or two about you, you're such a mystery."

"Yes but she wouldn't say anything flattering."

"Does that worry you?"

"Of course not she's only a child."

"At eighteen she's nearer to being an adult than a child."

"You don't understand. Rachel did the dirty on me. She had a child by another man while I was fighting in North Africa. I came back to find her gone. Not only that she took everything my furniture, everything and of course Jenny as well. Is it any wonder I feel so bitter?"

"But Charles it happens all the time. Of course it must have been dreadful but you have to go on, make a new life, put the past where it belongs, behind you." It was on the tip of her tongue to tell him about her child but somehow now was not the time. Charles' bitterness would despoil the purity of her memories. She didn't want to be bitter; she wanted to protect those golden days when the two people she had loved most had been her family.

"She made a fool of me." The anguish made Charles's voice rasp as the words were torn from him, "I can never forgive that."

"But my dear Charles, none of that is Jenny's fault."

"No but she looks just like her bloody mother. If she were not my daughter I would probably fall in love with her."

They stopped. Barbara turned towards him and spoke very quietly.

"That is the way to madness and destruction for both of you."

"I know," he whispered.

"I think it's time we got back." In silence they returned to Barbara's flat then Charles walked home alone.

*

Chapter 22

Jenny brushed her hair then back-combed it all into a halo round her head and applied a liberal layer of lacquer; tonight she wanted to look her best. William was taking her out for a meal. It was their last evening together as he was off to Stockholm in a few days. She wished she didn't feel so sad; she must put on a brave face and make sure the evening went well. She could do no more.

She put on her best skirt and her shantung blouse and wished that she could afford to buy more fashionable clothes. Her best shoes were low-heeled but as William said they were walking to the restaurant they would seem a sensible choice. He had promised a taxi back.

She reflected on this her first week living in luxury, all so different from what she was used to. At first the heating overpowered her forcing her to open her bedroom window wide or swelter in bed. William had been attentive, too much so, he had crept into her bedroom once George and Iris were in bed. She was frightened by her feelings and terrified that Iris or George would hear them then she would be thrown out in disgrace.

She was in turmoil, her body was taking control. She only had to look at William to feel the heat of sexual excitement, the situation was getting out of hand and she didn't feel she could cope much longer. Was this how Laura had felt? Perhaps it was a good thing William was going away; it would give them both a chance to cool down.

She went down to the living room where William was waiting.

"You do look nice," George said.

Iris looked her up and down. George was right, she was a very attractive girl when she made the effort. Iris recalled how Rachel had looked when she smiled at George in the Dorchester. Neither mother nor daughter was conventionally pretty but there was good bone structure and of course both Rachel and Jenny had such beguiling eyes.

"Do you want me to drive you to the restaurant?"

"I don't mind walking, Mr. Martin"

"You can if you like Dad."

"My son is becoming an idle toad but we can't have your hair ruined by the wind." George patted Jenny on the shoulder. "Come on it's your last night for a while."

Iris watched in silence as they left the room.

Laura stretched out on the settee; it was good to be home.
Mum and Dad had made such a fuss of her that the pain of the
abortion was receding with every day. After long discussions
about her future it had been decided that she should enrol at the
local college and try to get some qualifications in child care. With
some luck she might get in at the start of the September term. At
times she wondered if it was a wise choice; after all she had
destroyed a life, was she a fit person to work with children?

She sighed and had another look at the letter from Mark which
she had received that morning. It had been enclosed with a letter
from Miss Pritchard which explained that it had not been possible
for her to pass on Laura's address to him, only Laura could do
that. On the back of the letter from Mark was his name and
address – somewhere in Manchester. Laura was not sure what
she wanted to do. The first time she read Mark's letter she had
screwed it up and thrown it in the waste bin. She didn't want to
be reminded of all that had happened.

Miss Pritchard's letter explained that Mark had called at the
hostel as he wanted to trace her and another girl. He had been
turned away by one of the kitchen hands who had only
remembered Laura's name. Before she even read Mark's letter
she had known it was Jenny he wanted to contact, not her. She
unfolded the crumpled letter and reread it.

Mark had got a new job near his home in the North West. He
hoped that Laura was fully recovered and that if she had left the
hostel his letter would be forwarded. Then it came to the
important bit. Had Jenny been a resident at the hostel? He was
unsure. Was Laura still in contact with her? If so would she
please forward Jenny's address?

He explained about the meeting that didn't take place. Laura
had been surprised as Jenny had confided that she always arrived
early for a date. What had happened? He must be keen to go to
all this trouble.

"You're looking very serious, poppet." Mr. Johnson sat down
on the settee with a groan. "By Jove I'm not as young as I used to
be." He put his arm around his daughter, "Nothing wrong?"

Laura folded the letters quickly and smiled at him. "No
everything's fine."

He looked at her. "I wonder if we only appreciate what we
have when we come close to losing it?"

Laura wondered if her dad realised what he had said. She did lose it, the baby that is, by her own actions. Silence clogged the air, poor old Dad he didn't mean any harm. She must tell him about the letters, ask his advice.

*

After the taxi driver was paid William and Jenny ambled up the path. Her feet didn't seem to be in contact with the ground, it had been a relaxed, intimate, romantic evening. If she didn't think about Friday, maybe it wouldn't come. They walked into the living room where Iris and George were sitting.

"Had a good time, kids?" George asked.

"Oh yes, it was wonderful." Jenny sat down, her body felt boneless, she was floating. It was difficult to make her eyes focus so she closed them. That was a mistake as the room seemed to tip and lurch from side to side. She felt colour drain from her face and perspiration beaded her forehead. Iris watched her.

"I think I'd better go upstairs," Jenny said.

Iris saw George gave William a knowing wink as Jenny struggled to her feet.

"Take her up, lad, she might lose her way."

William grasped Jenny's elbow and steered her round the furniture. So it's amusing for Jenny to come back sloshed, Iris thought, she clicked her tongue in annoyance.

"The girl's not used to alcohol, she'll be all right."

Iris didn't bother to reply.

Upstairs William helped Jenny into her room. She clung to him, fearful that she might fall.

"Shall I help you get undressed?"

Jenny opened her eyes wide with alarm. "What would your Mother say?" she whispered.

William shrugged, "I'd better go down." He put his arms round her. "Am I going to get a good night kiss?"

She pursed her lips and closed her eyes; she clung to him as the room started to spin again.

"No," he whispered, "a proper kiss, later."

She opened her eyes and looked into his. What could she say, was this the right time? He was going away and there was the Berthe woman in Stockholm. She thought again of Laura and what had happened to her; it was a sobering thought.

"I don't know, William, I just don't know."

"I've got some Durex, please Jenny."

She felt icy cold and shivered. He put his arms round her, his

155

grip even tighter and kissed her hard. She heard footsteps coming up the stairs and pulled away breathless.

"You must go," she whispered.

William turned to leave as Iris walked past on her way to her bedroom.

"Off to bed, Mum?"

"No, just getting my book."

"Isn't it downstairs, on the settee?"

"Perhaps it is."

Jenny lay on her bed, this was awful; what was she going to do? She listened as William and Iris walked down stairs. Perhaps it was all her fault and it would have been better if she had stayed at the hostel. Everyone knew that young men put pressure on girls, William couldn't help it and he was going away. But men didn't want to marry easy girls and if she did what William wanted she would be easy wouldn't she?

She decided to get undressed, clean her teeth and go to bed. She would feel better after a good night's sleep. As she walked across the landing she could heard Iris's voice.

"Don't forget, William, while that girl is in our house we are responsible for her."

Jenny stood and listened to a low buzz of conversation between William and George, something about work and Stockholm. Feeling guilty at eavesdropping she scuttled into the bathroom, soaped her face, did her teeth and hurried back to her room. She heard footsteps and felt herself tense, it was William.

"See you in the morning, Mum, Dad, goodnight."

Jenny stood still, not daring to get into bed, and hoped hard that William would not come into her room. She was not ready. Minutes passed and the noise of people moving about got quieter. Jenny relaxed. She heard George call downstairs something about locking up so Iris was not going to bed yet. Jenny felt glad. William wouldn't do anything with his mother still awake.

*

Iris looked at her watch, twelve o'clock and her eyes were closing. Perhaps that last brandy she had after George went upstairs had not been such a good idea. She wanted to be alert. It didn't matter if she were late to bed as she could always lie in when the others went to work.

William was so obvious. Did he really think she didn't know what he was up to? She was sure she had heard moving about on

156

a couple of occasions but it might have been visits to the bathroom. She wondered what she would do if she heard noises coming from Jenny's bedroom. She hoped she had spiked William's guns and he would accept seduction was not on the menu tonight.

She closed her book and stretched, all things considered it was as well that William was going away. She and Jenny would have to do some very serious talking. She turned out the lights and went upstairs; she paused at her bedroom door, there was nothing to stop her checking on her own son. She pushed open his bedroom door; moonlight was streaming through a crack between the curtains. She tip-toed to the window and pulled the curtains together. The heavy breathing suggested that William was deeply asleep.

*

Jenny jumped with alarm and William clapped his hand over her mouth before she could make a sound. She swivelled her eyes to her bedside table, the clock showed that it was three in the morning.

"What are you doing?"

"Ssh," he whispered, "move over, let me get in."

"Your Mum and Dad might hear."

"Not at this time. Mum will be dead to the world and Dad wouldn't say anything."

Her sleep had been so deep that she now felt drugged and stupid. Her head was throbbing and she had a stale, unpleasant taste in her mouth. This was like the repulsive business with Jim. Love was supposed to be hearts and flowers and gentleness not all this grunting and hot breath.

William was trying to devour her, his tongue invading her mouth like a surgeon's swab cleaning a wound, pressing, probing until she felt she would choke. His body was heavy against hers and then he was on top of her pressing her down. His penis, hard and hot, pulsated against her abdomen.

"Please, William," she whispered, "please don't, I'm scared."

"What is there to be frightened of, I love you don't I? And I'm going away; you'd do it if you loved me." His whisper was harsh and hot in her ear. "Show me you love me, Jenny, please."

She felt her body go rigid with terror. All she could see behind closed eyelids was blood, oceans of blood and Laura slumped, ashen-faced, on the floor. The butcher's shop smell of congealed blood that had swamped Laura's hostel bedroom filled Jenny's nostrils again. Nausea pushed against her throat and she retched.

William stopped and in the gloom she could see his face, his eyes and mouth dark holes like a death mask. She felt tears on her cheeks.

"What's the matter?"

"I told you I'm frightened."

He clicked his tongue and Jenny felt like a stupid child who had annoyed a grown-up. He lay beside her and she felt his hand moving up and down. He groaned and grabbed her hand. "Just hold it, you're driving me crazy."

She placed her fingers around the stiff, hot, hateful thing. How can women want this inside them, she thought, letting it thrust deep into their most secret, delicate place?

She realised William was fumbling with something.

"Quick, help me put this on." He held the sheath and put it on the end of his penis. "Roll it down quickly. You'll be all right. I promise I'll be gentle; I won't hurt you."

Jenny felt paralysed. She could not escape, there was nowhere to go. He guided her hand and clasped it onto the rolled sheath.

"Roll it down for God's sake."

Terrified she rolled the rubber down until she could feel coarse, harsh, pubic hair against her hand. He checked it was in place and groaned as he rolled on top of her. He tried to force her legs apart but she could not, dare not relax. He thrust against her, his breath rasping in her ear.

"Please, Jenny."

"I can't," she sobbed, "I can't, it's wrong."

Without warning he rolled off her and though he lay beside her he was no longer with her. Without a word he sat up and fumbled with his pyjamas. He walked from her room leaving her limp with despair. Tears coursed down her face. Was it always like this, she wondered, was romantic love just make-believe?

She lay listening for any sounds. She thought William had gone into the bathroom and after a while she heard the toilet flushing. There was the sound of footsteps going past her room and into William's then a conclusive click of his bedroom door. She pulled the covers over herself and turned to the wall using her pillows to stifle her sobs.

*

Chapter 23

"I meant what I said you know."

"What about?"

"Meeting Jenny."

Barbara watched as Charles squirmed. She had been shocked by what he had said last week and had wondered if she should cancel the invitation for him to come for a meal. But what had he confessed to? He hadn't actually done anything, he had only said how desirable he would find Jenny if she were not his child. He wasn't the first man to feel like that.

"Why the interest in my daughter?"

"I'm not sure but she sounds to have had quite a lonely time, maybe I could be a friend. If Rachel is so unreliable perhaps the girl needs an older woman to confide in. Women and girls do that."

"She's apparently got her boyfriend's mother. Do you realise I haven't even met the people she's living with? Met the boyfriend and can't say I was impressed."

"What father is impressed with his daughter's choice of mate? Isn't it a case of poacher turned gamekeeper?"

"Perhaps so."

"My parents were less than impressed with Paul."

"Who's he?"

"Who was he, he was my husband."

"I didn't know you had been married."

"You haven't given me much chance to tell you a lot about myself."

"I hope my disclosures haven't been a burden to you."

Barbara laughed.

"I'm sorry; I didn't mean it like that."

"What a prickly person you are, I can see I'm really going to have my work cut out with you," she smiled as she stood up and went to the kitchen. "Better check it isn't going to be burnt offerings to go with your sack cloth and ashes."

Charles followed her to the kitchen. "I'm sorry. You know I don't mean to be a pompous ass but perhaps living on my own is to blame."

He watched her for a moment. "Anything I can do?" he asked.

"Open the wine, food won't be long."

"I'm not very good at this."

"What opening wine bottles?"

159

"No, offering a sympathetic ear. You know you can always talk to me about…well…you know…your past, if you want to."

"The past is a funny thing, you can't get rid of it and, if you let it, it can bugger up your future. I'm selective about my past. I want to cherish the good times and push the pain and grief into a corner of my mind where it will do no harm."

"Did you have good times with Paul?"

"Oh yes."

"So what went wrong?"

Barbara watched as Charles's face flushed with embarrassment at his own audacity.

"You don't have to say if you don't want to," he said.

She looked at him and wondered how often in the past he had expressed an interest in another person's life.

"Let's eat first and I'll bare my soul afterwards."

Charles smiled and carried the wine through to the table.

*

The television murmured quietly in the corner and Iris sighed, another evening with little conversation but plenty of time to think. She had said nothing about her suspicions regarding William's intentions on Thursday night but had noticed how subdued both he and Jenny had been on Friday. George had noticed nothing but then he never did. Now William was in Stockholm she could breathe a sigh of relief.

She wondered how much company Jenny would prove to be, she had hardly spoken all evening. She spent far too much time in her room or when she was downstairs usually had her head in a book. That wouldn't do at all, Iris thought. Perhaps the girl was overawed by the improvement in her life style.

Having seen most of Jenny's belongings it was clear not much was spent on clothes. That too would have to change, if Jenny was to be one of the family she would have to look the part. I'll take her shopping, Iris decided; they could go shopping together and have lunch afterwards. She glanced across at George who was sprawled in his armchair, asleep.

"Jenny," she said quietly, "get me a brandy, it's in the dining room." She held out her empty glass.

Jenny put her book down and also glanced at George. She wondered if Iris would have made the request if he had been awake. In the short time she had lived with the Martins she had observed the constant battle of wills between George and Iris, a

160

battle centred on her drinking.

Jenny was in a difficult position, her accommodation was of the grace and favour variety and depended on her not upsetting anyone. In order to please Iris she would cause George concern. She did not want to upset George as she liked him but she feared Iris more. Very quietly she left the room and poured what she hoped was an acceptable measure of Courvoisier.

Returning to her seat she faced the television but her thoughts were elsewhere. Neither she nor William had made any reference to his failed seduction. It was so unfair; he was behaving like a spoilt brat. If only she had someone to talk to. Everyone knew men didn't marry girls they slept with so that must mean he had no intention of marrying her. She was all right to be used and then discarded when a suitable virgin came along; she wondered if the dreaded Berthe was a virgin. He didn't respect her feelings therefore he didn't love her, Jenny's heart ached.

George stirred and sat up. Iris watched as his eyes went to her glass, she smiled at him confident he would say nothing.

"I've been thinking George, Jenny says she has a day's holiday owing to her, I think I should take her shopping to pick out some suitable clothes."

"That sounds like a good idea, what do you think, Jenny?"

"I do need some new things."

There's only one problem, she thought, I have very little money and Iris is bound to take me to expensive shops.

"You could do with a decent suit and a few dresses."

Jenny looked at Iris in alarm. Of course she was saving money now she didn't have to pay her hostel rent but even so she didn't have enough to buy all the things Iris was suggesting.

George laughed. "Don't look so worried, we'll give you an early Christmas present, some money to help with the shopping expedition."

Jenny grinned with both relief and gratitude. Iris watched. That smile will get Jenny a long way, she thought.

*

Barbara and Charles were sitting on the settee, one at each end. Barbara had removed her shoes and lounged against the cushions. Despite the space between them the atmosphere was relaxed if not intimate. Mellowed by wine and good food, Barbara watched and waited to see if Charles was prepared to probe a little into her past.

161

"You know I said to Gordon that I couldn't understand why you had never married, does he know about Paul?"

"Oh yes but he's very discreet. Perhaps he thought I might not want to tell you but there's no secret about it."

"I think Paul must have been a very foolish man," Charles stopped for a moment, "to allow himself to lose you."

Barbara smiled, "Maybe, maybe not. Anyway he's happy now."

"How do you know that?"

"Perhaps I'm just assuming but he looked happy the last time I saw him. He's remarried and his wife's expecting a baby."

Barbara swallowed hard. She felt herself tense; this was always the difficult bit. "You see our child died."

She heard Charles gasp but he didn't speak.

"I had a very bad time having Richard and was told I should not attempt to become pregnant again."

"My dear Barbara I am so sorry. I've blathered on about myself, I had no idea."

Barbara stood and walked to her bedroom returning with the silver photograph frame. Charles drained his glass and stood as though to leave.

"I'm imposing on your grief and that is unforgivable."

Barbara turned the frame to show a chubby-faced, smiling child with golden hair.

"This is Richard. The picture was taken when he was three, just before the accident."

"What happened?" Charles asked and sat down again.

"It was a road accident." Barbara worked at keeping her voice flat and even, all feelings squashed out.

"He'd gone to the park with his father and it was on the way back you see. They'd been playing football and Richard was bouncing the ball on the pavement but it rolled into the road." She paused. "The driver didn't see him." She drank some wine and heard the glass clink against her teeth.

Charles got the near empty bottle from the table. He topped up Barbara's glass and drained the rest into his own. They both sat down, this time side by side.

"When did it happen?"

"Seven years ago, he'd have been nearly eleven now."

Charles put his glass down and took Barbara's hands in his. She noticed that his face was drained of colour. Perhaps, she

162

thought, he is not as tough as he would have me believe.

"Paul was distraught, we both were. But he could not deal with his feelings of guilt and my grief. You see my tears were like daggers in his soul. He blamed himself and went over and over it, if only, if only."

"But it was his fault."

"Charles, Charles what has fault got to do with it? Would that have given Richard an extra day of life? It happened. All the wishing and hoping will not change that."

"Is that why you divorced him?"

"Because of the accident? In a way. We realised we would destroy each other if we didn't separate, that was the only thing left for both of us. So we parted and waited the appropriate length of time and divorced each other."

"And now he's married again, another child on the way. It's wicked for him to get away scot-free."

"Has he? He still has to live with himself."

"What has he left you with?"

"Memories, happy memories, I wanted to be a mother and I was. For me it was only a short time but they were golden days. Now I have a different life, I'm not unhappy it's just different from what I expected." She shrugged and stood up.

"That's quite enough of me, let's get this table cleared."

*

Jenny tore open the envelope, it was a letter from her father and as always it was to the point. He expected her to go to his flat for lunch on Sunday in two weeks time. They would be eating at one o'clock. She had not expected to hear from him, never mind be asked to visit. She must reply, by letter, and let George and Iris know.

Today was the day Iris was taking her shopping and Jenny viewed the expedition with trepidation. Supposing Iris suggested things she didn't like, would she dare to make alternative suggestions? She checked her Post Office Savings Book, she had twenty seven pounds which was hardly a fortune. George had given her another forty, what a nice man he was.

She pondered on how different life would have been if Dad had been more like George maybe Mum and Dad would not have divorced. She reflected on the relative difficulties of being a husband to Iris or Mum, in their different ways there was not much to choose between them.

163

She heard Iris calling so quickly gathered her savings book and purse and hurried downstairs.

"We'll go to Oxford Street there's so much choice there then we'll have some lunch."

They got into Iris's car and headed for town. Jenny had wondered if it would have been easier to go by Tube then there would have been no problem with parking. She suspected that Iris found public transport beneath her.

Jenny found being driven by Iris an alarming experience; at best her driving was flamboyant. The Ford Anglia swept in and out of the traffic and Iris's patience evaporated as they cruised round trying to find a parking space. With an air of triumph Iris careered into a small gap in a back street just off Oxford Street.

"Will it be all right here?"

"Of course, we're off the main road." Iris slammed the door shut and locked it.

"Now you have Selfridges, John Lewis, then Dickens and Jones. We'll go to Claridges for lunch; might as well make a day of it."

Jenny was overwhelmed; the big department stores had a magic about them associated with wealth and privilege to which she had no access in her own right. For entirely different reasons neither of her parents would consider entering places like this yet for Iris it was a normal part of life.

The morning passed in a flurry of dressing, undressing and staring at herself in mirrors. Agreeing with Iris when she wasn't sure, sounding unsure when she didn't like the garment under appraisal. I should be enjoying this, she thought, if I can't choose what I like what's the point?

After traipsing up and down from one store to another they agreed that enough was enough. Jenny now had a dark blue suit with a straight skirt and a shawl collar, a pink, tweedy, short-sleeved dress and a full skirted dress in dark green with a wide belt. Iris had treated her to a pair of plain black, court shoes with slender, high heels – higher than Jenny had ever had before. Iris had bought herself an elegant maroon dress and jacket with a turban style hat and gloves to match. Those items were put on George's account. Poor George, Jenny thought.

They walked back to the car to find a parking ticket under the windscreen wiper. Jenny said nothing while Iris ranted and raved and strode up and down wanting to know who had done such a monstrous thing. In the end she accepted the inevitable with very bad grace indeed, wrenched the ticket from the windscreen and flung it on the back seat of the car.

"What are these fools trying to do? They'll kill the trade in the West End if people can't drive in to shop. It's a disgrace, how dare they?"

Jenny slid into her seat and clutched her carrier bags. If only I could disappear, she thought. People passing had watched Iris's initial outburst and now with an ear-splitting crunch of gears the car shot backwards and stopped with a jolt. There was a tinkle of broken glass and Iris swore as she yanked the wheel round, crashed into first gear, shot forward and out past the car in front.

People shouted and gesticulated while Jenny stared out of the window not daring to catch anyone's eye.

"Get me a cigarette," Iris said, "in my bag on the back seat."

Jenny leaned across, got a cigarette from the silver case and lit it with the matching silver lighter. Her hands were shaking. They crawled down Oxford Street, turned into North Audley Street, past Grosvenor Square and Brook Street to arrive at Claridges.

Iris seemed unperturbed by the incident which had left Jenny mortified. She wondered how much damage Iris had done to the car she hit and how could she just drive off? Suppose someone had taken her registration number, supposing the police were told a younger woman had been in the car with her? Would she be regarded as an accessory to a traffic offence, should she tell George? She felt sick.

"Come on girl, get a move on." Iris was waiting to lock the car door. Having secured the car Iris set off at speed towards the hotel entrance and Jenny had to run to keep up with her.

Once inside Iris accosted the first waiter she saw.

"A large brandy, please then a table for two."

"I'm sorry, Madam, the restaurant has stopped taking luncheon orders. It's after two o'clock"

"Just get me a brandy then."

"Are you a resident, Madam?"

Iris swelled with rage. "I am Mrs. Martin, my husband and I regularly use this hotel for meals and accommodation for our business colleagues when they visit London."

The waiter nodded and looked embarrassed.

"We have recommended Claridges many times however that can be changed, get me the manager."

The waiter rolled his eyes and scuttled off. Jenny stood still and gazed into the distance aware that people in the foyer were staring and talking behind their hands. Iris lit another cigarette from the stub of her last.

A large, genial-looking gentleman approached with the frightened waiter in tow.

"My dear Mrs. Martin so good to see you, I believe we have a slight difficulty but nothing that we cannot sort out," he glanced at Jenny, "for you and your young friend."

Iris nodded and waited for what was her due.

"Now if you would like to follow me we can take you to a private room where we will provide a light luncheon, a selection of sandwiches followed by gateau and coffee."

He bowed and smiled as he clasped and unclasped his hands, he reminded Jenny of Uriah Heap. They were taken to a room with comfortable chairs and low coffee tables.

"I'll have a large brandy," Iris said then she turned to Jenny, "what do you want?"

A lime and lemonade, please."

The manager and waiter departed at speed leaving Iris and Jenny in a heavy silence. Jenny waited for Iris to speak, to explain or justify what she had done to someone's car. Iris drew hard on her cigarette and as soon as the waiter appeared with drinks, she took a large mouthful of brandy.

"You have to let these people know you won't be messed about."

Jenny nodded, sipped her drink and waited.

"Do you like the things you've bought?"

"Oh yes, they're lovely and I am so grateful you helped me choose, I couldn't have managed on my own. And the shoes, they will go with everything. Thank you ever so much."

"Don't say 'ever so' it sounds common."

Jenny blushed and stared into her glass. She remembered Grandma Cardew correcting the way she spoke but that had been years ago. She'd been a lady but Iris wasn't a lady, she was horrible. She glanced at Iris, I don't think I will ever like you, she thought.

The food arrived. There was a plate piled with dainty, triangular sandwiches minus crusts and Jenny realised she was very hungry.

"Another brandy, please waiter," Iris said.

166

He took the glass and left. Jenny glanced at Iris and felt a quiver of anxiety, she was being driven home by this woman and surely it could not be wise to drive after so much alcohol but she dared not say anything. She picked up the plate of sandwiches. Perhaps it would make things better if she could encourage Iris to eat something, to soak up the brandy, but Iris wrinkled her nose and carried on drinking.

"They do look nice," Jenny said and offered the plate again. Iris took two but lit another cigarette. Jenny sighed and started eating as there was no point in wasting them. The waiter reappeared with the brandy, bowed and shuffled away.

"Has your Mother always been so strange?"

Jenny swallowed hard.

"George found her very odd."

Remembering the meal at the Dorchester it struck Jenny that George had accepted Mum with less difficulty than Iris but there was no point in saying so.

"She was very ill some years ago and had to have brain surgery. I think it was called a lobotomy. I don't think they do it any more because it changes people's personality too much. She used to be all right." She couldn't tell Iris that Mum had always been alarming.

Iris nodded and ate one of the sandwiches. So far so good, Jenny thought, eat the other and I'll offer you the plate again.

"These are good, smoked salmon I think."

"Are you hoping to marry my son?"

Jenny felt the face redden. "I don't know. We haven't talked about it; perhaps we are a bit young yet."

"You have to be so careful with mental problems."

Jenny stared at Iris. There could only be one explanation for that remark, hands off my son, your Mum's barmy. What had kids yelled at her and Stephen as they walked to school? 'Your Mum's in the loony bin'. The sandwich she was eating turned to sawdust in her mouth and she blinked back tears.

Iris tapped a cigarette on her case and watched Jenny's reaction then she lit the cigarette and smiled.

"Have some gateau," she said.

But Jenny was no longer hungry, she shook her head. What did anything matter when she had her mother like an albatross around her neck?

"Coffee?" asked Iris.

"Yes please, shall I pour you a cup?"

If Iris wouldn't eat perhaps coffee would ensure that they both got home in one piece. Jenny watched as Iris drained her brandy glass and hoped she would not order another.

The manager appeared. "I hope everything is satisfactory, Madam."

Iris gave a brief nod, "Would you bring the bill, please." The manager turned, clicked his fingers and the waiter appeared on cue. Placing the silver tray plus bill on the coffee table he dipped his head low to Iris and waited.

Iris glanced at the bill and extracted a note from her wallet.

"Keep the change."

"Thank you, Madam. We hope to see you and Mr. Martin again soon."

He bowed low and left. Iris drained her coffee cup and stood. She stared at her reflection in the large, gilt-framed mirror; she patted her hair and smoothed her skirt. Jenny scrambled to her feet and followed as Iris swept out.

Back in the car park Jenny saw that the car's rear lights were broken and there was a nasty dent in the bumper. She didn't tell Iris. They set off and were soon in heavy traffic on the Edgware Road. At least when it's this busy we have to go slowly, Jenny thought.

Once past Lords' Cricket Ground and on to the Finchley Road the traffic thinned and Iris gained speed. Jenny could not believe how close Iris got to other cars without touching them and seemed oblivious to hooting horns and irate drivers who caught up with her at lights and indicated their annoyance with a variety of gestures.

Any conversation could cause a life-threatening distraction so Jenny closed her eyes and said nothing. As they turned into the Martins' drive Jenny wondered if her legs could still hold her upright. She struggled out of the car with her shopping.

"Let me carry yours in," Jenny said as Iris scrabbled in her bag for the front door keys. She had left the driver's door open and the keys in the ignition. With a sigh of relief Jenny collected Iris's purchases, the car keys, shut and locked the doors and went into the house.

*

168

Chapter 24

Laura showed her father the letters from Miss Pritchard and Mark. He scowled.

"Is this the man responsible for......."

"Oh no, Dad, he was really kind, he contacted Tony and told him that he must help me."

"I'd like to meet that young man."

"Who, Mark?"

"Well yes, he sounds a decent bloke. No, it's Tony I'd like to meet; I'd knock his bloody block off."

"I was the fool, Dad, and Tony just took advantage of my stupidity."

"Yes, well..." Mr. Johnson put his arm round Laura and hugged her. She realised in that moment that i was wonderful to feel so safe and loved. All the irritation that used to explode in her head whenever her parents told her anything had diminished to the point where she thought she could control it.

"So Mark wants to contact this girl, Jenny, wasn't she the one who found you?"

"Yes and I should have written to her, I said I would."

"Then do it, she's at the hostel isn't she?"

"As far as I know."

"Why not give her a ring now."

Laura dialled the number and listened as the phone rang and rang. She liked Mark and felt jealous of Jenny, plain, ordinary Jenny with rubbish clothes and no money. Why couldn't Mark have liked me, she wondered? At first she had thought she would not bother to contact Jenny or pass on Mark's letter but now she had confided in Dad, she had no choice. Just as she was about to ring off, she heard a voice.

"Baron's Court Hostel, Miss Pritchard speaking."

"Hello, Miss Pritchard it's Laura, Laura Johnson. Thank you for the letter but it isn't me Mark Ogden wanted to contact it's Jenny, Jenny Warr."

"I see. There's a slight problem as Jenny has moved out. But I do have her address. As you know Hostel Trust rules do not permit me to pass on any resident's new address."

"If I write to Jenny and enclose Mark's letter with it, would you pass on both?"

"Of course, my dear, all part of the service. And by the way are you fully recovered from your dreadful ordeal?"

"Yes, Miss Pritchard, and I'm going to enrol at college."

"Quite right too, I'm pleased to hear it, I wish you every success."

Laura returned to the living room and promised she would write to Jenny that evening. Mr. Johnson smiled and suggested that they walked down to the post box together as soon as she'd finished.

*

George walked into the kitchen, "What's happened to your car?"

"Some stupid sod boxed me in, had the devil's own job to get out."

"You do realise the bumper is going to have to be replaced and you'll need a new off-side light."

"Oh." Iris continued preparing the evening meal.

"You'd better not drive it again until it's fixed."

"How long will that take?"

"I'll ring the garage first thing; they'll probably come to collect it."

Jenny heard George's heavy footsteps on the stairs; she was sitting on her bed writing a note to her father accepting his invitation to a meal. George tapped on her door.

"Can I come in?"

"Yes, of course."

"Must have been a nasty bump you had."

George was watching her and she didn't know how much Iris had told him.

"It was a bit difficult for Mrs. Martin to get out of the parking space and I think she was annoyed about the ticket."

From his reaction she knew he hadn't been told about that."

"What did the other driver say?"

"The car was just parked, there was no-one in it."

"Did she leave her name and telephone number or anything?"

Jenny shook her head.

George loosened his tie and leaned against the chest of drawers.

"This is awkward but I must ask you, had she been drinking?"

"No," Jenny paused. "Not then..."

"I see." George turned and went downstairs.

Jenny remained in her room. I don't want to be with Iris, she thought, I shouldn't have come here, it has all been a dreadful mistake. The awful night with William wouldn't have happened if I had stayed at the hostel. Now I will be piggy in the middle between George and Iris.

She sat on her bed and tried to quell the feeling of panic. If she left here where could she go? She could not face food, she felt sick. She listened to voices downstairs in the kitchen, the conversation sounded tense though she could not make out exactly what was being said.

"Your meal's ready," Iris shouted.

"I'm sorry," Jenny called down the stairs, "but I don't feel very well, I don't think I could eat anything."

There was no reply from Iris so Jenny lay on her bed and stared at the ceiling. Perhaps she should write to William. He had already sent a letter to his parents perhaps he was waiting for her to make the first move. Perhaps she should apologise and tell him she really did love him and would prove it when he came home at Christmas.

She could hear raised voices, now there was a row going on downstairs. She heard her name among a stream of otherwise unintelligible invective. In the brief pauses she caught the lower tones of George trying to placate his incandescent wife. She heard the kitchen door bang followed by the clanging of saucepans. What should she do? She didn't want to be dragged into a screaming match.

There were footsteps on the stairs and Jenny prayed it wasn't Iris. For the second time George tapped on her door.

"You'll gather from the racket that Iris isn't in a good mood."

"I'm sorry. I suppose it's my fault."

"Not entirely although she's taken exception to your refusing to eat."

"I didn't know what to do; she just crashed into the car and drove off. Supposing someone reports her to the police. I was so frightened and she wouldn't eat anything and she had two large brandies and I kept offering her sandwiches and things, coffee, you know to soak up the alcohol. I didn't want her to have another accident. What could I do?" Jenny drew a shuddering breath.

George sighed. "I'm so sorry, it must have been awful for you but do you think you could manage a little? I know Iris can be difficult but from her point of view she's taken you shopping and now she's tired yet she's cooked a meal but you don't want it."

Jenny looked at George, his face seemed crumpled. All the trappings of wealth meant nothing when he had Iris to deal with.

"Will you come down and try to eat something; will you do it for me?"

"I'll try."

George smiled, put his arm round her and gave her a quick hug.

"Go wash your face and try to look cheerful, please."

The atmosphere in the dining room crackled with tension. George complimented Iris on the meal, Jenny apologised for causing a delay but Iris said nothing and pushed her food around the plate.

"When am I going to see what you girls have bought?"

"Shall I bring them down after the meal?" Jenny looked at Iris.

"And what did you get, dear?" George said, "I hope something nice caught your eye."

Iris barely acknowledged the enquiry but the tension eased and Jenny continued to put food in her mouth, swallowing was the problem.

"I managed to pick out some lovely things for Jenny and I treated her to a pair of shoes."

Jenny blushed at the implied rebuke.

"That was very kind," George said.

"I've never had such nice clothes," Jenny replied, "and shoes."

"Well I think a fashion show is in order, don't you?" George beamed first at Iris then at Jenny.

After the meal Jenny offered to clear the table and do the washing up. Standing at the sink she let her mind drift away from the tension that seemed to be a permanent feature of life in this house. She must write to William but somehow her feelings for him had changed. He hadn't written to her yet although surely he was the one who had behaved badly. She wondered if he was copying his mother or did he feel guilty?

She thought of Mark and sighed, was it fated that they should not meet again? Was there anything she could do about it, at least say sorry for not keeping the date, would that look too forward, pushy? Perhaps she could call as she knew where he lived. If she just put a note through the door, that way she could write her new address on the note and then it would be up to him.

"Is the model girl ready yet?" George stood in the doorway

and winked when she turned to answer.

"Two minutes," she replied.

As she left the kitchen she watched Iris walk downstairs in her new clothes. Jenny smiled. "Gosh, that looks lovely," she said.

"Of course, I've got an eye for fashion. Now hurry up and get changed."

Jenny scuttled upstairs, scrambled into the pink dress, turned to hurry back to the sitting room then turned again and put on the black high-heeled shoes Iris had bought her.

In the seconds it took her to change her clothes she had decided what she would do about Mark. She would go to his house.

As she slid her feet into the elegant black shoes she realised it would take time and practice to get used to such high heels. She walked downstairs with great care.

"Well, my dear," George said to Iris, "you have made an excellent choice, as always. I can see you two girls are going to have lots of fun shopping."

Iris smiled but Jenny felt uneasy for although she smiled, the air was heavy with hostility. After several changes of clothes and an avalanche of thanks and appreciation for all that Iris had done for her, Jenny felt drained. She tottered upstairs certain that she would be expected to wear her new shoes when she went to Dad's for lunch. She decided she would have to spend time each evening wearing them until she felt more confident.

She lay down on her bed and wondered how George had stuck it for so long. With Mum it was like treading on eggshells and coping with Iris wasn't much different. Jenny sighed, I must be positive, she thought, I will go to Mark's flat and leave a note. I'd better do it after work one evening before Mr. Martin goes on his next business trip. I shall tell them tonight that I have to work late, that will give me an opportunity to deliver the note without any awkward questions from Iris.

*

Mrs. Ogden collected the post. There was a letter with a London postmark, it was addressed to Mark. She went to the stairs and shouted.

"Letter for you, son, I think it's from that young lady you are trying to find."

After a thudding of bare feet down the stairs, Mark appeared. Mrs. Ogden laughed.

"Don't let this sweetheart of yours see you like this, she'd run a mile."

Mark gave his mother a loud kiss on the cheek and took the letter. It wasn't from Jenny.

"It's from Laura."

"Who's she?"

"The one who had the abortion, remember, I helped her with some money."

"And what's she got to say for herself?"

"Oh, you know, just saying thank you again and how I would always be welcome, and her parents would like to meet me."

"That's nice."

"You don't know her, spoilt rotten she is."

"What like you?" Mrs. Ogden ruffled Mark's already dishevelled hair.

"She'd better have passed on my letter to Jenny otherwise I'll go down all right, to give her a piece of my mind."

"I'm getting worried about you. This girl is becoming an obsession and that isn't healthy."

"I know but I've just got this feeling."

"Which Jenny might not share."

"Then let her tell me herself, I don't want someone else deciding for her."

"Fair enough, now don't you think you should get ready for work? I don't think turning up in your pyjamas would go down well."

*

Jenny arrived outside the house, note in hand. She pressed the bell for the top flat and waited; it was cold, dark and she was scared. She decided they must all be out and she would have to push her note through the letter box when the door unexpectedly opened.

"Well, well, well if it isn't Laura's frigid friend. Changed your mind have you? 'Cos you're too late, wouldn't touch you with a barge pole."

Jenny stared. It was the repulsive Jim who lounged against the door frame and leered at her.

"Is Mark in?"

Jim laughed, "He's left."

"Have you got his new address?"

"Suppose I have, why should I give it to you? Mark wouldn't

174

like that."

Jenny paused, Mark must be very angry because she didn't turn up. But would he have confided in Jim?

"I don't think he would mind, I was ill you see, so I couldn't meet him."

Jim watched her.

"I just want to say sorry and explain why I wasn't there."

Jim straightened up and grasped the door latch.

"Well tough luck because I don't know where the hell he is and do you know what, I don't bloody care."

With that he closed the door in her face. Jenny stood for a moment, it was fate, she and Mark would never meet again. She tore the note into small pieces and pushed them through the letter box; let Jim clear up the mess.

The journey home to Golders Green was horrible, as usual, and when she arrived she found Iris on her own.

"Letter for you and it isn't from William."

Iris passed the envelope over, obviously expecting to be told who it was from.

Jenny checked the postmark, Baron's Court. She ripped open the envelope and started to read.

"It's from the hostel, from Miss Pritchard, she's the warden there."

Iris arched her eyebrows.

"By the way, what have you got on my husband?"

Jenny felt the breath catch in her throat.

"What do you mean?"

"The other night, after we went shopping; I'm not your servant you know."

Jenny felt her face flush, she had no idea what she should say so said nothing.

"I took you out, something your parents seem reluctant to do. I chose things for you, I even spent my own money on you, and then I cooked a meal even though I was tired but you didn't want it."

"I did come down, it's just what happened with the car and everything," Jenny paused. "I was scared in case you got into trouble."

"But it only took a word from my husband and suddenly you were happy to join us. I repeat what have you got on my husband?"

"I don't know what you mean?"

"Are you trying to get off with him? You wouldn't be the first little minx who has tried to ensnare an older man."

Jenny gasped.

"I notice William hasn't written to you yet."

Jenny felt her heart thudding, the woman's mad, she thought, and she complains about my mother!

"I'm very sorry you think I would do such an awful thing. I'm not like that."

She turned and walked out of the kitchen, so angry she was trembling.

"But I bet your mother is," Iris shouted after her.

*

Chapter 25

As well as a letter from Miss Pritchard there were two others enclosed - one from Mark and one from Laura. After reading both Jenny's spirits rose, Mark had been trying to contact her. She sat very still and remembered their one and only meeting, it had seemed so right although she could not say why. He wants to see me, he isn't angry that I didn't turn up for our date and now, she thought, I have his address. She must write to thank Laura but she'd write to Mark first.

Her delight at hearing from Mark confirmed that she did not love William, perhaps she had been in love with the idea of love and loneliness had shielded her from the truth. Of course she might not fall in love with Mark either but she knew he would be a friend and at the moment perhaps that was all she wanted.

She had already written a chatty, sisterly letter to William and wouldn't mind if he didn't reply. At least Iris would be relieved that the romance with her son was over. Jenny wondered if she should say so but with Iris the less said the better.

Jenny re-read Mark's letter and smiled, although Manchester was a long way away they would manage to meet somehow. They would take one step at a time, there was no rush. She wrote to say how much she wanted to meet him and explained about being ill last time. She gave her address but decided not to include the telephone number. She thought it would be best if he didn't phone her, not here.

George had been away for three days and the evenings with Iris had been an ordeal. Twice Jenny had been sent to the local off-licence for bottles of brandy. It was fortunate that Iris liked watching the television because after the third drink she was not only incoherent she was also confrontational. At least, Iris's interest in the television ensured that any conversation was kept to a minimum.

This was the last evening they would spend alone and Jenny breathed a sigh of relief as she walked down stairs.

"When do you go to see your father?" Iris asked.

This was a safe topic, Jenny would ask Iris for some advice which was bound to please her.

"On Sunday, I was going to ask you what I should wear."

Iris smiled and put her cigarette and brandy glass down.

"The suit might be a bit formal, I think."

Jenny nodded.

"But have you got a decent coat? It won't be warm enough to go in just a dress."

"I've only got the navy one. It's very straight, I'm not sure the green dress would go underneath it, the skirt's so full."

"Wear the pink then, pink goes well with navy. What about shoes?"

"Oh, I must wear the lovely black ones you bought me."

"Have you a black handbag?"

"Yes, thank you."

"That will be fine."

"Thank you so much. I do appreciate all that you've done."

Iris held out her empty glass and Jenny went to the decanter for a refill.

*

Barbara was not sure whether to arrive at the time Charles had given or whether to go early and offer to help. He might view such an offer as a reflection on his ability to cope alone. Sod it, she thought, this is ridiculous. Besides, he was probably feeling nervous and Jenny would be too. It would be easier for both of them if there was a third person present.

She put on her jacket, picked up her handbag, bottle of wine and the potted plant she had bought. She glanced at her watch; she'd be there by twelve twenty, if nothing else she could set the table.

Barbara knocked at the door of Charles's flat and heard a loud crash and then an exclamation of anger. Seconds later the door was flung open.

"Don't look so harassed, I'll keep out of the way."

"No, no, come in, it's just that everything's at the critical stage!"

"Well, have a glass of that, to calm you down," she handed him the wine, "then go back to your kitchen, slave!"

He smiled and took the wine and her jacket. She walked into the living room and noticed, with amusement, that the table had been set; she should have known.

"It looks very nice, shall I put this," indicating the pot plant, "in the middle?"

"Why not, thanks, it's kind of you."

He disappeared into the kitchen.

"I hope Jenny isn't going to be late."

"If she's her father's daughter, she would rather die than be

178

late."

"Well her mother could never manage it, always late she was, be late for her own funeral, I expect."

Barbara pulled a face; it was like living with a ghost. He must think about Rachel all the time, obsession, that's what it was. She walked to the window and gazed out at nothing in particular. It certainly wasn't an inspiring view. Dust-bin sheds, neat and well painted but hardly aesthetically pleasing and a central yard, with washing lines, for the tenants.

One or two children were tearing round on home-made carts. They reminded her of Andrew; she turned away and went into the kitchen. There was a knock at the door.

"Must be Jenny," Barbara said.

"Will you go?"

Barbara looked surprised, "I think you should, after all she hasn't met me; it could be a bit of a shock. You go."

He shot out of the kitchen, muttering. Barbara sighed, how sad to feel like that about your own daughter.

Jenny took a deep breath as the door opened. "Hello, Dad."

"Good heavens girl, you've grown."

She blushed, "I think it's the shoes."

He had never allowed her to wear high heels, wouldn't have expected it, probably wouldn't approve.

"Come in, child," he said and took her coat.

Barbara came to meet her, she held out both hands.

"I'm Barbara, a friend of your father's. I am so glad to meet you at last; I hope we will be friends too."

Jenny felt a great surge of relief; it was going to be all right.

"You must excuse me; I need to go back to the kitchen." Charles rushed out.

Barbara rolled her eyes to the ceiling, in mock despair, Jenny giggled.

"Now come and sit down and tell me about yourself. Are you working or still at college?"

"I work at the Middlesex Hospital, I'm a laboratory technician."

"That must be interesting."

"It is, if you don't mind rats!"

"Do you, mind them, rats that is?"

"They're not my favourite animal and you have to be careful you don't get bitten. The professors I work for are very nice,

179

though."

"I'm a librarian, at the local library, at least books don't bite."

"Have you known Dad long? He's never mentioned you."

"Three or four months, that's all."

"Come along, food's ready." Charles raced in with two plates, piled high and dashed back for the third and a gravy jug. He opened the wine and poured two glasses.

"Now, are you going to be able to cope with those stilts you're wearing, if I give you some wine?"

Jenny blushed as she walked to the table.

"Don't be an old grouch, Charles. I think she looks very smart indeed. You didn't tell me you had such an elegant daughter."

Charles frowned and poured out a third glass.

"Come on now, eat up, you don't want it to get cold."

As the meal progressed Jenny relaxed. Barbara's light touch with the conversation made for an easy atmosphere. She told about some of the strange people who frequented the library which made them laugh and she encouraged Jenny to talk and would not allow Charles to dominate the conversation. She very gently poked fun at the slightest hint of pomposity.

Jenny felt more comfortable in the company of her father than she could ever remember. Barbara really was wonderful, she thought, she knows exactly how to handle Dad. I'll have to take lessons.

Barbara and Jenny remained seated after their meal as Charles insisted on doing all the washing up. Jenny was amazed to see that it was three o'clock. Usually her father's meals were over in a flash, army training he had insisted. Jenny had always assumed that if that were the case the entire British Army must be martyrs to indigestion.

"Once your Dad has finished crashing about in the kitchen," Barbara said, "we could have a little stroll. I'll show you where I live, it is quite near here. I know your Dad's not on the phone but you could have my number if you like just in case you ever needed to contact him in a hurry."

"Thank you that would be great."

She leaned back in the armchair and smiled at Barbara; the food and wine made her feel sleepy but very happy. She had been anxious about today yet it had gone like a dream.

"Now then," Charles said as he wiped his hands on a tea towel, "how about some fresh air and exercise." He pointed a finger at Jenny. "You'll get fat, my girl, if you're not careful."

"Well you shouldn't feed her so well," Barbara replied. "In any case we've already decided what we're doing. If you promise to behave yourself, we might ask you to come along too!"

Charles looked at Barbara, about to say something then changed his mind.

"Come on you old bear, get your jacket on."

Charles did as he was told.

They strolled down the road, Charles in the middle, Barbara on one arm, Jenny on the other. "This has been good," he said.

*

"Dad."

Mr. Johnson put down his Sunday paper, "Yes?"

"You know that man who helped me..... you know."

"The one who wrote?"

"Yes, Mark."

"What about him?"

"I thought it would be nice to invite him here after all the help he gave me, he told me he would like to meet you and Mum."

"I can't imagine why he would want to do that."

"Well, I think he likes me, he must do to have helped me like he did. I've got his telephone number, perhaps I should see if he could come here next weekend. I never had a chance to thank him properly."

"Ask your mother."

"But you wouldn't mind?"

"No, can I read my paper now?"

Laura hurried to the kitchen where her mother was cooking the Sunday roast.

"Dad says he thinks it would be a good idea to ask Mark here next weekend."

"Mark? Oh, he's the one who gave you that money. Where did you say he lives, Fulham was it?"

"He did but he's moved to Manchester."

"Why on earth would he want to come all this way?"

"I just think it would be good to say thank you properly and he's very nice, I'm sure you would like him."

"You can ask if he wants to come for a meal on Sunday though how he'll get here I don't know. Has he got a car?"

Laura didn't bother to answer she rushed upstairs and found

181

her address book.

Luckily he gave his telephone number as well as his address in the letter. She hurried downstairs and dialled.

"Hello."

"Mark, is that you?"

"Yes."

"It's Laura, Laura Johnson; I forwarded your letter to Jenny."

"Thanks."

"Mum and Dad thought it would be nice if you came down for a meal."

"That's very kind but it's a long way.....but do thank them anyway."

Laura bit her lip. "I'm asking Jenny too."

"Oh," Mark paused, "it all depends on the trains. I'll have to get back to you."

"Have you heard from Jenny?"

"Not yet," Mark replied.

Laura walked up stairs, deep in thought. She didn't really want Jenny to come for a meal but she must ask her now. She paused, she didn't have Jenny's address, she would have to write to Miss Pritchard and ask her to send the letter on. If she left it until Wednesday to write, Jenny might not receive it until it was too late. It wasn't her fault, Laura thought, Jenny should have replied to my letter sooner.

*

Chapter 26

Charles and Barbara said goodbye to Jenny who waved as they watched her go down the escalator.

"She's a nice girl," Barbara said.

"She's got a lot to learn."

"Haven't we all," Barbara replied as they strolled away from the station, "let's walk through St. Luke's gardens."

"St. Luke's is where I got married."

As no appropriate comment sprang to mind, Barbara said nothing.

"Her mother and stepfather opposed the marriage. I wasn't good enough, only a working class boy."

"That must have made things difficult for you both."

"They disinherited her, you know."

"She must have loved you a lot to go against them."

Charles snorted, "She had a funny way of showing it. It would have been better for me if she had listened to them, if the whole thing had been called off. It would have saved me a lot of heartache."

Barbara stopped dead. "But then you wouldn't have had Jenny."

"Well, she's going to turn out just like her mother. Look at her, no more than a child, tottering along in those ridiculous high heels, waggling her backside in that tight skirt, for all to see. I tell you Barbara I was shocked. If you hadn't been my guest I would have told her exactly what I thought."

He went to link his arm through Barbara's but she pulled away.

"You really are a sanctimonious, judgmental prig! If this is how you treated Rachel, I am not surprised she sought comfort elsewhere."

Without a word he turned to walk away but she grabbed his arm, forcing him to stand still.

"You have a delightful daughter who, I suspect, has had a thoroughly nasty time because you and maybe Rachel as well, have indulged in monumental self-pity."

"Do you think it's been easy for me?"

"Probably not but you were an adult making your own decisions. What about her? She didn't ask to be born."

"What can you know about it? I came back after the war to nothing....."

183

"Yes, Charles, you've told me but what support have you offered to Jenny during the painful transition from child to woman? What comfort, understanding and love, for God's sake, have you given her? She's your flesh and blood, Charles."

"What could I do? I don't know how to deal with a girl."

"Do you know, the one deep impression she left on me? A gut-wrenching loneliness, coupled with a desperate desire to please, so what do you do, Charles? Criticize."

"She did look like a tart in those shoes. Am I not allowed to have an opinion?"

"Of course you are but you must temper those opinions with love and kindness. I wear high-heeled shoes, does that make me a tart."

"That's different, you're an adult."

"Well I tell you this, Charles, Jenny is a very sensible young woman. She may not be twenty one yet but if you treat her as though she's a naughty child you will be the loser in the end."

"So what did I say that was so awful?"

"If you don't know there is no point in my trying to tell you. But comments that ridicule are wrong. She looked lovely and you should have told her so."

"You mean tell lies."

"Charles, you are driving her away. There is only so much any human being can stand. If she finds someone who can appreciate her and love her for what she is and not criticize her for who her mother is, then bloody good luck to her."

"Have you quite finished?"

"For the time being, yes, I can only hope that some of what I said has sunk into that gin-trap brain of yours; otherwise, my dear, there is no hope for you."

This time as he turned she made no attempt to stop him. He strode away, head erect, stiff-legged with rage. He walked past Sydney Street, which would have led to the gardens; he took instead the next turning. She watched as she walked slowly behind him.

"Don't think I will follow you," she said quietly, "you have a lot to learn and you will have to learn it on your own."

She wondered how an obviously intelligent man could be so blind. She felt a great weariness as she turned down Sydney Street and entered the gardens. There were some children in the playground as she walked past. She found a seat facing the massive, austere church. So this was where it all began.

*

George took Iris out for a meal. It had been a pleasant evening and Iris had shown she was glad to have him back; also she'd been able to discuss plans for her sister's wedding. Iris had explained that it was better for her to sort everything out as she was good at such things.

"That'll keep you busy, my dear," he'd said although he had wondered if Sheila and David wouldn't have preferred to make their own arrangements.

Jenny returned at seven looking happy and relaxed.

"Had a good time?" George asked.

"Yes, Dad seemed quite pleased to see me and I met his new girl friend. She was great, really great," she smiled.

"Did he like your new dress and shoes?" Iris asked.

Jenny hesitated; it would not be tactful to pass on what he really said.

"He thought I looked very grown up."

Iris nodded and, not for the first time, wished she were young again.

The telephone rang; it was a call for George from one of his suppliers.

"It's too bad having business calls even on a Sunday," Iris sighed.

"Can't make it before Wednesday or Thursday, only just got back, I'll have to go into the office tomorrow and Tuesday to clear up any problems there."

"Good God, he's hardly here before he's off again." Iris stomped into the sitting room.

Jenny decided to make coffee for them all. She heard George go into the sitting room and waited for the explosion. I'm sick of having to keep out of the way, she thought. While she waited for the kettle to boil she thought about the meeting with Dad.

Barbara was so nice and I've got her address and phone number, I'll call her soon once all the fuss dies down, I'll say how pleased I am to have met her. And Dad seemed better as well; perhaps that was Barbara's influence. Jenny set the tray and carried in the coffee.

"Since you two girls are going to have the house to yourselves on Wednesday and maybe Thursday, why don't I book a table for you, for one of those nights at the new restaurant on Golders

185

Green Road? You know that French one. After all I'm going to be wined and dined in Manchester. Which would you prefer, Wednesday or Thursday?"

Jenny looked at Iris, the decision must be hers. That would mean being in the car after Iris had been drinking. Jenny felt a tremor of concern but what could she do?

"Thursday, I think, George." Iris said without reference to Jenny.

"Fine, you might as well go there and back by taxi. Then you can relax and have some wine and even a brandy or two with your coffee. Be better than taking the car."

Jenny flicked her gaze from one to the other, fearful that Iris might interpret the suggestion as a reflection on her driving ability but there was no adverse reaction. That would make life a lot safer, Jenny thought. The only problem that remained was how on earth was she going to find things to talk about during a whole evening with Iris?

*

The letter arrived by first post on Wednesday. George had already left to catch an early train to Manchester. Jenny had taken the post and a cup of coffee to Iris before she finished getting ready for work. She was startled to hear Iris cry out and wondering if she had spilt her drink, Jenny rushed into the bedroom.

"Are you O.K.?"

Iris was sitting bolt upright in bed, ashen-faced.

"He's definitely going into the Army, after all I said. He's all I've got and now even he's leaving me." She started to cry.

Jenny rushed to the bathroom for some tissues. Obviously it was a letter from Freddie. So he'd done it, she thought, he had told her he would. Although Jenny had had little opportunity to get to know him she had been struck by his quiet determination. This was going to make things difficult. Iris would rant and rave and carry on of course and George would not be back until Friday.

She stood by the bed not sure what she could say that wouldn't make matters worse. Iris needed to speak to George but he would be somewhere between London and Manchester by now.

"Could you leave a message for Mr. Martin at the hotel? He's staying at the Midland isn't he?"

Iris turned a blotched and tear-streaked face towards her.

"How could he do it? I thought I'd persuaded him when he was home last time."

No, thought Jenny, he just went along with what you said for the sake of peace and quiet. Having made the only sensible suggestion she could think of and had it ignored it seemed there was nothing more she could do. She glanced at her watch. If she didn't hurry she would be late for work.

"I really should go now so will you be all right?"

"Go, what do you mean go?" Iris leapt out of bed and grabbed Jenny by the shoulders.

"You can't go, how can you leave me now? We must go to Freddie's school before it's too late; I've got to stop this."

"I can't miss work."

"I've always had to manage without my husband; it's always been the same. I've had to deal with everything while George has swanned around having business lunches."

"But wouldn't it be better to talk to Mr. Martin first?"

I've done everything for him and the boys and what thanks do I get. We even take you in, it was my idea you know, felt sorry for you and all you can think of is some tuppenny-ha'p'orth job. No body ever thinks of me."

Jenny tried to pull away. Iris's nails were digging into her flesh, it was like being in a vice. What was more alarming was the expression in the woman's eyes. She's mad. She had the same expression as Mum had when she was really manic. Jenny felt afraid of what Iris might do to her, she couldn't stay; she struggled to get free.

"Please let go of my arm because you are hurting me. Please ring the hotel then you can leave a message. That would be the best thing."

As Iris loosened her grip her face crumpled. Jenny hesitated, unsure whether to put an arm around the woman or escape whilst she could.

"Sit down for a while; you've had a nasty shock, drink your coffee. Mr. Martin left the hotel 'phone number in case you needed to get in touch. It's on the notice board in the kitchen, isn't it? I'll get it."

She rushed downstairs, grabbed the piece of paper and ran back upstairs again.

"Leave a message; ask him to 'phone as soon as he arrives. I'm sure everything will be sorted out."

She paused, wondering whether to point out how successful her Dad's career in the Army had been. Freddie could have a very fulfilling life. She knew that to do so would suggest that she approved of Freddie's plan. Deciding that discretion was most definitely the better part of valour, she said nothing.

Iris started to dial the number as Jenny finished getting ready.

"I'm sure it will all be sorted, see you tonight." Jenny said. With Iris on the phone now was the time to go; she started to walk quickly downstairs.

Iris shouted, "Don't leave me, take the day off. I need you here, don't leave."

Jenny ran across the hall, I've got to get away I can't stand this. She opened the front door and as she glanced back she saw Iris was following her. Surely she wouldn't come out in just her nightdress. Jenny almost ran up the path and turned left towards the station. To her horror, she could hear Iris screaming after her.

"You bitch, you selfish little bitch, all you think about is yourself."

Jenny glanced back, please, please, dear God, don't let her follow me. Iris was standing in the doorway; she was still yelling but a brisk morning breeze carried her words away. Jenny felt as though she were going to faint, her legs were shaking and her heart thumped. She had got away but it was only a temporary reprieve. She would have to go back tonight because she had nowhere else to go.

*

Iris slammed the door and stormed into the kitchen. There were Jenny's breakfast things left for her to clear.

"The slut, the lazy little slut."

With a single sweep of her arm, Iris cleared everything. The china broke with a satisfying crash as it hit the floor and marmalade oozed from its smashed jar.

"You can clear this lot up when you get back, you ungrateful little bitch."

Ungrateful that's what they all were. "No one cares about me," she mumbled and looked down. She had better leave the kitchen, the broken glass and china would cut her bare feet to ribbons. She went to the sitting room to get a cigarette. She fumbled with the packet but her hands were shaking so much she dropped it and the cigarettes spewed in a cascade across the floor.

She clutched at her chest and wondered if she were having a heart attack. What I need is a drink to steady my nerves, she thought, and got the brandy and a glass from the dining room. Brandy would do her good; everyone knew brandy was good for shock. She drained the glass and poured another hefty measure. She dared not go for a shower as that was bound to be when George would ring.

She wandered through to the living room and stared out of the window at the garden. The last of the summer's roses were turning brown at the tips. She remembered how she had put roses in Freddie's bedroom to welcome him home. He'd scoffed at her because she had shown how much she loved him but he didn't care, no one cared. She started to cry, how much longer will I have to wait for George? All my life is spent waiting, waiting for other people.

She sat down on the settee and let her head rest against the cushions. The brandy was helping to ease the ache in her heart. George even begrudged her that consolation, always going on about her and her drinking. If he were a better husband I wouldn't need to drink. He's the one who's driving the boys away; it's his fault I end up on my own all the time.

She jumped as the 'phone rang and glanced at her watch, it was ten thirty. She had been waiting hours. She walked to the 'phone with languorous step, let it ring, let him worry about me for a change, she thought. She lifted the receiver.

"Midland Hotel, Manchester, call for Mrs. Martin," said a young, cheerful voice, "putting you through now."

"Hello, George, George. You've got to come back at once, I've had a letter from Freddie, he's going into the Army, you've got to stop him." Her lips felt thick and the words seemed to jostle together.

"Listen, Iris, I can't come back. For God's sake don't be so melodramatic. No-one is going to pressgang him between now and Friday. We'll talk about it then."

"Friday, you expect me to wait until Friday, don't you care?"

"Yes, my darling, of course I care but I can't do anything right now. We can speak to Freddie; we can even go up to see him, if you like, at the weekend. But there is nothing I can do today."

"Bastard."

"Iris, listen to me please, I know you're upset. Wait until I get back then we can decide on the best thing to do."

"You're all the same, no one cares about me. Even Jenny, after all I've done. She went off to work, left me, she knew I was

189

upset." She started to cry down the 'phone.

"Look, I've got to go. I'll ring you at lunch time and we can have a proper talk. Now promise you'll have something to eat and some strong coffee. You've got to keep your strength up."

Iris slammed the 'phone down and went upstairs. George had been right about one thing, Iris thought. We must go to the school, speak to Freddie in person. We must point out that he has responsibilities towards his parents. He had no right to just walk away, that would be selfish. He must be told.

I'll have a shower now, that will make me feel better. She walked into the bedroom. The coffee Jenny had made was still there. Perhaps George was right. She drank the cold coffee in quick gulps but almost immediately her stomach seemed to be squeezed in a tight knot. She was going to be sick; she just managed to get to the bathroom in time.

On hands and knees, she retched and gulped as the brandy burned her throat. She slumped sideways, perspiration beaded her face. It's because I'm so upset, no wonder I'm ill. She shivered and pulled herself to her feet, staggered to the hand basin and splashed her face with cold water. She felt dreadful. Somehow I've got to speak to Freddie, I've got to explain. Her words seemed to echo through the empty house.

She turned on the shower and stepped out of her nightdress and once under the blessed stream of hot water she let the warmth comfort her shivering limbs. As water cascaded over her head and shoulders, she lifted her face and revelled in the heat of it on her skin. This will cleanse my soul, take away the pain. Everything will be all right once I've explained to Freddie then he won't leave me.

She turned off the shower and draped a towel round herself. Slowly she dried her limbs, taking infinite care, just as she had for Freddie when he was a baby, her baby; he'd always been hers. She dragged a comb through her wet hair. Can't be bothered drying it, she thought, I'll wear that turban I bought when I took Jenny shopping.

Just wait until she gets back, I'll have a few things to say to her. If she is going to stay here she'll have to learn how to behave herself. Iris walked back to her bedroom. Dress to kill, she thought, I know how to put on the style, I'll arrive looking like a duchess. I shan't plead; I shall tell him his father will not allow him to join the Army. That's it, his father is furious. I've come to warn him to change his mind while his father is away. I'm doing him a service, saving him from his father's rage.

She looked at her reflection in the mirror, not bad, not bad at all. Freddie will be proud of me; I know he won't want to let me down. She walked downstairs. She had a terrible taste in her mouth even though she had cleaned her teeth. She paused in the hall; perhaps she should just have a cup of coffee to settle her stomach. After all she had been upset and who would wonder at it.

She looked at the mess in the kitchen. If she were careful she could pick her way through the debris. Might as well have a piece of toast with the coffee, perhaps George was right. She sat in her hat and coat, sipping the coffee and slowly eating the toast. She had to admit the hot drink was soothing. Of course when she drank the cup Jenny had made it had been cold, that was probably why it had made her sick.

As she sat she talked through what she would say to Freddie, remind him of how pleased he had been when he realised he would just miss National Service. If he had felt like that why was he even contemplating joining up?

She thought about the other young men she knew of, the sons of acquaintances and business colleagues of George's, just a bit older than Freddie, they had seen fighting in Suez and Cyprus. Her hand began to shake. William had been so lucky not to have been posted abroad but would Freddie have the same luck?

She stood up and took a few deep breaths. She thought about the route George usually took to Mentmore School, just south of Dunstable. Of course he always drove, insisted he was not a good passenger; claimed he got bored. Iris wondered if he did not trust her driving but that was nonsense, she was an excellent driver. She tried to picture in her mind's eye they way they went. She hadn't taken much interest in the past preferring to look at the passing countryside. Still it would be all right, there was a road map in the car. She would find her way.

She was sure they picked up the North Circular and then headed towards Watford. From there it was through Hemel Hempstead and on, North West, through the Chiltern Hills. The countryside would be ablaze with autumn colours, she smiled, this was going to be her adventure.

She'd show George she could stop this stupid nonsense, wait until Friday, indeed she would not. She picked up her bag,

191

checked she had money and cigarettes then carefully picked her way back through the broken china and glass that littered the floor. She would stop at a country pub on the way back to have a bite to eat. She would take her time.

Let Jenny get back to this mess; that would make the point. She shut the front door firmly behind her, got into her car and set off with confidence.

*

Chapter 27

Although it was cold, the autumn sun shone in a clear blue sky, it was a day to lift the spirits and Mark whistled as he walked down the street. It was Wednesday and the weekend would soon be here. He had checked the train times and realised that the Sunday service would not enable him to get to London and back and still leave enough time, between journeys, to have a meal with Laura, her parents and Jenny.

He had decided he would travel down on Saturday, he could call at his old workplace, it would be good to see his ex-colleagues again. He glanced at his watch, there was enough left of his lunch hour to call them when he got back to the office, tell them his plans. One of them might offer him a bed for the night, if not he would find a bed and breakfast.

Once back at the office Mark was told Mr. Jones, the branch manager, wanted a word with him. Although it was not Mark's Saturday to work, would he be able to come in? Mr. Jones had a family crisis which he would have to deal with over the weekend. He was sorry and hoped it would not interfere with Mark's plans; Mr. Jones pointed out that everyone had to make sacrifices. He for one would far rather be at work than dealing with his cantankerous mother-in-law. Of course Mark would be left in charge and this would be valuable experience that would stand him in good stead in the future.

Mark managed to retain a fixed smile throughout the fulsome excuses. He did not comment on the telephone conversation he had overhead when Mr. Jones had been enquiring about the possibility of getting a ticket for Saturday's rugby match.

"Of course I'll come in, Mr. Jones," he said.

"Good lad, remind me to give you the keys on Friday night, you keep them over the weekend and make sure you're in early on Monday morning."

Mark walked out of Mr. Jones's office and thought how fortunate it was that people couldn't read each other's thoughts. There was no point in ringing his mates in London; he would have to travel down on Saturday evening after he had locked up the office. Another visit to the station was needed so he could see what later trains were available. He didn't fancy arriving in London late on Saturday night with nowhere to sleep and wondered if he could crash out at his old flat. The thought of being forced to ask Jim for a favour made him dismiss that idea.

As he had a driving licence perhaps he could borrow a friend's car, just for Sunday, and set off early. Was life so complicated? If he couldn't borrow a car, he might have to catch the earliest train on Sunday and thumb a lift back. But what if he didn't get a lift? If he didn't get to the office by half past eight, quarter to nine at the latest, no-one would be able to get in. The phone rang and with great difficulty Mark managed to put on his best office voice.

*

Jenny felt dreadful when she got to work and Professor Walker suggested that she should go home if she wasn't well. That was the last thing Jenny wanted to do. She was sent to the hospital's canteen and had a cup of tea after which she felt calmer.

She wondered what time George would be home and if she dared to stay out until she was sure he was back. But he might not come back tonight, hadn't he planned to be away until Friday? How could she wander the streets for hours or days even in this cold weather?

She remembered the paper with Barbara's address and phone number, she'd put it in her purse. She yearned to speak to someone who would be sympathetic and she was sure Barbara was just the person but she would be at work and Jenny didn't know what time Barbara's library shut. Perhaps she could go over to see her but if she didn't go home Iris would be even angrier than she had been this morning. Jenny sighed. She would just have to confront Iris when she got home; there was no point in getting worked up about it yet. However, she thought, it would be a good plan to 'phone Iris at lunch time to show she cared.

*

Iris arrived in a flurry at Mentmore School; she had no time to waste. Perhaps she would ask the Head teacher for permission to take Freddie out to lunch or afternoon tea. She rehearsed what she would say, there was nothing to fear, she would make Freddie see sense. Some half-witted careers teacher had put the lunatic idea into Freddie's head and the dear boy didn't want to hurt his teacher's feelings.

The approach to Mentmore was up a long tree-lined gravel driveway. The school was housed in a large stone mansion, surrounded by acres of park land where the boys were encouraged to take part in a wide variety of sports. This was what had made

George and Iris choose the school. Freddie was a keen sportsman and clearly enjoyed the school's facilities.

As her car crunched up the drive, Iris wondered if she should have rung to make an appointment. Surely not since this was a family crisis, besides they were paying handsomely for Mr. Brownlow and his staff to have the privilege of educating their son.

She stopped outside the main entrance, locked the car and walked through the pillared entrance. The large hall was cool and imposing, with plaques on every wall, in celebration of past pupils' successes. She noticed another more sombre plaque that listed past pupils who had died serving their country in the two World Wars. A cold finger of fear ran up and down her back.

No-one was about as she walked through the hallway, her high heels clacked on the polished floor. There was a sign on the left, 'Reception', with an arrow pointing down another corridor. She could hear a typewriter clattering as she knocked on a glass window. After a moment, the glass window slid open and an earnest looking woman, of late middle age, smiled at Iris.

"Can I help you?"

"Yes, I've come to see my son, Freddie Martin."

"Is the Head Master expecting you?"

Iris paused, she should have rung first.

"No, there's been a family crisis and under the circumstances I thought it best to come straight here."

The woman stared at Iris.

"Mr. Brownlow is a stickler for the school rules, I'm sorry but he takes exception to parents arriving unexpectedly without an appointment. He believes the school does its best to provide a good education and parents must abide by his rules with the same rigour as he demands from his pupils."

"So I'm not allowed to see my own son."

"I didn't say that but you had better see Mr. Brownlow first and I believe he is in a meeting at the moment with another parent who did make an appointment."

Iris gave a sigh of irritation, some people are power mad, she thought.

"How long will he be?"

"It's difficult to say, would you care to wait? There is a waiting room just down the corridor, on the right. Can I get you a cup of tea or coffee?"

195

Iris sighed, "Yes, I suppose so, coffee please."

She turned and walked down the corridor as instructed and feeling thoroughly exasperated sat in one of the overstuffed cretonne covered chairs. Must have a cigarette, she thought.

After a few minutes the woman appeared with a tray holding a coffee jug, cup and saucer, milk, sugar and biscuits. She placed the tray on the low table, in front of Iris.

"There is no smoking allowed, Mrs. Martin, I'm sorry. It is one of Mr Brownlow's very strict rules. We want our boys to be healthy in body as well as mind." She gave a faint smile and left.

Iris felt as though she had had her legs slapped and anger bubbled in her head as she ground out her cigarette in the saucer and poured herself some coffee. There was nothing to do but wait.

She sat, with increasing impatience, for Mr. Browlow to appear. After half an hour she started pacing up and down. This was ridiculous; she couldn't see her own son. She wondered if she should go back to that po-faced secretary to remind the woman that she was still waiting. After three quarters of an hour the door opened and Mr.Brownlow walked in.

"Mrs. Martin, sorry to have kept you waiting but it is usual for parents to make an appointment."

He walked towards her and after a perfunctory touching of hands he suggested they go to his office. He showed her to a seat and went behind the huge desk which dominated the room. Once seated, he clasped his hands on the blotter in front of him.

"Now, Mrs. Martin, what seems to be the problem?"

"I need to speak to my son."

He waited, smiling.

"It's a personal matter," Iris said, trying to keep the irritation out of her voice.

"I see. We do like to know if there are family problems. We don't like our students to have worries or concerns of which we are unaware. After all, we are in loco parentis and wish to support our students in times of trouble."

Iris took a deep breath, by now she was desperate for a cigarette.

"I received a letter from him this morning which caused me considerable concern."

She paused while Mr. Brownlow nodded and smiled encouragement.

"I understand, from that letter, that he has decided to join the Army," she paused again and Mr. Brownlow waited.

"His father and I are vehemently opposed to any such idea, his father in particular. He's away on business at the moment so I decided to come here myself."

"I see," Mr. Brownlow stood up, "I do interview all my six formers about their future plans. I saw Frederick quite recently but...." he smiled, ".... I will get his file, just to refresh my memory."

He left the room via a side door and Iris heard him open a filing cabinet in what must be a storeroom adjacent to his main office. He returned, sat down and flicked through Martin, F.'s file.

"Ah, yes, I saw him three weeks ago. Now he did talk about your husband's business, he is determined that he will not join it," he paused, "is that what you and your husband had hoped for?"

"Not necessarily, but not the armed forces, we had all agreed on that."

"All?"

"Yes, we had discussed it with Freddie and he had agreed."

"He's a very keen member of our cadet corps and you know he has always enjoyed the structure and discipline."

Iris wanted to scream. It must have been this stupid man, who had put pressure on her son, how dare he? She swallowed hard and took a deep breath.

"Maybe, but do parents and their wishes count for nothing? Is it not possible that we might know best?"

"Of course, parents have a considerable part to play in helping their children fly the nest and choose a career that is suited to their talents and inclinations. But, Mrs. Martin, I do think we sometimes have to accept that our children may want to do something that we would not choose for them. Is it not a matter of letting go and accepting, with love and understanding, their choice for their future?"

It was obvious, Iris thought, that the interview was a complete waste of time. They were all in it together; colluding to distance her from the one person she loved above all others.

"Can I see Freddie, please?"

Mr. Brownlow glanced at his watch.

"I'm sorry, but the sixth form boys are out of school on an activity day. They left an hour ago. We do not expect them back

197

until six this evening."

He sat with his hands resting on Freddie's file.

Iris leapt to her feet, eyes blazing; she must have only just missed him!

"I am so sorry to have wasted your precious time, please have the decency to tell my son that I have been here, I presume that is allowed."

Mr. Brownlow stood and extended his hand.

"I'm sorry I could not be of greater assistance."

Ignoring the proffered hand, Iris strode to the door, snatched it open and turned, "I bet you are!" she said as she slammed out, banging the door behind her.

Iris was shaking as she drove away. When she reached the end of the drive she stopped for that much needed cigarette. She had a good mind to take Freddie away from Mentmore, how dare that man be so condescending? He had behaved as though he knew Freddie better than she did.

Now what she needed was a drink, her nerves were in tatters. I'll look for a nice country pub, one that will make me a sandwich, she thought, and took pleasure in flicking her half smoked cigarette onto the hallowed turf of Mentmore School grounds. Engaging first gear she set off with a screech of tyres.

*

Jenny walked from the canteen and went to the public pay 'phone. Her stomach was knotted with tension; after this morning Iris was hardly likely to be sweetness and light now. Jenny dialled the number. Her throat was dry and she cleared it several times as she tried to sort out what she would say when Iris answered. The 'phone rang on and on and a wave of relief flooded through Jenny. Iris wasn't in. I can tell her I tried to 'phone to apologise, it would be best to say sorry even though it isn't my fault. I'll take her a bunch of flowers, pick some up at the station, on the way home, she decided.

*

Chapter 25

Iris stopped in Redbourn, a pretty village with timber-framed, thatched cottages and Georgian houses around the edges of the Common. The Blue Boar public house looked pleasant enough. She drove into the car park, locked the door and walked into the lounge bar.

It was very quiet with just a few customers sitting in dark corners. There was a faint hum of conversation and the smell of wood smoke which came from the huge fireplace that was piled high with crackling logs. She went to the bar.

"A large brandy, please."

The well-built, middle-aged barman finished polishing a glass, smiled and turned to the appropriate optic.

"Do you have sandwiches or anything?"

"Yes, Madam, cheese or ham? The ham's home-cooked."

"Yes, that would be fine thank you."

She picked up her glass and walked to an empty table by the window. The brandy made her stomach glow and she felt very hungry. She lit a cigarette while she waited for the food. After ten minutes a comfortably rounded, middle-aged woman, in an apron, appeared with a plate of sandwiches.

Iris smiled and then turned to the barman, "Another brandy, please."

"Double, Madam?"

"Yes, please."

She thought about events of the morning; she was sick to death of the way people walked all over her, she would just have to put her foot down. She would not be treated so casually. She glanced at her watch, one thirty, by now George should be wondering where she was, maybe even worrying about her for a change. As for Jenny, if she didn't buck her ideas up she could go, let her find someone else to wait on her hand and foot.

Glowing with righteous indignation, Iris finished her meal. She stood and relaxed into that delicious feeling that drinking just the right amount of alcohol always induced. She felt comfortable with herself, all the anger had gone; she was in charge now. She could sort things out. She settled her bill with the barman, waved a cheery goodbye and walked with studied care to her car.

She sat thinking for a moment. If she went back the way she had come there would be lots of traffic. She could go on the new motorway down to Watford then she would miss Hemel

Hempstead. She had never been on the M1; George always took what he called the scenic route. It would be fun on a motorway, she could put her foot down, it would be like the highways in the States. She started the engine, reversed and then drove out of the car-park. She must keep her eyes open for the motorway signs.

She drove with exaggerated care, demonstrating to herself what a fine and competent driver she was. Every gear change was executed with precision; she imagined she was taking the Advanced Driving Test. She might do that one day; that would be one in the eye for George. So deep in thought was she that she realized, too late, she had missed the sign to join the motorway.

She slammed on her brakes then glanced in her mirror; there was a lorry behind her. She wound down the window and waved the driver on. A spotty-faced youth, in the passenger seat, pulled a face and indicated, in a surly manner, that she needed to go to an optician. She ignored him, probably can't even drive, she thought, who was he to try to lord it over her, the stupid little runt.

Now she needed somewhere to turn round but there were no obvious turnings nearby. I'll do a three-point turn, she thought, that would be best and she started to manoeuvre.

Suddenly the deserted road become crowded with cars and lorries and Iris's car was straddled across the road. She felt flustered; she had been doing so well, why were these people harassing her? Stay calm, I will take my time, do a good job of it, I'll show you lot she thought, and put the car into first gear. In her haste she stalled the engine.

She jammed her foot hard down on the accelerator and tried the starter but now she could smell petrol. She must have flooded the engine. She could see there was a long queue of traffic in both directions and horns were blaring. The driver of the nearest car was getting out.

"What the hell are you doing trying to turn here?"

The sharp retort on her lips evaporated, a bit of charm might be better. She smiled in what she hoped was an alluring way.

"I'm lost, I need to get to the motorway, it's urgent. Please help me."

The man pulled a face, "Bloody women drivers," he muttered loudly enough for Iris to hear, "smells as though you've flooded it. Get out I'll see what I can do."

Another driver came to offer assistance.

"Want a push, mate?"

"She's flooded it."

Iris stood on the roadway and shivered, the euphoria had gone. The car was manhandled into the side of the road and after two attempts the engine started.

"Thank you so much," she said as the two men returned to their respective vehicles. She got back in her car, engaged gear and letting the clutch out too fast, jolted and jerked her way up the road. She could not control the shivering; she must be in a state of shock after all that had happened. She needed to get warm.

She pulled into the first lay-by she saw and turned up the heater. She lit a cigarette but after a few drags threw it away, she felt sick, she needed to get home. She saw the motorway sign ahead, her plan to go that way home was the best, she would get there quicker and be able to have a good hot bath.

Perhaps she was sickening for something. She would go to bed after her bath and let Jenny find her there. As George had said he would ring, he was bound to ring again. Iris hoped he was worried that he had not been able to make contact with her earlier.

The heater was doing its job, she felt better and the shivering soon stopped. The thought of sinking into a steaming bath spurred her on. She engaged first gear and drove down the slip road to join the M.1. She got to the start of the carriageway and out of the corner of her eye became aware of streams of traffic thundering past, they were really shifting. She wondered if she was doing the right thing after all but there was no turning back. She couldn't do a three point turn now.

She eased forward; waiting for a gap, she hesitated then lost patience and floored the accelerator. The car shot into the nearside lane. She saw a lorry coming up fast behind her. Just keep going, she thought, as she pressed her foot down harder. The gap between her and the lorry increased. She was all right now; she could ease up a little. She fumbled for her cigarettes on the front passenger seat. This was fun. She glanced at the speedo, eighty miles an hour, she laughed out loud. She imagined the look of horror George would have on his face if he had been beside her.

She managed to grab hold of a cigarette and groped for her lighter, lit the cigarette and sat back, she would soon be home. It was a good little car, bouncing along so happily, she should do this more often. She was lulled by the regular sound from the wheels as they rode over the concrete slabs that made up the motorway surface. It was a bit like being on a train, clackety-clack, clackety-clack. She yawned and wriggled a little in her seat, she must not get too comfortable. She could go a bit faster and get home sooner. She glanced in her mirror, there was nothing behind her so as she pulled out into the middle lane and put her foot down, accelerating hard.

She was beginning to feel very sleepy. Open the window a little, she thought; I need some fresh air. She took several deep breaths and her head cleared. As she started to close the window the front off-side tyre exploded. She had only one hand on the steering wheel which bucked and jerked out of her hand as the car careered towards the central reservation.

Confused, Iris pressed her foot down hard on what she thought was the brake as the car lurched onto the wheel's metal rim. She tried to grab the steering wheel with both hands and turn it. She could hear the screeching of brakes, it must be her brakes but the car wasn't slowing down, what was happening?

The wheel would not turn and she was being forced into oncoming traffic. It was then she saw the bridge, it seemed to leap towards her, squat, ugly, menacing, grey concrete. It loomed over her and suddenly it was all she could see, blocking out everything else, this monster was going to crush her. She opened her mouth to scream but blood thudding in her ears obliterated the sound.

The Anglia hit the bridge at forty five degrees. The sharp edge of the central support held fast and the bonnet of the car was crumpled down the whole of its length, dividing the front of the car into two equal but compressed halves. Iris watched as the front of the car seemed to disappear beneath her. There was terrible pressure on her legs and she heard a strange crunching sound, her legs were being squeezed, crushed. She supposed the sound must be her bones breaking. She looked down in surprise as the steering wheel came up to meet her, it too was crushing her; it was crushing her chest.

The windscreen shattered. Her eyes were open wide as glass flew towards her, she gasped when a long sliver penetrated her right eye. It didn't hurt but she was puzzled that she could not close her eyelid. She tried to lift her hand to brush whatever it was away but her arms were pinned down by the steering wheel which came closer and closer. There would be no room for her soon, no space left in her dear little car.

The pain in her chest was becoming unbearable. She heard that strange, crunching sound again; her ribs could withstand the pressure no longer. One by one they crumpled into razor-sharp splinters, waiting to deliver the coup de grace. Must breathe, must get some air, I can't stand this pressure any more, she thought.

In one, last, desperate effort she tried to expand her lungs and the slivers of bone slid, effortlessly into the quivering tissue and both lungs collapsed with a soundless sigh. Her head slumped forward, she needed to rest. The pressure of her face on the steering wheel forced the glass deeper until a glutinous stream of vitreous humour was released from her eyeball. This grotesque imitation of tears dripped slowly onto her still hands. The last sound she heard was the wailing of the car horn as the weight of her head depressed it.

*

Chapter 29

Jenny had stood for most of her train journey home. The butterflies in her stomach felt as though they had clogs on. She checked her purse as she left the station. She had just enough money for a reasonable bunch of flowers. The chrysanthemums had looked lovely with their russet shades echoing the trees autumnal foliage.

She walked slowly down the street, her feet dragging her nearer to the inevitable scene with Iris. I can't go on like this, she thought, Iris is making my life a misery. If William had been serious about her it would have been worthwhile to continue making an effort to get on with the woman. What was the point now? She accepted that her relationship with William was over so there was no reason for her to stay with the Martins.

As she approached the house she was surprised to see Iris's car was not there, she was usually at home when Jenny returned from work. She let herself into a house that was silent and clearly empty. The car wasn't due at the garage for repairs because Mr. Martin had sorted that out already. She stood in the hall not sure what she should do. Perhaps the best thing was to get a vase and put the flowers in water. She could point them out when Iris returned. Perhaps she should leave them wrapped and then grovel a bit. Iris liked arranging flowers.

She walked into the kitchen and stared at the wreckage. Of course, in the morning's furore, she had forgotten to clear her breakfast things. Considering the mood she had been in, Iris had obviously taken exception to Jenny's oversight. She sighed as she draped her coat on the back of the chair, stuck the flowers in the sink and went for the dustpan and brush.

She swept up the fragments of china and gingerly picked up the marmalade encrusted pieces of glass, shovelling the lot into the bin. The floor was sticky and streaked with coffee. She took the bin outside, emptied it and grabbed the mop and bucket on the way back. She had just finished when she heard the sound of a key in the front-door lock. She raced to replace the mop and bucket outside the back door, grabbed the flowers and went to meet Iris.

To her amazement it was George standing in the hall. He had removed his overcoat and was just standing there. The expression on his face made Jenny's heart lurch, something dreadful had happened.

"You haven't heard yet, have you?"

His voice was barely a whisper.

"Heard what?"

"There's been an accident," he paused, "Iris is dead."

A thin wail of horror escaped Jenny's lips as she fell. The flowers were crushed by the weight of her body; their petals scattered on the black and white tiled floor, like droplets of blood.

*

George rang Mentmore School later that day and then drove up to collect Freddie. William had been contacted in Stockholm and returned by 'plane that evening. Jenny had stayed in her room most of the time, unable to sleep, eating little. There had been much coming and going as the funeral was arranged. The three remaining members of the Martin family spoke in low voices which drifted upstairs to remind Jenny of her isolation.

She was ashamed that she could not leave them to their grief unencumbered by her guilty presence but where could she go? George knocked on her bedroom door, came in and sat beside her. His worried face was enough to make her start crying again.

"Is there no-one you can talk to? I hate to see you like this," he said.

She had shaken her head, no-one, I am a pariah, I am nothing, she thought.

"You must stop blaming yourself, it could have happened at any time."

She had sat very still, eyes so swollen with crying she looked as though she had been beaten up.

"Let me at least get you a cup of tea or coffee, you can't go on like this."

She nodded. Of course he was right, she felt drained.

"Shall I 'phone your parents?"

"It's all my fault, I'm so sorry, you see she asked me to stay with her but I went to work."

"I won't let you blame yourself," George put his arm around her. "Are you listening, my dear, it was not your fault."

That only made it worse. He should rant and rave at me for not staying with Iris, Jenny reasoned, after all she had asked, no begged me not to leave her.

"I was totally selfish and thought only of myself, I was so frightened, I didn't know what to do."

"We both know Iris had a problem. You witnessed that first

205

hand didn't you?"

Jenny nodded.

"It seems that Iris had been drinking before the accident; that was her decision. She took an awful risk with her life but it could have happened anywhere. It had nothing to do with you. If anyone is to blame, I am."

"But you were so good to her."

"Maybe not, perhaps I should have listened to her more, understood how unhappy she was."

Then George had hugged Jenny and given her his handkerchief to wipe away her tears.

"Now if you continue to blame yourself, I shall be very upset and you don't want that, do you?"

Jenny had nodded.

"Are you sure you don't want anything to eat?"

"I really don't think I could, not tonight anyway."

George patted her shoulder and went back downstairs where William and Freddie were finishing a meal their father had cooked. Jenny lay on her bed, in the dark, listening to the steady hum of traffic on the main road. She had tried to imagine how Iris must have felt when she knew she was going to hit the bridge. Apparently the police had reassured George that Iris would not have suffered; it had been over in a split second.

Despite all that George had said, Jenny could not stop feeling that she should have done more. Perhaps the fact that she had never liked Iris was why she felt so guilty now. If it had been Mr. Martin who asked her to take a day off work she would have done it. So what sort of person was she? Shallow. Only willing to help people she liked. Perhaps that was why the accident had come as such a terrible shock.

Although George had asked if he should contact her parents, Mum and Dad were the last people Jenny wanted to speak to. In their different ways, neither would have understood how she felt. She would have to leave here, that she knew, but it would not be to go to either of them. Of course there was Barbara, dare she ring her? Did she have the right to burden someone she had only met once?

George had been so kind but surely he would prefer not to have a lodger at such a difficult time. Jenny went downstairs to speak to him and found him slumped in an armchair in the living room. William and Freddie were in the kitchen.

"May I use the 'phone?"

"Of course, my dear, do you want to use the one in our room?"

They exchanged glances, it was his room now.

"Thank you."

She went back to her room and searched in her handbag for Barbara's number.

William and Freddie were washing up, talking quietly when George joined them; he put the kettle on the stove, glad that his sons seemed more comfortable with each other.

"I'm making a cup of tea for Jenny, that girl worries me, she's blaming herself."

"That's stupid," Freddie said, "if anyone's to blame, it's me. I sent the letter that started it all off."

George sat down, at the kitchen table.

"I think it's time we laid that particular ghost to rest once and for all, neither one of you is to blame. Your mother had a serious drink problem, you both knew that. You could say I'm to blame for buying her a car. What's happened cannot be undone; blame won't make a jot of difference. Will you take the tea upstairs, William? Try to comfort the poor girl."

William looked uneasy. "I'd rather not, Dad. You see I should have written and told her."

"Told her what?" George asked.

"Berthe told me to write but I kept putting it off, I don't want to say anything now when she's so upset?"

George watched him but said nothing.

"Will Jenny go on living here, after what's happened?"

"I don't know, I've asked her to contact her parents but she doesn't want to."

"It's a bit awkward really."

George raised his eyebrows.

"I don't think Jenny and I will be seeing much of each other in the future...., you see Berthe and I........" William's voice trailed away.

"I presume she doesn't know."

"I haven't said anything yet, it didn't seem the right time."

"Well, don't put it off too long, that wouldn't be fair to anyone."

William nodded. "Jenny's all right, but she's just a kid, Dad."

George stared at his son and wondered whether if it was Jenny who was a kid or William. William seemed a more likely candidate.

"You may not feel like saying anything over the next few days but I do expect you to do the decent thing before you go back. Now take this tea up and at least try to be kind to the poor girl." He turned and walked into the living room, sat down and closed his eyes.

As well as the tea William took some biscuits since he had not seen Jenny eat anything all day. He tapped on the door and walked in.

"Dad said you are blaming yourself. You shouldn't, you know; it wasn't your fault." He stood by the bed and Jenny sensed his discomfort. She realised at once that he wanted to leave the room as soon as possible I'll just have to talk for him, she thought, I've had enough.

"It's not going to work, is it?"

"What?"

"Us."

"Is that why you are so upset?"

Jenny looked at him, how arrogant, she thought.

"Us being apart made me see that we aren't really suited."

His look of relief told Jenny that no matter how sad she felt at that moment, for what might have been, he was really a weak man and she would probably have come to despise him.

"Thank you for the tea," she said, "I have a phone call to make."

William left without a backward glance.

*

Jenny took a deep breath and dialled Barbara's number. She tried to keep calm but the need to explain what had happened made her cry. Although she had not liked Iris, she had never wanted this. Perhaps it had been unhappiness that made Iris behave as she did. How sad.

Barbara did not recognise Jenny's voice at first but as she listened it became obvious that something dreadful had happened. Jenny kept saying it was all her fault and someone had been killed. Had Charles been in an accident, had he been injured, or was it he who had been killed? She hadn't seen him for weeks but surely she would have heard. She waited for the avalanche of words to slow and finally stutter to a halt.

"Jenny, Jenny can you hear me?"

"Yes."

"Listen, my dear, I realize you are dreadfully upset, but I couldn't make out what you were saying. Is it something to do with your Dad?"

"No, no it's Mrs. Martin."

Who the hell was Mrs. Martin, Barbara wondered?

"You know, William's mother."

"Right, what's happened?"

"She was killed in a road accident."

"Oh, you poor thing, no wonder you're upset."

"But it was all my fault, you see she wanted me to take the day off work, but I wouldn't, because I was frightened and she had this dreadful accident and if I'd stayed at home with her instead of going to work it wouldn't have happened....."

"Hush Jenny, hush, of course it wasn't your fault."

"But it was, she'd been drinking, that's what the post mortem showed. If I'd been with her she might not have had a drink. She just needed someone to talk to and I didn't listen, I just went to work and I bought some flowers to give to her, to say sorry, but she was already dead."

At this point, Jenny burst into tears again.

Barbara waited. "Do you want me to tell your father?"

"No, no he'll say it was my fault too."

"I'm sure he wouldn't." But perhaps he would, Barbara thought, Charles did have a facility for off loading blame. "What would you like me to do?"

"I don't know. I need to talk to someone, William and Freddie have come home and I just feel I'm in the way. They must hate me."

"Of course they don't." Barbara decided that a little briskness was required, "now first of all, what's your 'phone number?"

Jenny gave the number in a flat, exhausted voice, she felt like a puppet with all its strings snapped, she longed for sleep, just to escape into oblivion for a few hours.

"Secondly, when is the funeral?"

"Next week I think."

"Would it help if you came over to see me? Go to work tomorrow, that will stop you brooding, then come straight over. Tell Mr. Martin you think it best to leave them to grieve on their own. You can give my phone number if you like in case they need to contact you."

Jenny sighed. At last she had someone who wanted to take care of her. She wasn't alone any more.

"That would be so good," she said, "are you sure I won't be a nuisance?"

"Of course, you're bound to be a terrible nuisance but don't worry, my dear, I can cope."

*

Laura looked at the contents of her wardrobe; she needed to look her best on Sunday. She had already booked a hair appointment for Saturday morning and after that she would go shopping for something new.

Part of her felt guilty; she had sent the letter to Jenny but not until Wednesday evening. If it didn't arrive in time she would have Mark to herself. But these two people had been good friends to her, they were more than she deserved. There was only one thing to do, she took a deep breath, went to the phone and dialled the hostel's number.

"Hello, Miss Pritchard? It's Laura, I'm sorry to bother you again but have you received a letter from me today?"

"Yes, I sent it on."

"Oh, it's rather important and I didn't post it as soon as I should. It probably won't arrive until Monday and that will be too late. Can you contact Jenny and ask her to phone me?"

Miss Pritchard laughed, "Leave it with me."

Laura stood for a while and knew that she had, for once, done the right thing.

*

Jenny walked downstairs. She had slept deeply for the first time since Iris had died and felt quite light-headed. The house was very still. Now that she had decided that her time in this house was coming to an end, it was like being in a hotel. She was transient, just visiting, so she must behave with circumspection, take nothing for granted.

She presumed everyone was still asleep. She stood in the doorway of the kitchen and saw George at the kitchen table; she wondered if walking in on him would be an intrusion. He turned and smiled at her.

"Come in, dear, have you managed to get some rest?"

"Yes, thank you. I'm going to get off to work soon unless there is anything I can do."

"You go, it will do you good. I'll see you tonight."

"Do you mind if I don't come back? Barbara, that's Dad's friend has asked me to go to her place after work and stay the night. I'll give you her number if you like, in case anyone calls."

"I think that's an excellent idea, none of us are ourselves at the moment. Now you must have some breakfast before you go."

*

Jenny knocked at Barbara's door, she felt surprisingly nervous. She heard footsteps coming down the stairs and then the door opened and there she was arms wide, smiling such a glorious welcome that Jenny could feel her eyes filling.

"Come in, my dear, it is so good to see you."

They walked upstairs together and Jenny felt the warmth of belonging.

"You've had a horrible experience and if you want to have a damned good cry, I don't mind, I've got plenty of handkerchiefs."

Being given not just permission to cry, but positive encouragement, made it unnecessary. Jenny sat down on the settee and felt a sense of peace. The table was set, just because she was expected, it had been set beautifully with flowers and glasses, just for her. She sighed and let her head sink back into the cushions. Barbara sat beside her. There was no pressure, no recrimination, now everything would sort itself out somehow.

"Do you think it would have made any difference if I had stayed with Mrs. Martin, if I hadn't gone to work?"

"I honestly don't know. Did she drink much as a rule?"

"Yes, she and Mr. Martin were always at loggerheads about it."

"So what could you have done?"

"I don't know really. I suppose it's because I was the last one she saw, before she went off to Freddie's school."

Barbara pulled a face, "I think you are punishing yourself needlessly. I doubt that Mr. Martin thinks you could have done anything. I should imagine he's just relieved."

"What relieved that she's dead?"

"No, relieved that you aren't."

Jenny opened her eyes wide, that thought had not occurred to her. Of course, if she had stayed at home, she would almost certainly have been dragged to Mentmore School too! And yes, she would have either been killed or very seriously injured. She shivered.

"You see, my dear, then it would have been a double tragedy;

211

that would have made everything even worse. You have your life ahead of you. I don't know why Mrs. Martin had a drink problem; even her husband might not be able to answer that one. But what I do know is that she effectively took her own life, by accident or design and that was her choice. She could not be allowed to do the same to you and thank God, she didn't."

Jenny was too stunned to reply.

"Now then, my girl, I think it's time we had something to eat; you're looking decidedly peaky." She went through to the kitchen.

It was while they ate that Barbara brought up the subject of where Jenny was going to live.

"I assume you don't intend to go back to Dad."

"It wouldn't work and I suppose I would have to tell him what happened. Has he said much about me living with the Martins?"

"Actually, I haven't seen him for a while."

Jenny looked up with such an anxious expression that Barbara couldn't help laughing.

"My dear girl, don't look so worried. Our friendship does not depend on your father, I like you for yourself. I'm sure I don't have to tell you, he is an obstinate old cuss and I told him so. At the moment, he is stewing in his own juice. It will do him good; in the end, he'll be much more tender."

Jenny giggled. What a lovely woman Barbara was.

"So what will you do? I suspect Mum's out too."

Jenny nodded, "My stepbrother and sister would see to that."

"What about the hostel, if only as a temporary measure?"

"Of course, yes, Miss Pritchard said she could always find a bed for me."

"That's it then. You won't have to stay there for ever and when you are here on a visit I can always put you up, as long as you don't mind the settee."

"Why are you so nice to me?"

"I've told you, I like you."

"I'm glad."

"Right, down to business; I'm going to clear the table, you are going to 'phone this Pritchard person and then we are going to confront the dragon in his lair."

"What do you think he will say?"

"Haven't a clue but I'm not worried and you mustn't be either."

While Barbara washed up Jenny phoned the hostel.

"Miss Pritchard speaking."

"It's Jenny Warr, Miss Pritchard, I wonder if you can help me. You did say that you'd always be able to find a bed for me if I needed one and if it's possible I would like to move back."

"I'll just check."

Jenny heard the rustling of papers and kept her fingers crossed.

"There will be a vacancy in ten days, can you manage until then?"

"Yes, that will be fine, thank you so much."

"Before you go have you heard from Laura Johnson?"

"No."

"You had better phone her, do you have her number?

"No, I don't."

"Now I do not usually give out personal information but I understand from Laura that she wants to invite you to her house, this Sunday. Therefore I feel I can break the rules just this once."

Number provided, thanks given, Jenny went to the kitchen and gave Barbara the news about the hostel and asked if she could use the phone again.

"Mr. Johnson speaking."

"Hello, it's Jenny, Jenny Warr I met Laura at the hostel, could I speak to her, please."

"Ah, you're the young lady who's coming to lunch. I expect you need some directions."

"Oh," Jenny said. She heard Mr. Johnson shout and then Laura was on the phone.

"I'm so glad you called, Jenny, I thought I'd left it too late. Mark is coming for a meal on Sunday. I wanted you to come too."

Jenny's head was spinning, everything was happening too fast. She took Laura's address and said she would call back to confirm arrangements.

"Guess what?" she said to Barbara and recounted the tale of the party that wasn't, the repulsive Jim, Mark's lunch date that wasn't and William and Berthe.

"Good Lord, it's a wonder you've time to breathe. I presume you would like to see Mark again."

"Yes, he was so kind and I think we could be good friends."

"What a very sensible young woman you are. Friends are so important; romance can come later if it's right."

"Laura lives in Elstree and I'm not sure how I'll get there."

"We'll let your father sort that out; he can make himself useful. You have to keep these men in their place."

Jenny leaned forward and kissed Barbara's cheek.

"He can take me to lunch after he's dropped you at Laura's and we will pick you up afterwards."

They walked to the flats, armed with paper and pencil to leave a note if Charles wasn't in. Once at the front door, Barbara made sure that they were standing level, if not exactly shoulder to shoulder. Jenny knocked and they heard his footsteps coming up the hallway. Jenny looked at Barbara who smiled. The door was opened and Charles stared at them both for a second, but it was only for a second before he opened the door wider.

"What a lovely surprise, come in my dears, come in. I'll put the kettle on."

*

Chapter 30

Saturday was busier than usual and Mark had little time to think about plans for his journey south. There was no suitable train on Saturday evening and he had been unable to borrow a car so would have to rely on getting the earliest train on Sunday. There was still the problem that a restricted service meant there was no train on the Sunday evening; he would have to thumb a lift.

He had phoned Laura to find out how he would get to her house from the station. She had assured him that her father would be happy to pick him up once he got to Euston. She also said she had spoken to Jenny who confirmed that she would be able to come for lunch too. Apparently her father would drop her at Laura's.

If, as his mother claimed, he was in the throes of obsession, only seeing Jenny again might sort out his feelings. He could not make any plans for the future until then. Part of him wanted to write to Jenny to make his own arrangements to meet; he wasn't sure how wise it was to involve Laura. And there were so many other difficulties, was it all worth it? Perhaps I'm scared, he thought, scared that I will make a fool of myself again like I did with Denise.

Quite apart from the problems of getting to Elstree there was also the worry that he might not be able to thumb a lift home. The manager, Mr. Jones, would hit the roof if the office was locked and there was no-one to open up on time. But he must have another set of keys, Mark thought, he would have to hope for the best.

*

Jenny had breakfast with Barbara who then went off to work.

"Will you be able to amuse yourself today?"

"Yes, I've decided I will go to the house and collect some clothes for tomorrow; I can't go in this lot."

"Shall I ask your dad round tonight?"

Jenny hesitated. "Would you mind if I asked you not to. He was really nice when we went round but I'm feeling so churned up about everything."

Barbara patted Jenny's arm, "Don't worry, we'll have a girls' night in. After all we'll both see him tomorrow. I must dash; I'd better leave you a key."

Jenny cleared up and wondered if she should phone before she left for the Martins' house. If she did it would give William a chance to avoid meeting her. After some thought she decided he didn't deserve such consideration and so set off to catch the Tube.

When she arrived the house was empty, perhaps they had gone to the undertaker's. She ran upstairs and put the clothes she wanted and, of course, the shoes Iris had bought her into a large carrier bag. She hurried back downstairs and decided to leave a short note explaining she had been invited out by a friend and would return on Sunday evening.

Sitting in the train she had time to think about all that had happened. She knew people didn't, as a rule, change much as they got older but yesterday's meeting with Dad had been strange. He seemed softer, kinder and had, without hesitation, said he would be pleased to take her to Laura's. It could only be Barbara's influence, perhaps stewing in his own juice had had the desired affect. Jenny smiled and then saw that the man opposite her was smiling back. She blushed and looked away.

It would be nice seeing Laura again after the horrors of the abortion. Perhaps it had made Laura nicer too but, Jenny thought, what a terrible way to learn. Perhaps that was why Laura had invited her for a meal. Maybe she accepted that she hadn't behaved well and wanted to make amends. It was curious that Mark had been invited too.

Laura had said several times that she liked him. Was the meal an opportunity to show that she, Laura, was staking her claim to him? Jenny sighed, Mark the enigma, Mark who had been such good company. It all seemed so long ago now. She recalled how upset she had been over Jim's attempted rape. Mark had soothed her and she had relaxed, felt so comfortable in his presence.

Supposing when they met he just thought she was not interesting or pretty enough. Laura was pretty. Perhaps I am making too much of it, Jenny thought, after all that experience with Jim had been enough to make anyone's judgement dodgy.

She walked from the station and debated with herself whether or not she should have her hair done. She had not given the Martins her board and lodging money. Most of the cash she had was not strictly speaking hers. She hesitated outside a hair salon took a deep breath and walked in.

*

Mark rose early on Sunday morning but his mother was up before him.

"You don't think I'd let you go off without a decent breakfast do you?"

Mark smiled, "Good old Mum, what would I do without you?"

"Get into a terrible mess, I don't doubt."

Mark watched as she bustled about boiling eggs, making toast and brewing a large pot of tea. She is beginning to look old, he thought, she hasn't had it easy with Dad dying before his time yet she's never complained. He glanced at his watch; he would have to be off soon. He had such mixed feelings about the whole thing, perhaps he was just being a romantic fool.

He rushed out of the house and caught the Manchester bus. He would have to get a car; he couldn't go on like this. Besides with a car he would be able to take prospective buyers to view properties instead of always being stuck in the office. It would make travelling to London easier too because he would be travelling there wouldn't he?

Worried that he would miss the train, he ran up the approach to Piccadilly rail station. Out of breath he hurried to the ticket office.

"London Euston, please."

The man behind the grille smirked. "Ain't running, mate."

"What?"

"Been cancelled, leaves on the line."

"Damn., damn, damn," Mark said, "leaves on the bloody line."

"Here mate, not having any of that," and with a crash the booking clerk closed the ticket office window.

Mark turned away and walked back to the bus stop for his return journey. Now what, he thought. He'd better get home and call Laura to make his apologies.

*

Jenny was wearing the full-skirted green dress but hadn't brought her only decent coat back from the Martins.

"I shan't need it as Dad's chauffeuring me," she told Barbara who had lent her some pretty gold earrings.

Charles arrived on time, as expected, and this time did not make any derogatory remarks. He had a route planned having gone to the nearest phone box and called the AA for some advice.

Barbara sat in the front and read instructions from the sheet of directions Charles had given her. Watching them from the back seat, Jenny hoped that Dad would have the sense to keep hold of Barbara who had already made such a difference to both their lives.

They arrived and, once the Johnson's front door had opened,

217

drove off with Barbara giving a cheery wave.

"Who was that?" Laura asked.

"My Dad and his girlfriend."

"Thought you didn't get on with him."

"Well, I do now, sort of."

"I'd better introduce you to Mum and Dad," Laura said and took Jenny through to the kitchen where Mrs. Johnson was preparing vegetables.

"Now, is there anything you don't like?" Mrs. Johnson asked and waved her arm at the kitchen table laden with food.

"No, it all looks lovely, thank you for inviting me."

"Well, it's nearly ready; the chicken has got another half an hour."

Mr. Johnson walked in from the sitting room, "Thought I heard voices," he said, "you must be Jenny."

Introductions over Laura took Jenny upstairs. "This is my bedroom," she said.

Jenny gasped, "It's lovely," she said and remembered the stark, cold room she had had at Dad's.

"Mark called about an hour ago," Laura said, "he can't make it. He was coming down on the train but it's been cancelled. He left his number if you want to call him."

Jenny felt herself blush, "Yes, please, if you don't mind."

"Phone's downstairs, in the hall."

Laura listened as Jenny hurried downstairs then firmly closed her bedroom door.

Jenny stood with the receiver in her hand, what should she say to him? She dialled and waited as the phone rang at the other end. A woman answered, Mark's mother Jenny assumed.

"May I speak to Mark, please?"

"You must be Jenny, I've heard a lot about you."

Jenny felt herself blush.

"I'll just get him."

Then there he was; she'd forgotten what a pleasant voice he had.

"Would you believe it, leaves on the line the ticket clerk said."

Jenny started to laugh and she heard Mark, at the other end, join in.

"Shall we call it quits?" Jenny said, "I couldn't help being ill, and you can't help leaves on the line."

"So do we give up on the grounds the fates are against us?"

218

Jenny paused, "Oh no, don't let's do that."

"I'm glad that's how you feel."

Jenny felt her heart thumping, he really does like me, she thought, and I'm so pleased. Now I've got his number we can keep in touch that way until we can arrange to meet.

"What are you doing next weekend?"

"Nothing," Jenny said.

"Right, I will get a train down on Saturday and book a B&B for the night and go back Sunday, leaves on the line permitting."

He was so easy to talk to that she told him about Iris and William and Barbara and her decision to return to the hostel for a while. He told her about the job and his mum and going walking in the hills and having to work yesterday when it was really his Saturday off. It was all wonderful, she thought, and well worth waiting for.

She gave him Barbara's number and the Martins' too so he could contact her wherever she was.

"I will see you next week, my girl, even if I have to walk."

"I'll hold you to that," she replied.

She went back to Laura's room grinning. "Sorry I was so long."

Laura knew in that moment that she must forget Mark and be glad for Jenny.

*

During the drive back to London Jenny talked about the meal and meeting Laura's parents but didn't mention speaking to Mark. She would tell Barbara another time, when they were on their own. After collecting her things from Barbara's flat, Charles drove Jenny back to the Martins and on the way there they chatted about what a nice pub he and Barbara had visited for lunch. Jenny told Charles of her decision to move back to the hostel for a while.

"I never did like..." Charles stopped. "Glad you had a good time today, my dear," he said as he pulled into the kerb.

"Thanks, Dad, I'm so grateful for the lift and everything."

Charles smiled. "I think I'll pop in on Barbara on the way home, she promised me a night-cap once I'd seen you safely here."

He leaned over and kissed her.

"Take care, my dear, keep in touch."

Jenny stood and watched as her father's car drove away. She

smiled as she thought about how much he had changed since meeting Barbara. This had been the lovely end to an almost perfect day and next weekend she would meet Mark. She had lots to look forward to.

*

Lightning Source UK Ltd.
Milton Keynes UK
10 December 2010

164187UK00001B/78/P

9 781849 230506